The Magick
and
The Maker

Sharon K. Angelici

Write with Light Publications Colorado, USA

ISBN: 9798503713756
Library of Congress Number: 2021937803

DEDICATION

For my husband, my daughter, and my son. You inspire me and I'm grateful for the minutes, days, and years of living this adventure called life. I adore you. I'm glad you are mine and so grateful for all of the ideas you brought to the project. They say write what you know and that's why there's so much love in this story.

To Taylor, Thank you! Your cover art is the love story.

For my Aussie family, my Minnesotans, my rainbow support team. Thank you for every mile traveled and every Woo Hoo. Your encouragement helped make book two a reality.

To Hillary, only love and always be brave.

Kathy and Kelly thanks for your creativity and enthusiasm and all the extras you bring. The pinches weren't just for you.

For Christina, a true friend and champion. Thank you.

Diana, I miss you and I hope you get your ethereal copy.

To Dad, I love you and I'm so happy you get to hold my stories in your hands.

For Mom, I wish you'd have known this part of who I am.

CHAPTER I

Home

"Will you quit daydreaming and hold the Dagger of Doom?" Shay slapped the punch-style dagger into my hand as she flipped the pages in her book of spells.

I was daydreaming. We'd spent all morning looking at books. I'm sure you know there are 26 letters in the English alphabet. Did you know there are over 450,000 entries in Webster's dictionary?

My girlfriend has over seven hundred books on the shelves in her house. Until we started sharing space, I had about twelve, and that included the six manuals I kept from my college welding courses.

I've never been much of a reader. I certainly never expected to understand Nordic runes written in the blood of a demon. That wasn't ever a goal, but I've also never been much into research.

Most people try to design life well into the future, but that's not me. One day at a time was working out just fine until landing in this town of Bannock. With a name like Wildwood Blackstone, it would make sense that I'd resist planting roots. Moving ten times in as many years made temporary feel permanent, but this tiny ghost town was changing everything.

Nothing in my 28 years prepared me to be standing on a circle scorched in concrete, staring down at the heavy line of salt smothering it. If you asked me six months ago to spend hours researching how to read ancient runes, I'd have told you that blacksmiths don't need that skill set. One day I'm forging hot metal and welding farm implements; the next, I'm a pagan apprentice with the ancient powers of transmutation. If that isn't enough, my girlfriend, Shay, can out-witch me with her eyes closed.

She was also the law enforcement officer in command of the department's only K-9 unit, which made me partly responsible for the giant German Shepherd who responded to commands in Latin. My life was rather weird, but it also held a level of excitement I didn't know was possible.

"Wil, can you quit daydreaming and focus on the Dagger of Doom." My girlfriend tapped the palm of my hand.

I relocated to the small historic *ghost* town of Bannock after receiving a grant to restore their 19th-century carriage house. At the time, I thought it was the perfect location. I'd work as a welder by day and a blacksmith by night; set up shop, teach classes, and do demonstrations. I had no idea what was waiting for me.

In the first few months, I discovered the truth about my new hometown and, in the process, found adventure in magick. I wasn't playing tricks or pulling rabbits out of hats. I was using the forces of nature to alter the space made by the monsters in this town. Yes, I was a demon hunter, a skill I didn't know I had, and that's why I was standing in the center of this ring of salt.

"Wildwood?" She yelled to get my attention. "You're not here with me. I need you to focus on the Dagger of Doom please."

"I thought by now that name might wear off." My first forged creation using material left behind after a demon attack was the punch-style dagger I was holding in my hand. At the time, I was a novice to magick and all of the protections it could afford. It was during a cleansing ritual when I feared the demon content of my creation that I'd recklessly called it by that name. My misplaced fear amused Shay, and it had subsequently become the Dagger of Doom.

She was thumbing through an ancient tome about demons. "Wildwood, as long as that's your dagger, the name stays. It's a perfect reminder of the power of knowledge."

"Are you saying that I was dumb to call it the Dagger of Doom because I didn't understand your magick?"

She pushed the book up against her chest. "You just crammed an awful lot of assumption in my mouth." She turned and held the page in front of me. I saw my reflection in the polished cuff she wore on her wrist. "If you're interested, I found the reference."

I grabbed her around the waist. In a police uniform, my girlfriend was commanding but wrapped in her deep-purple cloak; she was utterly irresistible. "I'm interested in a lot of things, but you haven't told me how Benton is?" I rested my chin so I could read over her shoulder.

Shay was a ten-year veteran of the Bannock police department up and out at the break of dawn. When her schedule permitted, she returned to my workshop in time for early evening blacksmithing at the forge. Yesterday she'd spent a few hours with her friend and retired training officer, Reggie Benton. It had been only a few short weeks since the attack in Reggie's bar, and her recovery was slower than expected.

"If I said I was avoiding that conversation, would you make me talk about it?" She tucked her finger in the book, closing the cover and holding the text against her chest. I felt the muscles of her shoulders stiffen as she tried to withdraw from my embrace.

I pulled her closer to whisper in her ear. "She's like a mother to you. Watching someone suffer, someone you love. I know it's hard."

Shay took a deep breath. Her exhale slow as she leaned back in my arms. Her reaction was not a surrender but a compromise. "I'm not trying to keep you out of it. I'm just not experienced at sharing the difficult parts of my life."

I covered her arms with my own. She didn't know much about the partnership of love, but she was a consummate student. "I'm patient. I'm also here for you, so when you're ready, I'll listen."

"Please keep telling me that. It's good to hear."

I understood that Shay trusted me but growing up in the foster care system left scars, and she had more than I cared to count. I knew, if I gave her time, she'd share when she was ready. I tapped the cover of her research. "Tell me what you found."

She opened the book again. We'd spent the last few weeks testing and researching my recent creations in the forge. Benton had given us four pieces of demon remains that I'd transformed into weapons infused with the original demon's power. Our punch daggers came from a class-two creature that was my first contact with the sub-humans in this town. It was after that encounter when Shay confessed everything she knew about Bannock and its history of monsters.

The Dagger of Doom and its matched punch dagger taught me the lesson that demons turned to metal. Not only did everything I stabbed burst into a ball of flame, but they were indestructible. Benton shared her knowledge about demon guts and pieces, presenting me with the four chunks I'd forged. The cuff on Shay's wrist made the most horrible sound, freezing the unprotected where they stood. The folded ribbon candle holder we created together burned a blue flame that illuminated my workshop walls, the same walls covered with demon-blood-inked Nordic runes. A few days ago, we'd forged the final project: a short-handled throwing axe.

The book she was holding in her hands was the final incantation she'd use to bless our latest creation. Shay was my teacher, and after these months together, I felt like we'd shared a lifetime. What seemed impossible, standing in her presence, was if I would ever understand the practice of magick.

I felt the gentle tap of her finger against my temple. "Where are you, Wildwood Blackstone?"

It wasn't difficult to get lost in the extraordinary confidence of Shay Pierce when she was about to bless our altar and perform a purification ritual. In fact, it was beautiful. She was also patient with me when I asked more questions than she could answer. "I'm just thinking."

"Care to share?" She held out a small jar of salt. I touched her wrist, lingering on the scar wrapped around her hand. Shay had fourteen stab wounds on her body, left behind after a violent childhood attack. She was so much more than a magick practitioner. She was a miraculous example of survival and perseverance.

I followed her around the circle. "I was just thinking, that so far, everything has been right on the edge of terrifying."

"That's just because it's new. Stick with me, sweetheart, and the edge won't seem so scary." She held the hatchet up so I could see it. "Can you focus for the next half hour so we can go play with our new toy?" She flipped her grip, spinning the handle toward me.

"Yes, ma'am." I took the weapon from her hand. The leather felt comfortable in my palm as I slashed the air. "This has great balance."

"It must be that the maker has some talent."

"It must be." My right eye closed with a wink.

"You ready to walk the circle with me?" She pulled her punch dagger from the sheath, striking it against the candle holder. The spark turned to a blue flame as it met the wick, and she whispered. "Offer of fire, take the flame, perform the task we call you to."

We stepped together around the ring on the workshop floor. She chanted her blessing as I made a clear line of salt at our feet. The first rule I'd learned, salt is essential when creating a sacred circle.

She sat in the center of the ring, "Find true north and set the flames." I held the candles against my chest, carrying all four as I followed her direction. I set the first. "Good, light it, please."

I followed the edge clockwise, leaving a single taper candle burning east, south, west, and north again. I stepped with care, knowing that every motion mattered. Every whisper had intention. She was asking the goddesses and gods to be present for what we were about to do, and it was sexy as hell.

"Cleanse this axe with purposeful intention, purify the energies of this blade to protect and vibrate the skills of Macha." She held it in her hands, sprinkling water and salt over it. "Spirit of earth and air; bring strength and truth. Release the hindering forces housed within this weapon." She waved the blade in front of her body. "Forged from fire and called to be and do my will I cast away evil." She passed the axe from handle to blade through the candle flame. "My obeisance to truth and the boundaries of love and nature, for good to call out evil." She poured the cup of moon water over the tool reciting, "Blessed by the goddess to be true, in love and honor, dispelling evil. In peace and trust and in all that is my faith." She looked at me as she said the final words, nodding encouragement for me to repeat them. "So mote it be."

"So mote it be." I whispered.

Her eyes were a gorgeous shade of green, and the blue flame from the candle only enhanced their intensity. The first few minutes after an incantation were my favorite part. She smelled of incense and sacred oils, but the most dramatic experience was the surge of energy the earth sent in response to her words. I felt it through my body, warm and radiant, like the rising sun embracing the morning dew. But it went deeper, cycling through my skin and over my soul.

"You're getting very good at the staying quiet and focusing energy part." She waved me into the circle. "Want to come to sit with me while the candles burn?"

That was the silliest damn question. "Yes, of course, I do." I positioned myself in front of her, face to face, but she was not pleased.

"You're kinda far away." She held one beckoning finger in the air, summoning me closer.

"So demanding." I scooted until she pulled me against her.

Shay's arms came around, and I leaned into her body. "That's better."

"You can't be comfortable."

Her laugh was a whisper against my ear. "You in my arms is the most comfortable I've been in my entire life."

We sat in the sacred circle, holding each other until the candles burned to the floor. The blue flame of our forged demon candle holder waved in the darkness. I studied the map on the wall written in demon's blood. We'd discovered the map not so very long ago, determining it was a depiction of our small town. My carriage house was at the center, stamped with a symbol identical to my own blacksmithing maker's mark. We had unanswered questions about the map and its origins. Waiting for Regina Benton to heal hindered much of our progress.

"So . . ." I hesitated but asked again. "Benton?"

Her arms squeezed before falling away. "She's not good."

I grabbed Shay's hands, holding them in my lap. "I thought she was improving?"

"The concussion affected the tremors, and last night she had two seizures. If that wasn't bad enough, the infection in her arm keeps spreading, and she stopped responding to the last option of antibiotics."

"Oh, Shay." I knew what this meant, but we were both in denial. "Are they still talking about amputation?"

"They're talking about a lot of things, but Benton isn't having any of it. She just wants to go home."

"Is it safe for her there?"

"Probably, but I can't think about her safety and yours."
She held me a little tighter, and I couldn't deny the vibration
of energy passing between us. Her love was an extraordinary
combination of delicate ferocity, and it was all I could do but
hold tight to the tangled delight of being hers. Shay's soulful
voice had a way of making the dangers in our life fade. I
believed her when she said she would protect me, but I also had
to consider Benton. Who would protect her, and what would
she share with the people who loved her?

"You said she had a family. Do they know about the
demon-hunting blood running through her veins?" Shay's
body tensed in reaction to my words. I regretted the attempt at
humor.

"What did you just say?"

Shaking my head in apology. "I was trying to be funny."

"No, that's not what I meant." Shay shifted her hips to
stand, getting tangled in her cloak. I rolled away to help her up.

"What are you thinking?" I asked.

Shay walked out of the workshop and into the office. "The
blood. It's the key. There has to be a toxin the doctors don't
know about." I followed close behind her. Shay stopped fast,
turning around. She pressed her palms to my cheeks, planting
a hard, fast kiss on my lips. "You are so damn brilliant!" She
turned back to the table, flipping through the stacks of papers.
"Benton had a list of the class-one venoms. Jeez, it's been weeks."

"Are you saying that the attack . . . someone tried to poison
her?"

"Yes. I can't believe I didn't think of it sooner."

"I can. I mean, you've been worried about Reggie's
concussion more than the cut on her arm." Shay's behavior was
almost frantic as she picked through her reference books. I

wondered what she wasn't telling me about demon venom. "How can I help?"

She tossed a binder at me. "Look in here for everything class-one with venom." There were more than 100 pages in the notebook. Benton must have studied handwriting or gone to a knuckle-whacking religious institution because her penmanship was beautiful. I thumbed through the first twenty pages scanning by the class-four and onto the class-three specimens. The more I studied the pages, the more I encountered a recurring doodle. I interrupted my girlfriend's research. "Shay, have you ever seen this drawing before." I pointed to the image appearing on more than half of the pages.

Her finger traced the lines. "It looks a bit like a maker's mark." She rolled my wrist over and held the page beside it for comparison.

"I guess it does. Different, but it could be the mark of another Maker." I shrugged. "Can we research our research?"

"That'll have to wait until later. We need to figure out what's keeping Benton in the hospital." Shay focused on whatever thoughts were running through her mind. She had three stacks sorted out on the table before I had a chance to read the class-one list in my notebook. "What did you come up with?"

"Shay, I think I'm the wrong person for this job. I could only find two." I unclipped the binder holding the pages together. "This one and this one." I laid the cover sheet for each demon profile in front of her.

"You're perfect. These are perfect." Shay was on her cellphone before I could look up from the table. "Dani, I've got a lead on Benton's infection."

I couldn't listen to the conversation on the other side, but I could hear the hope in Shay's voice. "I think it was some kind of poison." She walked to the computer in the corner of the room, lifting the printer's cover to scan an image of the pages. "I'm sending you two profiles. Get them to the right people, and let's treat this as attempted murder and not a simple assault and robbery. Someone wanted Benton out of the way."

Shay finished emailing the pages. I wasn't sure what to do, so I waited. Watching her move through my office was almost as intriguing as watching her mind work through the problem. "Dani is headed to the hospital. She's going to arrange a blood test."

"Do you want to go see Benton, tell her what you've found?"

Shay was already hanging her cloak on the hook, searching for the keys to her squad car. "Yes, will you come with me?" Her question didn't require an answer. "Dexter." The massive German Shepherd came down from the apartment upstairs and sat in front of us, waiting for the lead to attach to his collar.

"Let me run up and put on my uniform," Shay said.

"I'm not going to be disappointed about that." I held my hand to her; instead of taking my own, she dropped the leash in my palm and ran up the stairs taking two at a time. I could hear her shoes hit the floor and a few seconds later she was in front of me closing the last button on her shirt.

"We need to run. I left the squad parked at my house." Shay wasn't a fitness enthusiast, but she did have a routine. I didn't. I never ran or lifted weights, but I didn't need to, my job was enough for now.

The three of us running down the street must have been a sight; a full uniformed police officer and a Kevlar-covered K-9 unit chased by a scrappy Doc Martin-booted wild-haired blacksmith. I could tell that Shay and Dexter were holding back to stay with me, and it was a gift that we lived only a few blocks apart. I felt a sense of relief when her bright orange door came into view.

I adjusted the leash, waiting for Shay to let us inside. The dog went through first, running down the hall, dragging me to the back porch. "Dexter, slow down." His paw scratched at the metal plate, and I opened the door to let him out into the backyard.

"He likes his yard." Her chin rested on my shoulder as we watched the German Shepherd dance around in the grass.

"Almost as much as I like you." I turned to kiss her, wrapping my arms around her, if only for a moment.

Her lips touched mine. "I need a different shirt. Will you let Dex in when he's ready?"

"Yep." Shay was about to put on what I teasingly called her superhero costume. I understood what the uniform meant to her, but growing up in foster care, being shuffled around by social workers and cops, didn't instill that same sense of pride and trust for me. Shay and I grew up in that system. I avoided every level of it, but Shay, her near-death assault, led her someplace very different.

I was lost in thought until Dexter's bark startled me from my musings. "Sorry, buddy." I filled his water dish, setting it near the door. I saw the backpack full of gear on the chair.

"You're a little daydreamy right now?" Shay was behind me, whispering in my ear. "I called you twice."

I shook my head. Shay draped her uniform shirt over the back of the chair. From the hips down, she looked like a cop in her well-pressed pants and strait-laced spit-shined boots, but it was the tight-fitting BPD t-shirt snugged over her breasts, that made me forget about the bottom half. "I was just thinking about you."

I'm sure she could tell by the smile on my face exactly what I was thinking. "I was hoping you'd bring me my vest."

"I guess my plan to watch you get dressed worked out."

The Velcro tore away from the front of her bullet-proof vest. She was never on duty without protection. She slipped it over her torso, and it was at that moment I realized why she always pulled it away from her side. "Does it rub on the scars?" I blurted out the question without thinking about her reaction.

Shay was startled until she read the concern in my eyes. "Yes, it's a tough spot. The seam rubs, and I don't feel it unless I've been very active."

My fingers tangled around her vested shoulder, pulling her closer to me. "I love you, superhero." I kissed her hard, making sure she understood that I cared about every bit of her.

"I love you too."

I stepped away, tossing the uniform shirt to her. "Put that on before I can't contain myself."

She adjusted the Velcro one more time, and Dexter's ears perked up. "You ready to go to work, Dex?"

I watched the buttons of her shirt close over the body underneath. Even though she would never admit to it, her courage, bravery, and tenacity made her the perfect superhero. She tucked in her shirttails and secured the duty belt around her waist. The department-issued baseball-style hat was the finishing touch, and I was pleased to watch it all come together on her body.

Dexter sat very still as she wrapped him with a much smaller but equally important vest. Shay dangled the keys on her finger. "Ready to roll?" The dog barked before I could respond. They were an adorable team.

CHAPTER II

Hagalaz

The hospital was a forty-minute drive from Shay's house, giving us time to arrive well before noon. The car ride felt long mainly because of the silence as Shay focused on the road ahead and I'm sure she was thinking about saving Benton's life. I didn't mind the quiet. I hadn't been out of Bannock since our last visit to see the retired cop, so I enjoyed watching the wildlife pass outside the car window.

Her cell phone buzzed, and I leaned closer to hear the voice on the speakerphone as Shay relayed her thoughts. "Pierce." She answered.

"It's Forrest. How far out are you?"

"I'm only a few miles away. What's the status?" Shay's questions were concise, poised and her rigid body language matched the conversation.

Dani was equally precise with her words. "We've got your scans. The medical team is running a few tests right now."

"What did they find?" Shay asked. "I was thinking it could be the venom of—"

"Just get here, Pierce. They moved her into isolation on the third floor. Someone will meet you at her old room and bring you here." Dani explained.

"Roger that." The call ended, and I didn't know what to say.

"Are you okay?" I asked, but I was certain she was not.

Shay looked at me. "I don't know." Her eyes turned back to the road, and I could see the city limit sign. We arrived at the hospital a few minutes later, and an officer was waiting for us outside of Benton's room. It was clear they had results from the blood tests and that Shay's guess was accurate.

"Are you planning to take Dex inside?" I wasn't sure where I fit in this investigation. I was Shay's girlfriend, but I didn't know Benton that well. Would she want me in the room during their inquiry? Did I have anything to contribute? I wasn't a law enforcement professional, and all of my childhood triggers were tripping as we approached the hospital room. I could feel the heat flush my cheeks and the sweat fall to the corner of my eye. Her hand touched my shoulder.

"Are you alright?" Shay was a keen observer.

I wasn't, and I didn't want to hide it from her. I also didn't need the burden of my past slowing her down. "I'll be okay. It's just a lot of cops and a lot of unknown."

"I promise I'll take care of you." She hugged me, giving little concern about who saw us or what their opinion might be.

"I know." I took in a deep breath, blowing it out with a puff of my cheeks. "I'll be okay."

"Why don't you take Dex for a walk? Keep your phone handy, and I'll come to find the two of you when we're finished."

I didn't judge myself for feeling relieved. I avoided hospitals almost as much as law enforcement, and Dexter was the perfect companion as we walked around the grounds. I relaxed as we strolled through the gardens, admiring the flowering landscape surrounding a building filled with the injured and sick. I looked up at the windows, wondering what desperate decisions they were making inside Benton's hospital room.

I dropped down against the base of an oak tree, the perfect spot to sit. Dex laid his head in my lap. Perhaps I was grounding myself in anticipation of what might come next, but after a morning that started with Shay in my arms, a dog in my lap felt like a quick backward slide. I thought about the silent moments we'd shared in the last few weeks. Me watching the powerful witch Shay had become and Shay sitting on the upturned five-gallon bucket while I transformed scrap metal into pieces of art. The more I thought about it, the more I realized that we just shouldn't work, but somehow, we did.

I'm not sure how long I sat before falling back into the fresh-cut grass, but when I settled, Dexter rested his head across my abdomen. I was protected in a way I couldn't understand, not yet. My eyes closed as my hands drifted to the grass beside me. The earth's energy moved across my palms, and rhythmic waves echoed through my body; Dexter rolled against my arm as if to draw strength from my source. It was a bond I hadn't experienced, and I let the connection rise and fall. It was like a song I'd never heard, and for a moment, it felt like this massive German Shepherd was doing light work with me.

A feather-light kiss touched my forehead as the weight of the dog lifted from my body. "The two of you make an adorable pair." I didn't open my eyes, basking in the sensation of Shay's voice and her touch.

I wiped my arm over my face, trying to remove the haze of energy that lulled me to sleep. I was glad to feel Dexter tug at the leash. What a statement to be asleep in the middle of the day with all of the drama around us. "Hi, Shay."

"Hi, yourself." The dog was vigilant as if taking sides. "I see Dexter wore you out."

"I'm not sure who wore out whom, but he's a good companion." I rolled to my side, attempting to stand. Shay held out her hand to help me to my feet. In a quick second, we were face-to-face, but I wasn't sure how to read her expression with her sunglasses over her eyes. "How did it go?"

She looked away. "I learned a couple of things about Benton today that I'm not sure how to process."

I touched her chin, tipping her face so I could lift her sunglasses. I knew when she was about to cry, her eyes glazed like emeralds underwater. It was beautiful and heartbreaking at the same time. "Will she lose the arm?"

Shay nodded. "It's looking like, yes, the damage is done. According to the doctors, the necrosis is irreversible. Benton is sure she can handle what's coming." She leaned against the trunk of the tree.

"What does that mean?" I asked. I stepped closer, looping a finger over the waist of her duty belt.

"That's the unknown that has become known." She ran her finger against the groove of the tree's bark.

"Shay, you aren't making a lot of sense, and that's usually your strength in a crisis."

She took the dog's lead from my wrist, transferring it to her own. "Benton told me she has been treating herself with some mysterious anti-venom for the last few weeks." Shay reached to hold my hand, leading the three of us toward the parking lot. "There's a lot to share with you, but Benton knew about the poison."

"How?" I felt her fingers squeeze my own.

"She said it was the seizures." We walked toward her squad car. "She let me believe that the assault and concussion caused them, but today she told me how it happened." Shay opened the back door, letting Dexter jump in the rear seat. She unclipped the leash and looped it back and forth in her hand. Shay rested on her forearms, leaning over the roof of the car. "Benton doesn't think she's going to survive."

I reached across the car. "Oh, honey."

She ducked down into the front seat, knocking her hand radio to the floor. "I need a minute." She clipped the mic to the dashboard. "I thought we were driving here to save her arm, not her life." She started the engine but didn't put the car in gear. She sat looking out the windshield at nothing. "I don't know how to lose another woman who . . ." Her voice trailed off as her hands fell to her lap.

Grief. It frightened me. "What can I do?" I asked, reaching for her hand. She was quiet for the longest time, staring out the window.

Her voice was soft, fragile, as she asked. "Have you ever wondered why it's always so hard?"

"What do you mean?" I shifted my body against the door of the car and reached across to hold her hand.

"You and I, we have almost the same story. Whoever put us on this planet left us behind. The people that the rest of the world call family, they didn't want us." She pulled away from me. "I'm not sure how to lose her. Losing Mama almost broke me, Wil."

I stared at the scars on Shay's hands. "I can't fix Benton, I wish I could, but you won't have to face it alone, Shay. Not this time."

She closed her eyes to force back the tears. She didn't say a word, putting the car into gear, leaving the parking lot. Unlike our hopeful drive to the hospital, a shroud of sorrow fell over our return. I thought about her life without me. Had she searched for answers? Maybe I should tell her that I had.

"I tried looking for my biological family." I blurted the words I decided she should know.

We were waiting at a stop sign. "Really?" She turned to look at me. "When? What did you find?"

I'd never spoken to anyone about my experience. I wasn't sure if it would be comforting or add to the day's pain. "Earl gave me some cash when I turned twenty-one. It was enough to get me through for almost a month."

"That's hardly enough time." Shay glanced at me before focusing on the road.

"I started at the hospital." I wasn't sure how much Shay remembered about my personal history. "I was told . . . well, Gran told me I was abandoned in a bathroom with my name scribbled on a piece of paper."

"That sounds like a place to start. There has to be a record, some files or documentation?"

"Nothing." I shook my head. "It wasn't true. When I asked for my records, they gave me an admitting document. I was an unknown newborn."

"Where did the note with your name come from?" I slid against the door as Shay turned off the highway.

"They couldn't tell me. I think it was something Gran made up to comfort me."

"That doesn't make sense."

The drive home felt faster, and I was happy about it. Talking about my childhood was never easy. I hoped one day to leave it in the past. "I talked to my caseworker. She didn't have much either. Whoever gave birth to me didn't want me to know."

Shay reached across the car to hold my hand. "Did you get any names at all?"

I looked at the scars on the back of her hand. I pulled the cuff away from her wrist, revealing the zig-zag marks left behind when she'd fought off her attacker. She opened the palm of her hand to me. We'd rarely talked about life before Mama Pierce's. "That's the point. There aren't any names to find."

She took a deep breath and blew it out. "So, here we are, quite the pair," Shay's voice broke as she spoke.

I rubbed the scar on her hand. "This makes it easier," I said.

"The scars?" Her hand tensed.

"Yes." I squeezed her fingers, keeping her close to me. "But not the ones you're thinking."

"You really are something, ya know."

It was impossible to miss the bright orange door on the front of Shay's home. I could see it from the end of the block. "I wish I had answers," I said. "I'm not going to lie, but I've made it here, and I've got you. Now that I think about it, I'm not sure why anyone else matters."

Shay kissed the back of my hand before saying, "We can be great together, you know."

I nodded. "I do know."

She put the car into park. "I'm going to change, and then we can go over to the apartment."

"Would you rather stay here tonight?" I asked.

She shook her head. "I think I'd rather be in a place that doesn't remind me of Benton."

I nodded because saying sorry would only compound the pain. We were talented women, Shay and me. She could think her way through anything, and I had hands capable of putting broken parts back together. The two of us should be unstoppable, but sometimes not knowing where you're from is an obstacle to where you want to go.

I read once, in ancient times, when priceless treasures broke, that craftsman would put them back together using golden paste. The artists saw each imperfection as the perfect opposite, and the precious metal transformed the broken into treasure. I wished that for my girlfriend. More than anything, I wanted to paint each tiny, stitched dimple and every ridged scar on her body. The stroke of my brush a reminder; so that she would see herself the way that I did—a perfect human treasure.

She wasn't gone for long when she stepped out on her front porch, still wearing her uniform, a duffle bag thrown over her shoulder. She must have read the questioning expression on my face as she opened the door for Dex. "I have to go to the station. I hope you don't mind."

"You're the driver." The trunk lid opened, and she dropped her bag inside. I waited to hear the reasons for our side trip, but

Shay didn't offer anything more. It would have been almost as fast to walk to the station from the house, but her car's computer and notes carried the details of her visit with Benton.

She pulled her car into the assigned spot in the department lot. "You want to stay in the car or walk over to the shop? I don't know how long this will take."

I shrugged my shoulders. As much as I wanted to understand the police station's inner workings, I needed time to adjust before hanging around would feel comfortable. "I think I'll take a walk. What about Dex?" I asked.

"I'll take him in." It was that simple. She walked around, opening my door, letting me out. "I'll come to the carriage house when I can." Dexter jumped out of the back of the vehicle.

I leaned against the car, waiting to kiss her. "I'll be there. Do you think we'll have time to play with the new axe?"

Her eyes lit with excitement and she flashed a beautiful smile filled with promise. "I'm counting on it." Her hand touched my face. Her lips touched my own. I watched her walk away, satisfied to get the off-duty side of this extraordinary woman.

~~~~~~~~~~

"They aren't even going to investigate!" Shay's arm whipped the axe toward the painted target, burying the blade deep in the slatted surface. "Nothing!" She yelled. "It's like Benton is protecting whoever poisoned her."

"So, it was intentional? there's no doubt?"

I was standing three steps behind Shay, and her backswing still felt dangerous. I was trying to understand her complicated world. How she balanced law enforcement with demon-fighting? How she could investigate human pain inflicted by demon evil.

I'd spent the last few hours building what I considered a stable two-by-four wall to withstand a few slings of our untested demon-steel hatchet. The sleek axe head looked like a native tomahawk without the added ornamentation, but right now, all I could see was the polished steel buried deep in the bullseye.

"I can't get an answer from anyone," she said through the grind of her teeth. I kept my distance as my fiery redhead walked toward a target peppered with gouges. Shay anchored her foot against our temporary test spot, working the axe head from the splintered wall. I kept the handle lean, and the grip wraps rough, making it easy to swing and release. She'd taken over our test, throwing our demon blade and using it to release her anger after the police station debriefing. Work-related frustration was a new side of this woman, and although I was happy she was finally sharing her work, she was losing the intention behind our afternoon fun. Shay planted her feet on the floor and flipped the leather grip like a tennis player waiting for a serve.

"I'm so pissed." Her motion was fluid, twisting in a blink. She launched the blade again, burying it in the blood-red center.

"Shay, hon." I reached for the loop of her pants, tugging her into my arms. "Wait." She resisted before relaxing into my embrace. "Stop for a minute and talk to me." I felt the flex of her shoulders against my chest. There was confident power behind her athletic build, so I held a little tighter—her energy seeping with a level of emotion that was new to me.

She pulled away. "I can't talk. I just need to throw the hell out of this axe."

"Are you forgetting something?" I asked.

She ripped the blade from the target again. "I'm trying to, yes."

I planted myself on the floor in front of her. "No." My arms crossed over my chest, preventing her from throwing our weapon. "You forget that this is *our* test run." Shay dropped her head. I could only imagine the thoughts running through her mind as she stared at our newly forged axe. The current situation was a bit of a letdown. Did she forget I was part of the team? Did she forget about me completely?

She flipped the handle in the air, rotating the grip so I could take it. "I'm ruining it, aren't I?"

The leather wrap was warm in my hand. "Maybe just a little."

"I'm gonna stand right here behind you and let you give it a throw."

I stared at the target in front of us. "You mutilated my wall."

"At least it isn't on fire."

"Good point." My fingers flexed as I adjusted my grip before throwing it across the room. In my defense, I'm not a weapons specialist, nor have I ever trained one bit on how to throw a hatchet. My inexperience was evident when the over-rotation forced the weapon to bounce back. Shay stepped in front of me, covering my body with her own as the blade skipped across the floor. It was funny and pathetic at the same time, and I knew this was going to follow me forever.

"Nice shootin' there, sweetheart."

"Well, maybe I'd be better if you didn't hog all of the fun."

"I'm pretty sure you need a lesson or two." She walked over to pick the axe up off the floor.

"What if we test it without throwing it?"

"One mishap and you're ready to retire?" Her arm came up with the axe head in her grip.

"Nope." I held my hand to her. "No matter how much we throw it, we're not getting anything different."

She slapped the axe against my palm. "What's your plan?"

"I think we've determined that throwing it into a wall isn't activating the powers. I forged the axe from a class-one demon. Shouldn't it be melting flesh or something?"

Shay was smiling at me, shaking her head. She walked to the desk, returning with the notes she'd written. "Class-one demons have a killing poison or venom and an organic weapon." She flicked the wedge of steel in my hand. "We have no idea what demon we've forged, only what part." She made a gesture with her hands, showing the length and girth.

I dropped it to the ground. "Why'd you have to say it like that and do that with your hands. It just sounds dirty."

She laughed. "No, your mind went and made it dirty."

"Do you think it matters that it's from a spire?" I asked.

"I do, yes." Shay was walking away, much like Benton in research mode, but I didn't think this was the time to point it out. Her hand held the demon tome we'd spent the last month creating. "The axe could be infused with any kind of energy."

"Any kind?" Demon fighting was a brutal reality to adjust to, and the world that Shay lived in was nothing like I'd known. After moving to Bannock, I pinched myself about a lot of things, mostly when I couldn't believe that Shay was my girlfriend, but I also did it to confirm that demons were, in fact, real.

"Evil, Wil." Her hand came up to my cheek. "Don't worry. You're safe with me." Her thumb rubbed against the tiny scar on my face, evidence of the danger demon encounters could create. I closed my eyes. Shay Pierce was the absolute best medicine. "Maybe we should put it all together?" She never stopped working on the problem.

"Put what together?" I asked.

"The demon weaponry?"

She was back on task, picking up the axe and laying it on the workshop table. She pulled the cuff from her wrist, and the punch dagger laced to the ankle of her boot. I didn't think I could love her more until the blade sparked across the candle holder, lighting the blue flame. Shay was the most magickal human being I'd ever known. "Dagger of doom, please?"

"Damn, woman, I was just basking in the magnificence of your street cred, and you have to go and doom me."

She fanned her hand over my creations. "Look at this. Your work is beautiful. If anyone should be basking, it's me."

"Mutual admiration society." I pulled the punch dagger from my hip, laying it beside her own. "Maybe we can get patches."

She was walking away again, but this time I knew where she'd gone. I heard the lid of the trunk squeak open and a few seconds later drop back in place. "Hats, we can get hats." She played along.

I grabbed her, pulling her against me. "Do you have any idea how much I love you right now?"

"I do." She laid the athame on the table. "It's the mutual part." We stood in front of the forged weapons. "Let's run through each of them."

I picked up my first creations. "Punch daggers." I waved them in front of my body, slicing the air. "They cut everything, are indestructible, and start shit on fire."

She nodded. "They also have intuitive reflection."

I turned to look at her. "They have what now?" Her observation was news to me, as was the concept of intuitive reflection.

"You remember when Benton left the package at the house? When I cut the top of the box?" I nodded. "I was testing a theory."

"What theory was that?"

"Intention." She waited for me to react, but I didn't have a clue what she was referencing. "When I cut that box, I set the idea that it would cut clean."

"So, you're saying that you can talk to the Dagger of Doom?"

"Yes, I'm saying that we can talk to the Dagger of Doom, and we can talk to my dagger, but not in words so much as in intention."

"Like telepathy?"

"Like . . ." She took her dagger from my hand and sliced through a piece of paper. "Intuitive reflection." It didn't catch fire.

I shook my head. "Do you think I'll ever understand half of what you do?"

"Eventually, you'll understand it all, and then we'll be an unstoppable force." She kissed my cheek. "Right now, I want you to stab the target with the Dagger of Doom. Let's see if you can control the power of destruction."

I walked toward the wall. Even though I'd just built it, Shay had shredded the red center with the accuracy of her axe throws. "Maybe I'll just hit the wall since the target looks like tinder."

"Think about stabbing the wood but not burning it." She winked at me. "Hit it hard, babe."

I adjusted my grip on the contoured bone handle, enjoying the perfect match to the size of my hand. I braced my wrist for the impact, preparing to hit the wall but not destroy it. The blade cut in, bursting to flame as I withdrew. "Nope." I smacked the fire with my other hand. "Grab the ladle from the quench bucket."

Shay scooped a cupful of water, splashing it on the tiny fire. "You have to be the boss, Wil." She demonstrated by smashing her dagger into the wood. She buried the demon-steel to the back of her knuckles, but when she stepped away, nothing was burning.

"How did you do that?"

She whispered in my ear. "You have to believe, Wildwood."

I was not a complicated person. I had simple tastes and more straightforward ideas. I didn't hide who I was or how much I didn't care about the complexities of life. This situation was pissing me off. "Is there anything that you suck at?" She ignored my question. "I thought I was believing."

"Stop for a second and think about what you just said." She squared her shoulders to mine, looking into my eyes. "Tell me you love me." She flashed a smile.

I didn't hesitate. "I love you."

She rested her hands on my shoulders. "Do you believe what you just said?"

"With every muscle I used to say it."

Her hand came to my abdomen. "With your gut?"

"Yes."

Her fingers hovered over my cheek before tapping my temple. "With your head?"

"Yes." I smiled, understanding where this exercise was going.

She put her hand in the center of my chest. "Your heart?"

I nodded, closing my eyes.

"You have the potential to become a powerful witch, Wildwood. You have to believe it as much as I do."

"You really are a witch." I opened my eyes to the most beautiful combination of power and love in her shining smile. "You make me believe anything is possible."

"We are proof that anything is possible."

I'm not sure how I got so lucky to have this woman in my life. "I'll practice believing I won't start the world on fire with my Dagger of Doom. What's next, hero?"

"We can put a pin in intuitive reflection for now and move on to the powers in the athame."

"Fairy steel."

She grabbed the research materials. "Have you added anything else about fairy lore?"

"As an athame, with fairy spirit, this should carry some strong energy for doing good." I said, not completely confident with my answer.

She agreed. "More focus on the concept of intuitive reflection, sweetheart." Magick was frustrating. Mostly it was my lack of understanding magick that was frustrating. Concepts put into action shouldn't make me feel so dumb. I flipped the note pages over, slapping them with my hand. "Be patient with yourself, my love. It'll come with practice."

"How is it possible that ten minutes ago you were shredding that wall with the axe, and now you're the voice of calm in my storm."

"I don't know."

I laughed. "You really are perfect, aren't you?" I put my hand over her mouth. "Don't say anything. Just give me this." She kissed my palm. "*You* are some kind of superhero when it comes to kissing my fears away."

She turned her head. "I love you. I just want you to be happy. I want all of this to work, and if I get to kiss you in the middle of everything, I don't know how it gets better than that."

"Neither do I."

"So, shut up, kiss me, and trust the learning process."

"Yes, ma'am." I saluted her, planting a kiss on her lips.

"The next few times we set up the altar, we can test the athame. What about the wrist cuff?" she asked.

"That's probably the easiest. Freezes everyone when something strikes it."

Shay picked it up, fitting it around her wrist. "Remember testing this?

"How could I forget." I remembered Shay laying her hand on the table and yelling, *"Hit me."*

And I shook my head and yelled. *"Oh, hell no!"*

"Don't be a chicken." She'd taunted and yelled for me to hit it. At the time, the idea of hitting Shay was more traumatic than the fear of how the demon steel might behave. I had no intention of hitting Shay, ever. Not even to test the object she was wearing.

But she stood from her chair and walked to the stand beside the forge. She took the largest hammer I owned from the rack. Dexter was right beside her, and before I could make a move to stop it, the massive weight slammed against the cuff. I saw the vibration, and the room went silent.

At the time I could tell she was speaking, but I didn't hear a word. I was frozen by some kind of magick, a force we still didn't quite understand. It took a few minutes before I could hear the faint sound of her voice screaming my name.

We decided never to do that again and although she still wore the cuff, the magic inside was still quite a mystery. We noted in our diary that it freezes the unprotected and that we would test it in the future.

"Maybe we should hit it with the axe?" Shay suggested and I thought it was worth a try.

I held up a finger. "Wait, let me cover my ears."

"Dexter!" she yelled for her K-9 companion.

The dog was drawn to the center of the sacred circle in my workshop; the ring formed after Shay's ritual, sealing a gatekeeper demon beneath the concrete. I wondered what the dog felt as he slept. Did he communicate with the ethereal world? Was he cosmically connected to the monster trapped beneath the circle? I wondered if I would ever know the answers. He was beside her in a few seconds, and she clipped his lead to the collar. We didn't know why but the impact of the pounding on the cuff made him wild.

I covered my ears with the muffs, gripping Dexter's lead in my hand.

Shay tightened her grip on the hatchet. With the full force of her upper body, she let loose on the demon metal wrapped around her wrist. Dex went wild, and I watched Shay freeze in anticipation. Her shoulders lifted in a shrug. "Nothing."

I didn't hear her words, but I understood. She held up a finger for me to keep my ears covered. When she gave me the thumbs up, Dexter relaxed to the floor. "No reaction at all?"

"The cuff reacted the same. Is it possible that the axe is just an axe?"

I took it from her hand. "You're the expert. Maybe it'll take some time to figure out."

"Maybe it will."

I picked up the candle holder, swishing the blue flame in front of her. "We've still got our demon shine-light." I walked toward the north wall of the workshop. "Maybe we should visit a few of the locations on the map?"

Shay held up her pencil sketch, a perfect reproduction of the glowing image in front of us. "Do you remember the mark we found in Benton's research?" She walked away as she continued talking. "Maybe we should find out what it is?" Shay held the notebook in the palm of her hand, swiping through the pages. "Here." She tapped the tiny X surrounded by a circle

"Do you think it's the same person who wrote on my wall?" I used the light of our magick candle to illuminate the image in our notes.

"Maybe." Reaching for the candle, she dropped her notebook in my hand. Shay held the light closer to the reproduction of Bannock painted on the wall. "The map isn't to scale, but the buildings are pretty clear. If we start here, at the carriage house, we can use it to orient ourselves and find the rest of these places."

"We can guess that up is north-facing by the representation of that tower."

Shay walked away without a word, returning with a tiny laser pointer. The red beam shot up to the map. "Yep, that's got to be the city building. It's the only one with a tower."

"Let's do this." I grabbed the five-gallon bucket, stacking a step ladder on top. "I'm going to put the flame here so we can stand further away."

Shay took a few steps back, sitting down on the workshop floor. "Oh my goddess, my girlfriend is brilliant."

I huffed my breath across my fingers and rubbed them on my shirt. "She really is." The original artwork in front of us was haunting. Killing in self-defense was justified but slaughtering demons to use for storytelling seemed extreme. Why was the blood source necessary? Who would use the blood of a demon to tell their story? Why would anyone need to hide this information on the carriage house wall?

"If we look at the history of Bannock, what order were the buildings constructed?" She asked as if I knew anything about it.

"Have I ever told you how much I hate the research part of being your girlfriend?" I sat down beside her, resting my chin on her shoulder.

"Nope, not until just now."

"Damn, I guess I was keeping that in my brain," I whispered in her ear.

She turned her head to look at me. "Have you registered for your library card yet?" Shay asked as she pushed up from the floor.

"You're kidding, right?"

Her laugh made it very clear that she was serious. "I want to run over and grab a few books about Bannock from the library and maybe some architectural drawings from the archives." She held out her hand, pulling me up from the ground.

"I've got a project idea. Why don't you get the books, and I'll make a little mess while you're gone?"

"You're going to work without me?"

"It was going to happen sooner or later." I kissed her. "Go get what you need, and I'll be right here when you get back."

"I'll only be gone for a few." She pulled her hair into a ponytail. "I love you."

When Shay said 'a few,' it meant hours, not minutes. She was aware of almost everything but time. As I set to work at the forge, I was beginning to understand that the workshop's wall was information central, and my project idea would make life a little easier. I opened the gas valve, sparked the igniter, and filled the forge with flames. The perfect distraction I needed was a hammer to hot metal to offset the piles of unknown research ahead of me.

As predicted, I had a few hours, and I was just finishing the final touches on my project. I was torching the edges so the hot wax would seal the metal stand. I'd turned the half-inch round steel into a giant lollipop, forge welding a tripod to create a freestanding pedestal for our demon candle holder. Placed in front of the wall, together, they fit perfectly in the room.

Shay was looking at her watch. "You made that while I was gone?"

"You were gone a very long while." I looked at the watch I wasn't wearing.

"That's cute." She dropped her pile of books on the worktable.

"Tell me what you found." I pushed the pile over so I could read the titles. "*Bannock Then and Now*, written by Jacob Kota." I wiped my forehead. "This should be a real page-turner."

"The librarian assured me that this book is full of local stories written by a local historian."

I opened the cover, looking at the date of publication. "Copyright 1958. The book is over sixty years old."

"His foreword, on page three," She thumbed to it. "He discusses how writing these stories will keep the founding families from abandoning the city."

I turned to the back of the book. "You're the only person to check this out, ever." The card was a shade of yellow I'd only seen in framed documents at a museum. "You think the author is still around?"

"The librarian wasn't very helpful with an answer to that question. I think we might look for him, though. He's a funny guy."

From the outside, the book looked to be about 150 pages. "How much did you read?"

"I skimmed the entire thing."

"Skimmed?" I shook my head. Her vague description was telling. "You read the whole thing, didn't you?"

She shrugged it off. "It's a weird memory thing. I see the page all at once, and it's just there. I had no idea it was unique until the academy."

"Let me guess. Everyone wanted to be your study partner."

"Hell no, I didn't let a single person know."

I was surprised by her confession. "Really?"

"It would have been terrible." Shay started making notes of her own. "We have to memorize so much material. Do you have any idea how thick the state statues book is?"

I had no idea what the state statutes book was, but it must have been impressive. Her comment made me wonder about her life as a police officer. "Can I just ask you a question?"

She stopped writing, looking up from her paper. "Sure."

"Are you happy as a cop?" She started to answer, but I amended my question. "I mean, a regular cop minus the magick and demons?"

She dropped her pencil to the table. "I can't separate them because it's been a very long time since they have been uniquely separate experiences. I've been a witch since the day you held me in Mama's field, and I've been a police officer since the moment I stepped through the academy door."

"And you're happy?"

She walked away, stopping to look up at the blue flame wall. "Before they read your name at the city meeting, I was content. Bannock isn't much of a town for human violence and criminal activity. The townspeople made me feel welcome to stay here and live a good life." I could see that my innocent curiosity sparked something else. "I was comfortable." Shay reached behind her head, pulling her hair from the elastic tie. She looked at the palm of her hand, staring at her scars. "When I heard your name, something changed." I kept my distance, respecting the space she'd made between us. "All I wanted was to see you again, and I hoped . . ." she hesitated, "I hoped that we could be friends."

"Did you hope for more?"

She shook her head, walking back to the research. "I didn't even know if you were a lesbian."

"I'm not."

Her eyes went wide. "What?" She smiled, shaking her head when realization hit. "I didn't know if you were into women."

"Bisexuality leaves all the doors open." I winked at her.

"Left them." She bumped my hip with her own. "Past tense."

"Past tense, yes, but always a bisexual." I continued reading the history of my new hometown. "So, you are happy now?"

Her arm came around to rest on my hip. "I am, more than I thought possible."

The silence that followed was a reminder of how comfortable Shay and I were together. There was no competition, just two people filling in the gaps. She flipped the pages back and forth, making notes. I tried to put the buildings in order by their construction dates in the early and mid-1800s. Our current city map was more detailed than the mining town scribbles in Mr. Kota's book, but one spot on the map matched Shay's drawing from the carriage house wall.

"Here it is again." I pointed to the circle that resembled my maker's mark. "It looks like this was the…" I squinted to read the title.

Shay leaned in closer. "Mill, it was the mill."

"Not far from the mine."

"It would make sense. That's where the original blacksmith would have been. It's closer to the action."

"This probably is a maker's mark." Shay pulled her hair away from her face. "Want to go on an adventure?"

"Hell yes, I do."

It was close to sunset on a very long day, and I wondered how much we would accomplish after dark. Shay looked at her watch. "What if we have some dinner and make a plan to explore the mill tomorrow?"

"You're on seven to three for work?" I asked

"I am."

"You think you can wait that long?"

"I can if you can." She bumped my shoulder.

I walked away from the worktable, climbing the stairs to the second-floor apartment. If you looked at my original restoration ideas, the demolition and reconstruction were complete. Meeting Shay and loving a demon hunting witch required me to make adjustments to the sketches.

Shay foraged through the refrigerator, juggling items that would make grilled cheese and ham. I was already setting the table.

"Do you think we will find this Kota guy?" I asked, filling Dexter's bowl with food.

The buttered slices of bread sizzled as Shay dropped them in the hot pan. "I've been here almost ten years, and the name doesn't ring a bell."

"It's a dead-end before we've started?" I patted Dexter's shoulder as he came in for a drink.

Shay turned around and waved her spatula at me. "The first rule of investigating, don't answer a question until you've asked it." She turned back to the stove.

"The first rule of dating me, don't be a smartass unless you want to get carried off to bed and kissed into exhaustion."

Shay stopped cooking and clicked the burner off on the stove. She didn't turn around. Her hands pressed against the cooktop. "Are you some kind of Neandertal?" I had no way of preparing for what came next, but when she turned to look at me, there was nowhere to run.

I balled my hands into fists and pretended to bang my chest. My heart was pounding with excitement and a tiny touch of fear. The woman standing in front of me was a force; her red hair, wild around her face, matched the fire in her soul: her emerald eyes, sleek and feral radiating uninhibited desire. I swallowed hard with anticipation, staring down at her hands, excited to feel her talented fingers caress my skin. As a lover, I was her only, but the way she ravaged me, with every part of herself, made me hungry for more.

I didn't run or make a move to avoid her advances. I wanted her with the same level of passion. She took three purposeful steps before wrapping her arms beneath my own. My legs came up as she pushed us both against the kitchen wall. Being loved by this woman might just cost me everything.

~~~~~~~~~~

I felt her kiss against my lips, heard a whispered, "I love you, see you later," and that's all I remember until the buzz of my cell phone woke me. The bedsheet twisted around my hips, and I rolled onto the loose knot in my hair. The woman wrecked me, and I was better for it. I answered the phone. "Lo?"

"Are you still in bed?" Shay was a machine.

"I absolutely am."

I could hear the sound of a car in the background. "If I didn't love you so damn much, I'd hate you right now."

I wriggled my fingers to comb through the tangles in my hair. "Did you call me to wake me up or harass me for sleeping through your exit this morning?"

"I called you to share some info I found, but maybe I should just come over and see you."

"You never have to ask." I didn't plan to leave my bed until after twelve o'clock. In my defense, I didn't have to punch a clock, like Shay. Until falling in love, I didn't answer to anyone for the way I lived my life. Maybe I was a bit laid-back, but it was hard work keeping up with officer and superhero, Shay Pierce. I should have known she was coming before her body walked through the bedroom door. The bedsheet was still around my hips, and my body positioned as Shay had left me, but my view was better. She threw her cell phone on the edge of the bed, crawling up my legs, kissing her way up my body until her lips found my own. Experienced or not, Shay listened, and heard, and touched me without ever laying a finger against my skin.

"Hello, love." I could feel the flex of her arms against my own as she hovered over me.

"Hello back." She tried to lean away, but I grabbed the collar of her shirt. "Where do you think you're going?"

"Nowhere, now." She could have held herself in that position for hours, but I kissed her and let her go.

"Sit." I pushed myself back against the head of the bed. "Talk."

"So bossy." Her body armor shifted against her duty belt, and I watched as she pulled it away from her torso. "Would you like to know what I found out about your favorite author?"

"My who?" I said, confused. In my defense, I was half awake and hadn't touched a sip of coffee.

"Jacob Kota. The best-selling author of *Bannock, Then and Now*." The smirk on her face was adorable.

"Oh, please share." I patted the bed beside me.

Shay pointed to the empty spot. "If you think I'm lying in this bed wearing my uniform, you're out of your mind, woman."

"You were already here."

"You snooze, you lose." She sat on the chair by the door. The radio on her shoulder crackled with noise.

"You have to go?"

"Not at the moment."

I threw my legs over the edge of the bed, taking my time to find a shirt and pair of shorts. Shay waited, not shy about watching my every move. "You going to tell me what you know about my favorite author?"

"Whenever you've finished making my heart rate go wild." She shook her head, clearing her thoughts. "I did a quick internet search, and it looks like he died a few years ago."

"Oh, that's kinda sad. I'd hoped to meet him."

"It is." She unfolded the printed page from her notebook. "He was kicked by a horse."

"You're kidding, right?" I read through the article. "He was alone." I looked up at her. "This story is so tragic."

"I pulled the police report. A witness found Jacob in the barn days after his death. The coroner was his friend, had to identify the body."

"That's horrible." I handed the page back to her, sitting down on the edge of the bed. While Shay had been dressed and ready for hours, I still wasn't prepared to face the day.

Shay stood beside me. "It is."

I laced my fingers in the loop of her duty belt, pulling her into my body. "Are we still going on an adventure to the mill?"

"I'll be here right after work." She leaned in to kiss me. "I'm looking forward to it."

"Are you leaving?" I held her closer.

"I have to, love." She kissed me one more time.

I fell against the bed, crawling back under the covers. "I'll see you later."

"You will." She looked back over her shoulder. "Oh, and if you feel the need to eat, there's something in the fridge for you."

Those were the last words I remembered before falling back to sleep.

CHAPTER III

History

I slept for most of the morning without moving an inch. I couldn't recall the last time slumber brought such rest, and I would have stayed longer if I didn't need to get ready for my tour of the mill. I tumbled off the mattress and did a terrible job making the bed. I filled the oversized claw-foot tub and soaked longer than necessary, reaping every bit of the reward from installing the vintage treasure. After, watery tip-toe footprints trailed to my closet, pooling to rest beneath me. I didn't know what to wear for our adventure, so I settled on something simple, jeans and a t-shirt.

I wasn't paying much attention to the time as I walked into the kitchen, noticing the pan on the stove and the dishes drying in the rack. I opened the refrigerator door to find a grilled cheese sandwich with a note on top. "Eat. You're going to need the energy," was written in pencil with a tiny smiling heart where her name might have been. Shay paid attention, not just on the job. She listened to the details of me, of who I was, and she always made me feel like nothing else mattered.

I warmed the sandwich in the pan, not bothering to sit before taking a bite. I wanted to look at Jacob Kota's telling of my new hometown's history, so I sat at the worktable eating and reading. I was downloading old photos referenced in the book onto my phone when Shay walked into the shop. Her presence in uniform was never disappointing.

I heard the Velcro, turning around to see her down on one knee, removing the tiny vest from Dexter. I could tell by the look on her face that she was setting me up. "I'm glad to see you made it out of bed."

"I figured I'd catch up on my favorite author." I ran my hand through my hair, noticing it still wasn't quite dry.

"He's funny, right?" She pointed at the book I was holding.

"Hilarious." I didn't read the same level of humor, but her enthusiasm was adorable.

Shay walked away, climbing the stairs to the apartment. I was quick to follow. She hooked the K-9 vest on the wall before going to our bedroom to take off her gear. "So, I got a call from Benton after I left." She said, unbuttoning her shirt.

"How is she?"

Shay draped her uniform over a double-wide hanger. "About the same, but she wanted to know if we found anything else." I wasn't shy about how much I enjoyed watching my girlfriend undress. "I updated Benton about the map and about our plan to head out to the mill."

"Do you think that was a good idea?"

"I had to get some answers, and I needed her expertise."
Shay looped her vest on the hook, sitting down to take off her
boots. "She said we should be careful walking through the old
building. No one uses it anymore."

"Be careful in a rundown building? That seems like an
obvious precaution." I leaned against the door, watching the
pants slide down Shay's legs. I wasn't thinking about anything
else after her foot slipped through.

"You might want to put on long sleeves." I heard her
making words, but they were slow to translate as the shirt came
over Shay's head. It didn't matter that she was naked beside me
every night. Maybe it was that our relationship was new or that
she was more than I'd dreamed, but I couldn't imagine a single
day going by without wanting her this way.

My eyes zeroed in on a red patch under her arm. "Babe, this
looks so chafed." The scar appeared more irritated than usual.
I reached over, touching the skin.

Without thinking, she pulled away. "It's fine."

I walked into the bathroom, returning with a small
container of salve. Her reaction wasn't personal. I understood
her trauma. Shay was attacked by hands she trusted, so she hid
from human touch. One day she would know that she didn't
need to hide from me. I wasn't letting go without giving Shay
the care she needed. "This is a home remedy." I waved the open
container under her nose.

"Lavender?" She guessed.

"Among other things." I dipped my finger in the jar. "Lift
your arm, please." Her hand raised over her head, draping
across the back of her neck. "Very good. Even superheroes need
to be careful." I dabbed the salve across her scar.

"That's cold." Her body shifted away as she let out a quick hiss. "You know I've been doing okay for over ten years."

"Well, you have *me* now." I huffed against my fingertips, warming the icy salve. I massaged the skin around the old wound. Without thinking, my palm rested against her abs, and her body relaxed into my touch.

"Lucky me."

"Damn straight, lucky you." I stood, planting a kiss on her lips.

She reached around my back, holding me in her arms. "Did you discover anything new from Jacob's book?" she asked.

I tossed the tiny jar of salve on the end of the bed. "Nothing new, really, but if you consider this guy funny, I think we need to sort out your sense of humor."

She laughed. "Are you ready to have some fun?"

"I'm so excited; I can't stand it."

She rubbed her hands together. "That's perfect. I've got a great plan."

"Does it include pants and a shirt?"

She pushed me away. "It does." I watched her pull on a pair of jeans, a cotton T, and an old flannel. It was more than fashion that made her a superhero. She laced her boots and pulled up her pant leg to slip the punch dagger into the gently worn leather. She bumped me with her hip as she passed. I closed my eyes. This woman knew exactly what she did to me. I could imagine every curve hidden beneath her clothes, relive each tender swell, and still, I thought I could slaughter demons with her with my bare hands. Everything about this woman tilted my world.

I'd made a brief list of things I thought we should take, but Shay was already dropping papers and notes into a backpack.

She tossed in a box and a small leather wrap of 'magick essentials;' that's what she called them. With my limited knowledge, I could only guess what they might be.

She pulled her hair back into a ponytail. "The mill is a few blocks away. Walk or drive?"

"Hon, it's Bannock. Everything is a few blocks away."

"True . . . walking it is." She grabbed the leash from the table. "Dexter could use the exercise."

I took the candle holder from the stand, handing it to her. I held her wrist long enough to slide the cuff around it. "Take care of this, please." With the magick essentials, daggers, candle holder, and bracelet, it felt like we were gearing up for a battle.

"Throw the candle in the backpack, and I'll grab the taser and my baton."

"Are you expecting trouble?" I hesitated to ask.

"This is me being me."

"Trouble?" I persisted.

"You never let up, do you?"

I took a slow, deep breath. "I'm new to this demon thing."

Shay whipped the backpack on her shoulders. "I won't forget how new you are, not for a single minute. I promise."

There was no doubt that Shay would put herself between my safety and her own. That was true to the person she was, not only because she loved me. Dexter was excited to go out the door, unaware of a destination. He just wanted to run.

"Are we in a hurry?" She asked. "Maybe we should go by the house and let Dex loose." It was a statement more than a question, but I didn't want to put our exploration off any longer.

"There's not much traffic after Center Street. Maybe we can just take him off his leash?"

She thought for a moment. "He'll be a mess, but the fields on Willow will tire him out."

That was our plan, and Dexter loved it. The grass was tall enough to lose sight of Dex, but the massive dog was bounding over the waving sweet grasses like a puppy. As he darted between us and the field, I could see his shaggy black and brown fur covered in a tangle of dirt and tiny burrs. I wasn't looking forward to brushing him out.

I reached to hold her hand. "This is kinda like a date."

She looked down at our tangled fingers. "If you're into demon-hunting, it is exactly a date."

I kissed the scar on the back of her hand. "So, what's the plan?" Shay held up her notebook, showing me a blank page. "That's not much of a plan. You said you had a great one."

"I figure we go in and walk around. Maybe take some pictures and use the candle to check for runes. That's all I've got, aside from the warning Benton gave us."

"That sounds like a plan."

"It's in my head." She laughed. "I just didn't have time to write it down."

Bannock proper was less than a few square miles, and the walk was long enough for us to enjoy the time together. I wasn't sure what I should expect when we reached the mill. It was standing, and that was the only positive thing I could say about it. I held up my phone, comparing the original black and white image of new construction to the run-down building in front of us. I touched the jagged mortar gluing the mismatched stones together. It was stable for a two-hundred-year-old building, but I was still hesitant to enter.

"Do you think we can even open the door?" Standing in front of the rundown structure, I lost my desire to go inside.

She dropped her backpack to the dirt, pulling out a small pry bar. "That's what this is for."

"You're just going to muscle your way in?"

"I'm not sure yet." She wiggled the wedge against the door frame.

"That's comforting." The first-story windows had boards nailed across their frames, but I could fit my hand between and wipe across the rippled glass, giving me a distorted view of the inside.

"Dexter." She called the dog to the front steps. "*Vigilant ad me.*" She whispered the Latin command, asking the dog to keep watch over us. Although I wasn't fluent in the ancient language like Shay, her K-9 was trained to respond to Latin directions. One day I hoped to know more than the dog.

"This is going to be so disgusting." I could see the abandoned grist mill's giant stones and what looked like centuries of spider webs.

"Think, old dirty adventure, hon." Shay pressed against the pry-bar squeaking the boards away from the door frame. I considered helping, but it was more exciting watching her work without breaking a sweat. "Maybe you should light the candle."

"Do you think we'll find demon runes in here?" I asked as I dug into the backpack, pulling the candle holder from the bottom. I struck my dagger across the forged handle, and the blue flame came to life.

"Benton seemed to think we would." She slammed her body against the door, letting loose a spiral of dust and cobwebs.

"She did?"

Shay hit the door once more. It slammed wide against the inside wall as she shouldered it open. "Benton had plenty to say about this building and even more to say about you." She waved her hands, swiping a dangling spider habitat away from her face.

"She did... about me?" I leaned against the doorframe while Shay surveyed the entrance. The first floor looked solid under her feet. The tongue and groove floor had gaps between, shrinking from age, but Shay moved without hesitation as she stepped on the occasional squeaky board. I followed her shoe prints stamped into the years of settled dust.

"Benton seems to think that the marks on the carriage house wall link you to this town. She had a thousand questions, but I'm not sure you have any answers."

"Because I don't have a family history?"

"Mostly, yes, but she doesn't believe in coincidences, and neither do I." Shay came back to take the blue flame candle from my hand.

"Where do we start?" I asked.

She waved the light in front of us and stopped at the foot of the north wall. "Here... we start here." My jaw dropped at the sight of the wall. From floor to ceiling, a spattering of illuminated runes lined the stones in front of us. Shay sat down on the floor, opening her notebook to record everything she could. "Can you hold the flame closer for me? Start in the right corner."

"Why the right?"

"They're written backward." She answered without looking up from the paper.

"How can you tell?" I stretched to my tiptoes, following the edge to get close to the ceiling.

"Years of practice." Her grin gave it away.

"Smartass. No, really. How can you tell?"

"There's directionality in the way they've written the characters." She stood beside me and snugged the notebook to her chest, pointing at the wall. "Look at this one." She lowered the page so I could see what appeared to be half of a letter B. "The peak of this rune is like an arrow, giving a focus to how I should read it. Since it's going to the left, we start on the right."

"Seems simple enough."

"Sure, if you don't read them." She laughed, not at my inexperience but the naivety of my description.

"So, not that simple?"

"This single rune can take on no less than four meanings on its own, but if it's being used as a cipher or hiding a message. It could be a thought, feeling curse, or a blessing."

"That's a lot to put on a single rune."

She sat back down. "Or it could stand for the *TH* sound in a word."

I lowered my arm, forgetting about the flame in my hand. "Seriously?"

"It also represents the thunder god."

"Thor?" I asked.

"That's the one." She looked up from the paper. "Candle, please."

I followed the face of the wall, lighting each rune written in the blood of a demon; this reality didn't escape me. "Why do you think the author used demon blood, and how is it that we magically built a candle holder that could reveal it to us?"

Shay set her pencil and notebook on the floor. "Are you nervous about all of this?" Her attention shifted away from the wall as she directed her focus at me.

I shook my head, setting the candle on the floor. "I'm not nervous, it just feels like all of these random individual things are coming together here, and I don't know why it points to me or this." I turned my wrist over, revealing the tattoo on it. "How is my mark here? How is this possible?"

She traced the symbol on my skin, looking into my eyes. "I don't know... *yet*." Shay pressed both of my hands to her heart. "But I promise I'll do everything I can to figure it out." Her words were sincere, and so was the kiss that followed. My eyes were closed as she stepped away. "Stop distracting me so I can work." She picked up the candle holder and put it into my empty hand.

"*I'm* the distraction?" I pointed at my heart.

She smiled, playing me like a fiddle, pulling her tasseled bow across the strings of my heart. Shay was already writing in the notebook.

I built a makeshift table from an old crate and a stack of papers to hold the candle, which released me to wander around the room. I'd never been inside a grist mill, and I wanted to explore the building. The massive grinding stones were off their pedestal, removed when the mill shut down. I'd read this much in Jacob's history book, but little more explained where all of the pieces had gone. The cylinder where the giant stones once rested looked like an ancient trap, and I felt like a mouse. I looked back at my girlfriend. "Have you ever been in here before?"

"I've never had a reason to, no."

I leaned over the edge. "Hello!" The echo through the grain chute drilled home that this wasn't a playground.

"Please be careful. Don't expect anything to be solid enough to hold your weight."

My feet hit the floor as I stepped away from the giant base. "You say that now?"

"Just before you decide to climb inside the dragon's den." She looked up from her sketch and winked at me.

I blew her a kiss and followed the stairs down to the ground floor. It was dirtier than the first, and I was cautious about where my feet landed. The peaty combination of earth and water infused the walls around me. I tapped my finger against the door of the milling vent, happy it was holding back the river water on the other side. The propeller basin was dry. As much as I wanted to drop down inside, I had no way of climbing out. In working condition, every piece of this mill could crush me without pause. The foundation walls were stone and mortar, solid enough to hold the two stories above. I marveled at the carpentry over my head, noting that massive cobwebs were stringing between the primitive rafters. This mill was the precise level of abandonment you would expect to find in a ghost town.

"Wil." I jumped at the sound of Shay's voice. "Come take a look at this."

I navigated the stairs, more comfortable with their stability after exploring what was beneath them. I dropped to the floor beside Shay, draping my arm around her back and over her hip. "What'd you find?"

She transferred the pages to my lap. "Jacob Kota."

I wanted to pretend that all the scribbling on the pages made sense, but they didn't. "What do you mean?"

"Our favorite Bannock author is, in fact, the original scribe of these runes."

"How's that possible?" I asked as I attempted to calculate his age in my head. "He'd be over a hundred years old."

"One hundred and thirty-six to be exact."

"How's that possible?"

"It's just not." She said.

I watched our blue flame wave across the wall, flashing the runes like a neon sign. The small mining town of Bannock was beginning to reveal some of its secrets. "Read the wall to me."

Shay raised the flame to shoulder height, moving it from segment to segment of the runic scribbles. She paused before reading the first words.

"*Like those who came before, to those who will follow.*" Her voice changed, taking on a serious tone.

"*I charge you this.*

We are the makers, the bearers of the mark.

We are before, and we are after.

We are meant to be until the time of the flame."

I felt heat rise from my hands, traveling to warm my heart. I closed my eyes, letting the sound of her voice and the words spilling from her lips tumble over my body.

"*Charged with creation are they who wield the hammer.*

Charged as a protector are those who emerge from the fight.

I am until you are."

As soon as she said the words, I knew it was a spell. Shay was reciting a sacred incantation, and it was about to knock me off my feet.

So mote it be."

I don't recall anything after hearing her final words. I was already lying on the ground. The first thing I remembered was the pressure on my chest and Dexter licking my forehead and cheeks. Then, it was Shay leaning over, listening to the beat of my heart, her hands shaking my shoulders as I gasped to catch my breath. My eyes struggled to focus but I could see the fear reflected in Shay's face. "Oh hell, sweetheart. Are you okay?"

I rolled to my side, trying to take in a breath of air but instead gulping in the dust of a hundred years. "I'm... I don't know." I gasped, trying to fill my lungs. "What just happened?"

Shay pulled me into her lap, holding us together. "Oh hell, I don't know. I was reading the runes." She paused. "I think I was about to finish, and you must have collapsed. I was on the floor. It felt like something hit me, and when I rolled over, you were just lying there."

My chest burned from shortness of breath, coughing to fill my lungs, unable to say another word.

"Shh, take a second. Don't try to move too fast." Shay held me, unaware of the slow, steady rocking. I coughed against her shoulder, struggling to pull air into my lungs. Eyes closed, she whispered a spell over and over across the top of my head. I felt a rush tickle the hairs of my arms, reminiscent of my first demon encounter. Shay stopped rocking, she felt it too, and with no effort, she lifted us both to our feet. "We need to leave, right now, Wil."

A silent nod was all I could muster as I leaned against her body. She was carrying me pinned against her as I tried to make my feet move. She sat me against the wall just outside the door of the mill. "I'll be right back. I can't leave our gear behind."

I had no way to measure time or to know just how long I was sitting outside the mill building, but I saw things I couldn't explain. The first vision was a tiny flying creature that I thought was a massive dragonfly. It was not. When it landed on the back of my hand, my jaw dropped. It was, to my disbelief, the first fairy I would ever see. It was plump and flaming yellow, and it was beautiful as its delicate flittering wings caught the sunlight.

Maybe it was there as a warning. I'm not sure. Dexter laid beside me, mindful of Shay's call to be my protector. When I reached to pat his head, I felt bony horns where his ears should be. I shook my head, trying to clear the foggy thought. Was Dexter a tiny dragon? Now I knew I was hallucinating.

"Dex?" His nose rested in my lap, snorting out a fluffy puff of smoke. I followed the trail up to the next apparition, a beast of a giant, but I'm sure it wasn't *a giant*. I closed my eyes, trying to wish it all away. When I opened them again, a vast face was peering into my own. I reached for the dagger of doom, and the creature turned as if my miniature blade would cause it injury. I closed my eyes, hoping that the unexplainable supernatural beings would stop their introductory parade.

Shay was shaking me again. "Wil!" I was afraid to open my eyes. "Babe, you've got to stand up."

"I'm not sure that I can." I was having a hard time raising my hand.

"Dexter, *auferetur.*"

I felt myself rising off the ground. I was half sure Shay was carrying me, but even her familiar touch didn't seem real. I sensed my body resting in the tall grass, and Shay's ear pressed over the center of my chest. When I finally opened my eyes, the sky was almost dark. Shay hovered above me, one hand on the earth and the other on the center of my chest. She was grounding me, us, just like I'd taught her when we were teenagers. I tried not to think why. "Shay?"

Her eyes shot open, looking down at my face. Tears streaked her cheeks as I read the terror in her stare. "Wildwood, oh goddess. I thought you were gone."

I tried to sit up as her arms came across me. "What's going on?"

"I don't really understand." She said as I relaxed against her body. "It was a spell. A damn powerful spell."

I wrapped my arms around her waist, feeling her soaked shirt. "Why are you wet?" I took my first glance at our surroundings, realizing she'd enveloped us in a makeshift altar. The melted candle had burned enough to tell me a lot of time had passed.

"We can talk about that later." She started collecting all of the tools from the ground. "You've been out for almost an hour." She handed me a bottle from her bag. "Drink this."

I took a few sips. "I don't understand."

"There's too much to put together." She threw the backpack over her shoulder. "Do you think you can walk?"

I nodded. I took a sip from the bottle. "What is this?" I could see tiny flakes floating inside the clear glass container.

"It's basically moon water. It's something like a recovery drink." She tipped the bottle to my lips and encouraged me to finish before helping me to my feet. "Okay, love. We have to get out of here."

I felt unsteady, but she was there beside me. It was the slowest walk we'd ever made together, mostly because I needed to sit every few minutes. Dexter zippered around us, guarding every angle. Until this moment, I'd never seen him in advanced protection mode, and he looked utterly feral. I expected her to take us to the carriage house, but we ended up at her bright orange front door.

She carried me inside and into the shower. She stripped us out of our clothes, and I relaxed as the heat of the pulsing water pelted my skin. I was beginning to feel a sensation in my body, something more than the anxiousness of fear. My eyelids felt heavy, and I fell against Shay for support. I lost control, surrendering to the constant, unwavering safety of her presence.

My next waking thought was the weight of a stone over my heart. I felt the cold fabric of a bedsheet draped across my skin and smelled the scent of burning herbs. I was in Shay's bed. It was nighttime, but the shadows of blue and yellow flame lit the room. I felt her hand come to my chest, and she jumped when I reached to touch her.

"Wil." The sigh was loud, and the release of fear was palpable.

"Shay." My voice was dry and scratchy. I hardly recognized it as my own. I tried to sit up as the chunk of crystal rolled onto my abdomen. My girlfriend sat covered in notes and books, and I felt them smash against my body as she pulled me in for a hug.

"Tell me you're alright." She said.

"I'm not sure what I am at the moment." I choked through the smash of her shirted breasts against my face. I let her wrap around me, feeling myself return to what was real. "Don't say anything. I'm pretty sure I'm not ready to know what happened in the mill."

"I don't think I could give you an answer that doesn't scare the crap out of me." She confessed.

I rolled over, looking at the pile of notes. "What is all of this?"

"I was trying to figure out what happened to you."

"And?"

"That innocent writing on the wall at the mill..." She hesitated before holding up a piece of paper. "It was a spell. Someone left us a spell, and if I read this right, you and I just received one hell of an ethereal present."

I held up my hand. "Wait. Stop. I need a clear head before you try to put anything else into it." I stretched to sit, throwing my legs over the side of the bed. The dog was at my knees. "Dexter." His furry eyes popped up to look at me. "Are you a dragon?"

The room fell silent. "What did you say?" Shay asked

I closed my eyes, trying to block out the memory. "It's nothing. I just thought I saw your dog breathe smoke."

Shay climbed across the bed and stretched over to look at her K-9. "You think he's a what now?"

"I'm woozy. You're going to laugh at me."

She dropped down on the floor. "I promise I won't laugh, sweetheart. What did you see?"

I rubbed my face, trying to shake the fogginess from my head. "When I was outside, at the mill. I think I saw a fairy, and a giant and Dexter had horns, and he didn't breathe fire, but smoke came out of his nose."

"At the mill?"

"I think so." I scratched the sides of my head, pulling my black hair away from my face. It was still damp, so at least I knew the memory of a shower was real. "I'm having a hard time with reality at the moment."

"I don't think that you are." She walked around the bed, picking up a notebook from her pile of papers. "Turn to page eleven."

I took Reggie's book in my hand and felt something very different as I thumbed through it. The empty spaces, so curiously void, were now magically filled with tiny characters, diagrams, and notations. "Where did you find this?"

She sat down on the bed. "It came in the box of notes from the bar. It's from the day after the attack."

"We went over all of that stuff," I said. "I know my memory isn't as good as yours, but I didn't see any of this."

"Look at page eleven."

I couldn't read as fast as Shay, but I skimmed over each word. "Reggie, did this?"

"She was aware of everything."

I looked over at my girlfriend. "Did you know?"

She was shaking her head as she stood. "I had no idea."

I held the pages up for Shay to take. "How could she send us there?"

Shay threw the book across the room, the loose pages scattering off in every direction. "I don't know. I need to see the rest of her files, but they're at the carriage house." Shay was standing in front of me, half-dressed, her red hair untamed around her face, her eyes wild with rage.

"Not like this," I said as I held my hand out to her.

Shay's fingers touched my own. "Benton knew about you all along."

I led her into my arms. "She knew about us, the Magick and the Maker, too."

"She used us." Shay kicked the paperwork off the bed onto the floor.

"Maybe we shouldn't jump to conclusions."

"I don't think we need to jump, Wil. I think we've already been pushed." That was the last thing she said before resting her head against my chest. Shay was my protector. She'd carried me away from danger, just as she'd promised. What she didn't know was that the threat was the direct result of the person she trusted as a mentor and confidant. Tomorrow we'd get answers even if we had to shake them out of Regina Benton.

CHAPTER IV

Betrayal

I loved Shay's bed almost as much as I loved her. It was like sleeping on a cloud and her arms around my body created the perfect cocoon. I was so content, I almost forgot about the world we'd just discovered. I slept without dreaming, which I thought was comforting, considering that my last hours awake felt like a crazy nightmare.

"How do you feel?" Her voice was a whisper across the skin of my neck.

I pulled her closer against my backside. "Rested, I guess."

"That's good."

"Did you sleep at all?" I already knew the answer, but I asked anyway.

"Not really."

I rolled over. Looking into Shay's eyes, I could see the truth. "Not really at all, hmm?" I touched her temple and pushed the hair away from her eyes.

"I feel like my world is falling apart."

"I can understand that." I heard the alarm clock buzzing its first alert. "Are you off today?"

"Fortunately, yes." She flipped her hand over, slapping the clock.

I pulled her against my chest. "Good, come here and sleep. Just for a few minutes." She rolled away, turning off the alerts on her watch and the side table alarm. I expected her to get out of bed, but she didn't. Instead, she laid down, curling into my shoulder. Shay let me care for her, and although she didn't sleep, she rested in my arms, and that would have to be enough.

"I didn't know, Wildwood." Her confession sliced through the silence.

"I believe you, Shay. You don't have to feel responsible for this."

"But I do." Her fingers rolled the hem of my t-shirt. "I was at the meeting. I told them to choose you. I'm the reason you're here."

"Are you sure about that?" I whispered across the top of her head.

Her hand stopped moving, pressing against my hip just enough to look me in the eye. "What do you mean?"

"Maybe, just maybe, bringing us back together was the plan all along."

Her eyes closed. "They used me to get to you?" The words were so soft I struggled to hear them.

"It worked, didn't it?"

"Yes." Shay rolled away, sitting up to leave the bed. "When did my life stop being my own?"

I didn't have an answer to her question. "Maybe we should go take a look at the rest of Benton's research?"

"Do you think it goes all the way back to these?" She turned around, holding her scarred hands out in front of her body. I watched Shay, wrinkling her forehead, wondering about the thoughts rolling through her mind. "How could they know? Was Mama in on it too?"

I didn't have a clue where our history began. Was abandonment part of the rite of passage? Did all of our suffering bring us to this moment? "Shay, I don't have the answers."

"Have any of our choices ever been our own?"

"Babe." I grabbed both of her hands, squeezing them to get her attention. "Stop." I looked into her eyes, searching for what was impossible to give.

"And loving you?" she asked.

I dropped her hands. "No one could have changed my love for you." I held the side of her face, never taking my eyes from hers. "Your blood is a part of me." I showed her the faded scar across my palm. "We made that choice. No one else."

Her forehead dropped against my own, surrendering, if just for a moment. "You're the only person in the world I can trust."

"And that's always going to be true." I watched as the vulnerable haze in her eyes transformed into fury.

She pushed off the bed. "I need to find some answers." She collected the paperwork piled up near our feet.

"Let me feed you first."

"There's nothing in my refrigerator." Her hands didn't stop moving as the papers fell into the backpack beside the nightstand. Her t-shirt and pants slipped over her body with the efficiency of a firefighter called to action. My girl was focused. "Dex."

I heard the tap of paws before I saw his furry face, closing my eyes to the memory of his dragon impression. "Did I tell you about the things I saw?"

Shay nodded. "You did, and I'm not underplaying any of it. We know fairies exist because we made the athame from them and I've seen them once or twice. We know demons exist, so why not giants?"

I pushed my head through the top of my shirt. "And dragons?"

She smiled at me. "Dexter is not a dragon, my love." She clipped the lead to his collar.

"Dexter is a dragon."

"It's not possible." She pecked my cheek with a kiss, and she was on the move.

I followed them out the door and down the street. Shay could tell I was watching the K-9's every move. If I saw a fairy and saw a giant, why would her partner's metamorphosis be any different? "Do you think that the spell transformed him, too?" I skipped to catch up with them.

She looked down at the panting animal. "What?"

"Well, Reggie led us to the mill so we would reveal that spell. We found it, and because I'm the Maker and you're the Magick woman, we are bound to some kind of prophecy? What if Dexter is, I don't know, a sort of familiar?"

She stopped walking, frozen in place on the sidewalk. At that very moment, I wished that I could see inside her brilliant mind, but that was not a power I possessed.

"Damn." Dexter looked up at her.

"You think I'm right?" I couldn't hide my smile.

She held her hand to me. "I think I don't know what to think. Not right now."

We were less than a block from the carriage house, and I knew that once we arrived, I would lose her to the piles of research on our kitchen table. "Will you make me a promise?" I asked as I tugged her arm, pulling her closer to me.

"What kind of promise?"

"That I won't lose you because of this?" I couldn't read her body language or guess what was circling inside her. She didn't say a single word as the dog lead dropped to the ground. She kissed me like it was our first, and nothing about it felt like the last. She didn't care where we were or who saw us. Without a single word, she made it clear that I wasn't going to lose her. She couldn't have said it better.

Her forehead rested against my own. "I'm here, with you." Her hands gripped my bicep. "When you feel like I'm not, remind me."

That was our promise, one to the other, to be partners in a relationship that went beyond any magick. We both turned toward the road as Dexter went wild with barking.

Officer Dani Forrest pulled up in the police cruiser. "Hey, Pierce." She yelled through the passenger side window. "We need to talk."

Shay stepped off the sidewalk, walking around to the driver's side. I couldn't hear the conversation, but I could tell by Shay's finger grip on the vehicle's roof that the information wasn't positive. She double tapped the top of Dani's shoulder seconds before the car pulled away.

Shay was crying.

Whatever Dani said shifted her solid ground. She picked up Dexter's lead, and without a word, Shay continued walking. I waited. It was almost ten seconds before I stopped in front of her. "Remember five minutes ago when you said I wouldn't lose you?" She didn't say a word. I grabbed her chin, pivoting her to look at me. "What did Dani say to you?"

The fire in her green eyes stared right through me. "She said that Regina Benton slipped into a coma last night. That after seventy minutes on life support, her heart stopped beating."

"Reggie's dead?"

"And so are all of the answers." I would never know if Shay's tears were for the loss of a mentor or the betrayal of a friend. I didn't react or attempt to ease the pain. Shay was learning to let me in, and I had to give her the chance to do it. I opened the door of the carriage house, pushing into the darkness of the shuttered space. It felt cold, emptier somehow. Dexter was off his leash and back to his favorite spot, the sacred circle on my workshop floor.

"Where do you want to start, Shay?"

"I guess I should go through Benton's paperwork." She dropped the backpack on the floor by the table. "What I want to do more than anything is punch her in the face, and then I realize that wishing for that makes me a horrible person."

I turned on the shop lights over the forge. "No, it doesn't. It makes you human, and Reggie hurt you. You have every right to feel the way that you do." I walked around the forge; a space that should have felt familiar but was now foreign to me.

Shay noticed my hesitation around the anvil. "What's wrong, Wil?"

"What makes you think something's wrong?"

The creases around her eyes deepened as she smiled, "I know you."

I couldn't prevent the silly smile that tightened the cheeks of my face. Of course, Shay knew me, and of course, she would notice my hesitation in a space that I loved. "I'm looking at the anvil, at the floor." I bent down, grabbing a handful of scale from the ground. "There's a blue powder mixed in with this." I sifted through with my finger, separating the tiny blue flakes from the dark grey.

"Grab another handful and bring it over here." She tapped the top of the worktable before running up the stairs. She returned a few seconds later with a small metal box.

"What is that?"

She opened the battered container, removing a plastic frame with five tiny built-in test tubes, each containing a shaded graph for color comparison. "Remember when I tested the ground for salt?"

How could I forget the memory of my introduction to her world of magick? "I remember. As if I could forget any of that."

"This kit tests for the presence of magical beings and demons." She filled each tube with a squirt of fluid from a rainbow of small rubber bottles. Shay used a tiny spoon to scoop pieces of the scale from my palm.

"It looks like you use it a lot?"

"This kit came from Benton." The mention of her name made her pause. "She gave it to me when she retired."

"I'm sorry, love." I emptied the flakes from my palm on the table. "We can wait to do this if you need time to see her family. Ask them questions?"

"I think I have enough unanswered questions to work on." She looked up at me. "Besides, there's no one to see right now."

She shook her head, clearing the distractions. "I'll be okay." Shay sprinkled anvil dust into each tiny tube, snapping a cap on top until she filled all five. She gave it a few quick shakes and set it back on the table.

"Now what?" I leaned closer to look.

"We wait."

I stood behind her, whispering in her ear. "For what?"

She unfolded the card inside the box and leaned against me. "This is a chart of known demon biochemistry." She folded the page, pressing it to her chest. "Technically, you shouldn't even be seeing this."

I laughed, pulling her tighter against my body. "Really?"

"The existence of demons in Bannock has always been written off as a ghost experience. Word gets out, remember?"

I drew an imaginary X over her chest. "Cross our hearts. I'll never tell a soul what you're about to show me."

"You joke, but this is serious shit."

"Trust me. I get the seriousness." I pointed to the test kit on the table. "Explain, please."

"Your anvil dust is something I didn't think to explore. You said forging didn't leave behind demon scale, so I let it go." She picked up the test tubes. "With everything we've experienced in the last 24 hours, I think I know what this means."

"Tell me, please."

She turned to hold the tubes up to the light. Four of the samples changed to a dark shade of very different colors. "Tube one shows signs of a class-one demon. Tube two shows signs of a class-two demon." She shook it a few more times. "Nothing in the class-three, hmm." She turned to see my face. "Did you forge a class-three?"

I shook my head. "I don't think Benton gave me a class-three sample." I took the test tubes from her hand. "Are you telling me that the blue flakes are demon scale?"

Shay walked away, pulling the notebook from her backpack. She thumbed through Reggie's papers. "Damn, Benton." She whispered before running back up to the apartment. I was becoming accustomed to her tendency to disappear mid-sentence. I left Dexter sleeping in his sacred circle. I turned off the lights and walked up to my apartment. I found Shay on the floor of the kitchen, spreading documents everywhere. I watched her fan through volumes of information. I couldn't help but notice the appearance of more notations and previously empty pages now filled with Benton's observations. I picked up the demon tome, thumbing through the latest facts. Was this disappearing ink? Written in blood? "There are notations here." I held up the open page to Shay.

She stepped around her layout on the floor, holding out her hand. "What's it say?"

I ran my finger across the page. "There's something about the anvil dust."

"May I?"

I passed the book to her, and she thumbed through the pages. From front to back, she scanned the new text. "This is impossible."

"What is?" I closed the book in her hands. "You have to narrow it down, please."

"First, I need to sit." She dropped into the kitchen chair. "Do you remember the day that you met Reggie?"

"In the bar, sure. We had burgers. Yes, I remember."

"She was setting me up."

I pointed to Shay. "Setting *you* up?"

"She wrote it all down. According to that." Shay pointed to the book I was holding. "As soon as Benton knew who you were, what you would become . . . She was after the anvil dust you were going to create."

"But I hadn't even met a demon. Forget about the idea of forging one and making scale." I looked at the notes, turning to the page about my gatekeeper. "Benton was a collector?"

"She was so much more than that." Shay took the book from my hand, closing it on the table. "She was me."

"What? What do you mean she was you?"

Shay thumbed through the pages. "Look, Reggie Benton was the last living Magick of Bannock," Shay explained. "The Magick is a guardian, protector of the settlers but most important champion of the Maker."

"Maker? Like me?"

"Yes, the force of all elements sworn to protect this town are also sworn to protect you."

My mouth fell open. What could I say? Shay's arms hit the tabletop just before her head slammed down in defeat. "Sending us to the mill, that was her idea, right?" I asked. I started listing the events leading up to our spell. "And she wanted the two of us to be there together, right?"

Shay confirmed again with a nod.

"Was she trying to help us or hurt us?" I asked.

She rubbed her hands across her face, frustrated to tears. "I don't know."

CHAPTER V

Chaos

The days that followed felt like weeks as we stitched together the history of the Magick, also known as Regina Benton. The Chief of the police department encouraged Shay to take her bereavement time which allowed us to focus on the past. Doing research wasn't my strength, but it grew on me for as much as we had accomplished. Knowledge, in this case, was empowering.

Benton's confidential documents held volumes of secret notations, and we poured over them one by one. The ends were coming together about Regina Benton and her intimate connection to the supernatural world. Every journal read like a user's guide. Every notebook transformed to become a portal to the underworld, a paranormal organization where Benton belonged.

Shay gave up making scribbles and handwritten notations and transferred everything to her computer. It was tedious and frustrating, but the ability to cross-reference was going to make a difference. Time was the barrier. It always felt like we just didn't have enough.

I was sorting through the last folder of sketches. "I need a break." I stood up from the table, coming around behind Shay. Her fingers were fierce against the keys of her keyboard. "Can we take a break?" I asked.

Her hands stopped, but her fingers hovered over the keys. "Yes, I probably should."

Leaning in closer, I noticed the bold side notes. I could see that my girlfriend was drawing some sad conclusions. "You think Benton meant to hurt us?"

"Until I find anything different, I have to believe that she was after the demon dust from your anvil."

"To what end?"

Shay gripped the screen of her laptop and folded it closed. "Let's take Dex for a walk, and I'll explain what I've put together."

The gorgeous German Shepherd had moved from his favorite spot downstairs to the floor beside the kitchen table. "Let's go, Dex," Shay called his name, and his entire body came to attention. I had the leash in my hand, but he ran to Shay. She dropped to one knee and whispered something I couldn't hear.

"Spellcasting?" I asked.

She looked up at me. "Not exactly."

I stood with my hands on my hips. "Okay, give it up. Tell me what you said."

Her cheek raised into a half-smile as she scratched the top of Dexter's head. "I just asked him if he was going to breathe fire." Dex cuddled into her palm, encouraging Shay's attention.

I slapped my hands together. "So, you do believe me."

She pointed to the stack of papers and file folders across the room. "Almost every notebook, file, and cryptic correspondence on that table is unbelievable, but it's also the foundation of my life." She stood up. "I have to have faith in the impossible if I'm going to figure out what's happening to us."

I stepped closer to Shay and kissed her cheek. I lowered myself down in front of her dog and ruffled the fur around his ears. "Who's a fluffy dragon?" His head flopped against my hand.

"Oh my gosh. You're incorrigible." She pushed her knee into my shoulder.

I looked up at my girlfriend. "Aren't you even a little bit excited?"

"Not yet."

"Not yet? Are you kidding me?" I clipped the leash to the loop on his collar. "Your K-9 partner is a freakin' dragon. Dragons are the stuff of dreams."

"Take this slow, love." She walked down the stairs, yelling back over her shoulders. "He's a dog first."

I looked at Dexter. "Come on, dragon."

It was a beautiful day, and we'd missed most of it huddled inside, hovering over the books. The dog led our walk, extending the stretch of his leash to its entire length.

Shay tugged to slow him down. "He's taking us somewhere."

"To his secret cave?" I joked.

"Stop." Her arm came around my waist so she could whisper in my ear. "You might want to restrain your enthusiasm in public. Not everyone can see fairies and giants."

I covered my mouth, speaking through my fingers. "Oh, right."

"It's okay, and I understand the excitement."

It was only a few blocks from the carriage house to Dexter's destination. He stopped when we reached the corner across from the bar. The front door was open, and I could hear the sound of people inside. We hadn't been around anyone since the news about Benton. "Do you want to go in, Shay?"

"Maybe for a few minutes."

I followed her lead and Dexter's. It was evident that showing up was a morale boost for Shay's coworkers and friends inside. It was four o'clock in the afternoon, and many of them were already drinking. Shay dropped the leash in my hand before hugging a very tall, gorgeous woman waiting just inside the door.

Shay pulled away. "Dani, this is Wildwood. Wildwood, meet Officer Dannielle Forrest."

The woman held out a hand. "Nice to meet you. Shay's told me a lot about you."

"Dannielle, you're the collector?" I gave her hand a shake. Her grip was firm as she clasped mine with both hands. There was something in her energy. I couldn't define it, but I knew in an instant that we could be friends.

"That's right, mostly just rocks, though."

Our hands fell away. "Funny, Shay talks about you, mostly when it comes to rocks." I didn't know what else to say. The dog gave a hard tug on the leash, so I let him lead me further inside. Shay stayed at the door, talking to her co-workers.

I avoided the crowded entryway and wandered to the back of the bar. It was easy to tell by their body language and demeanor that most of today's patrons were part of the department or connected somehow. There was a black stripe stretched across the badge hanging on the wall behind the bar. I knew enough to understand it was a symbol of respect to honor retired police officer Regina Benton. I stopped at the rail to order a beer from Diana and sent one down to my girl. Shay blew me a kiss, and I turned around to inspect the rest of the room.

The only other face I recognized was sitting in the corner, drinking what looked like a martini and scrolling through her tablet. I hesitated before crossing the room.

She looked up as if knowing I would approach. "Wildwood Blackstone. I'm surprised to see you in here so soon."

I pulled out a chair and sat across the table from her. "I'm not sure I know what you mean, Assistant Mayor Peters."

She stirred the olive skewered toothpick around in her glass. "Your trip to the mill."

The tiny hairs raised on the back of my neck and her words sent chills over my body. "To the what now?" Playing it cool was not a quality that I possessed.

My flustered reaction amused her. "I think Regina would offer insight if she were here."

I didn't understand what Andrea Peters was suggesting. I didn't know Benton's involvement well enough to respond, but I wouldn't have because I didn't know Andrea's motives at all.

Just when I thought I could hold my own, my superhero arrived. "Are you fishing for information or planning to share some?" Shay's hand rested over my shoulder in the most protective and marginally possessive way.

"Officer Pierce, nice to see you again." She turned off the screen on her tablet and waved an open palm inviting Shay to sit. "Why don't you join us?"

Shay pulled out a chair. "What do you know about Benton, Andrea?"

"Do you have super hearing, officer?" She held the glass to her lips, taking a small sip.

"Don't play games. I heard enough." The tension was palpable as I watched the conversation volley back and forth between them.

Andrea dabbed the corner of her mouth before setting the martini glass on the table. "I was just about to ask Ms. Blackstone what she discovered the other day at the mill."

Shay launched herself across the table, knocking over the assistant mayor's drink and our bottles of beer. Dexter was on his feet, barking at Andrea Peters. "What the hell do you know about what happened to us?" Shay gripped the table, hovering inches from Andrea's face.

"I think you might want to take a step back, Officer Pierce." The crowd in the bar went silent, watching the intense exchange between the two women and the ferocious snarling dog.

Dannielle came up behind us, holding the chair that Shay kicked to the floor. "You okay, Pierce?" Cops had a way of changing the mood in a room with just the tone of their voice.

"What the hell is she doing in here, Dani?" Shay snapped her fingers, and Dexter was at her side as if the entire scene was wiped clean.

"Jeez Pierce, she was at the hospital when Reg died." With a gentle but firm hand to the shoulder, Dani coaxed Shay back to the chair.

Shay turned around to look up. "She was what?"

"It's true," Andrea explained. "Regina called me that afternoon. She told me some things that you might find interesting." Her eyes glanced over Dani, dismissing the unwanted guest. "I'm sure this conversation is private. Would you mind, Officer Forrest?"

Dani looked at my girlfriend. "You good, Pierce?"

Shay tapped the hand with her fist. "I'm good, D."

She turned, with her arms in the air, and walked back to the crowd at the bar. "Nothing to see here, people. Just a tiny misunderstanding. Let's have another round for Reggie!"

"Yes, perhaps another round since mine seems to have made its way to the floor." Andrea wiped the top of the table with her napkin, leaving a streak behind. The tiny paper cloth wasn't thick enough to absorb the mess.

I stood, planning to replace the drinks. Shay held up her hand. "I got it. Give me a second." She turned toward the bar.

Andrea pointed at the martini glass with her eyes. "Dirty." I wasn't surprised that she preferred her martini that way, but I found it amusing she would demand such in the current setting. I watched my girlfriend at the bar how she combed her fingers through her hair before pulling it back into a ponytail. Cop-mode activated. Carrying beers in one hand and the martini in the other, Shay returned to the table where I sat shamelessly anticipating what was coming next.

"Your dirty." Shay slid the drink across the table before handing me a beer. "You're not." Her kiss was deliberate but quick.

"Are we going to continue to play these games, Officer?"

"I don't know, Peters. You're bursting to say something to me. Why don't you just spit it out?"

I touched Shay on the forearm. "Maybe we should just go?" I thought I understood the past lingering between them, but this was something else.

"You know, Officer Pierce, maybe you should listen to your friend and just go."

"Maybe you should tell me why you were at the hospital with Benton?"

Andrea's face flexed with a superior grin. Her motion was slow, deliberate as she picked up her handbag. She was in no hurry as she unzipped it to remove a large, padded envelope. "This is from Regina." She held up a hand before Shay could ask any questions. "I have no idea what's inside." The block-style letters on the front read *Shay Pierce*. "I'm only the messenger."

Shay's finger traced over the letters of her name. "It's her handwriting."

Andrea interrupted. "This file is from me." She pushed a yellowed with age folder across the table.

Shay looked surprised. "What's in it?"

"Read Regina's letter, and then when you're ready, look through this." She tapped the thick folder. "If you take a minute to understand all of the sides, you'll realize we don't have to be enemies, Officer Pierce."

Shay sat frozen, unable to respond to anything she'd just heard.

"Babe." She turned toward the sound of my voice. "Are you okay?"

"Yes, I'm good." She placed Benton's letter on top of the file. "We should go."

There were no goodbyes or handshakes as we walked toward the door, but Dexter resisted leaving the bar. "Come on, buddy." Shay tugged at his leash. It was the first time I'd ever noticed the animal defy her command. Shay reacted and gave Dex permission to work. He led her toward the tiny closet-sized office in the back of the bar. "Where are you taking us?" The light inside was on. "Hello?"

Dexter pushed the door open with his nose and sat in front of the desk. "What'd you got, buddy?" He pawed at the bottom drawer. I pulled the handle, but it didn't open.

"Should we be in here?" I stared at the framed pictures and plaques on the wall. The office was private, and I wasn't comfortable inside.

"Dex thinks we should, and apparently he's on duty, so where he goes, I follow. He's trying to tell me something."

"About the desk?" I asked.

Shay set down the file folder and opened the padded envelope from Benton. "Close the door. I don't want anyone to hear us."

I wasn't sure I should be here, but if anyone had a right to sit in Benton's chair, it was Shay. She tore the envelope open. Benton wrote with single stroke block lettering, perfect form similar to the style taught in the drafting lab at trade school. The letter was too long to read aloud, so Shay scanned through it. As if following directions, she peeled the padded layers apart to reveal a tiny key.

"Why all the mystery?" I asked.

Shay held up the key. "I think Benton was trying to heal herself."

"I don't understand. She never left the hospital after the attack."

"She sent things to the carriage house for her; to help her." she explained.

"Things?" I asked.

"Fairies." Shay passed the letter to me, and I started to read through it. "Don't worry about the details now. You can read them later." She unwrapped the tape from the teeth of the key and slid it into the lock on the desk drawer Dexter was still guarding. Shay had to lift and shake the drawer until it opened. An old leather bag covered the contents, and Shay pushed it back into the gap of the desk.

"Holy shit!" I covered my mouth to silence my voice.

The drawer was stacked full of Benton's stash of demon steel. The pieces on top were the size of an office stapler but weighed twice as much. As she sorted through to the bottom, where the samples were double in size, one round indentation caught my eye. "These are all stamped with the mark of another maker."

"We need to pack all of the bricks. We're not leaving a single piece behind."

"Shay, wait a minute. You have to slow down." I didn't know what to think, and I had no idea what to do.

She didn't stop moving around the room. "I can't." She pulled a leather pack from the back of the drawer. "Benton had a plan."

One by one, she dropped sixteen pieces of tagged demon steel into the bag. All of the pieces together must have weighed more than fifty pounds. She tucked the file folder into the backpack's pouch and folded the letter, sticking it in her front pocket and pitched the pack over her shoulders like it was featherlight.

"Want to tell me about that bag, superhero?"

"Later." She kissed me on the cheek and, without straining, stood to full height. "Is there a scroll of paper in there?" She turned around and pointed to the pocket on the side.

I squeezed the heavy leather. "Feels like it, yes." I unhooked the button to double-check. "Looks like, yep."

"Good." She locked the drawer, dropping the key into her pocket. "Let's go."

Every confrontation inside the bar in the last hour seemed like an improbable gateway into our new magick-filled world. From the details of the letter, Benton knew she was dying. She understood that nothing could stop the poison inside her body. Forcing us together, sending us to the mill was meant to speed up the transformation process.

The truth in all of it was that Shay needed protection and coming into my power as the Maker was essential to her survival. The Maker and the Magick were always a pair. Each day an endless list of questions came with loving Shay. Up until now, it felt like we never uncovered any answers. We knew from the letter that Benton was on our side, and with her last breath, she was trying to guide us.

Surviving my childhood meant lying to myself all of the time. The most significant lie was that I was safe and okay, and tomorrow would be better. It'd been a long time since I chanted that mantra but walking out of the bar triggered my need for that childhood comfort.

Shay reached for my hand, aware of my body's posture and the flight or fight instincts that were seizing my nerves. "I got you. We will be okay."

The only obstacle between us and the exit was Officer Dannielle Forrest. Dexter maneuvered himself in between tables and people, blocking anyone from getting closer.

"You two leaving?"

"I need some time Dani," Shay explained.

Officer Forrest tipped her chin up at the badge behind the bar. "Benton was a good one, Pierce."

"Better than we deserved." Shay waved off her incoming hug. "I'll see you at the station tomorrow."

Dani nodded. "Good to meet you, Wildwood."

I shook her hand. "You too."

Dexter was already out the door and on the sidewalk, pulling us with him. I was beyond curious about the backpack my girlfriend was wearing. Why was it in the drawer? What did Benton want Shay to do? Was she our ally all along? I tugged on the shoulder strap. "The backpack, it's magick, isn't it?"

She turned to look at me. The spark of delight in her eyes and a heart stopping grin on her face said it all. "It is."

"Damn that Regina Benton. She put this together for you, didn't she?" I tucked my hand in my pocket.

"All of it." My girlfriend raised her eyes toward the sky.

"Tell me what the rest of the letter said. I know you read it all."

"She called me kiddo." Shay hesitated, trying to push back her emotions. "I hated it the first time she did it. Kiddo. It made me feel inferior like I was a child. Now I understand that she wanted me to feel like I was part of her family."

"That's tough for us."

"Not anymore." She grabbed my hand. "Even when you and I were apart, you were my family." We walked the last few blocks to the carriage house, releasing Dexter to wander through the workshop. "Watch over us, Dex." He dropped down in the center of the circle.

"Do you think we need to lock up the backpack?" I asked as I followed Shay to the table.

"Nothing's coming in here without our permission." Shay opened the top of the bag, removing each piece of demon metal one at a time. I turned them around, lining up the maker's marks and sorting them by the class number written on each.

I picked up a block, the size of a pound of butter. It weighed five times as much. I turned it over and pointed it at Shay. "What am I supposed to do with these?"

"Benton had some instructions for the two of us." Shay pulled the folded letter out of her pocket, shuffling to the third page. She read it out loud.

"I know this is going to be hard, but there are things you need to know that I wish someone had shared with me. I have to tell you that being partnered with you was not an accident. I knew you were the Magick the first time we met. The scars you wear are proof that you can manage what's to come. When the time is right, you'll see everything as I have.

I've hidden a key between the layers of this package. Use it to open the drawer of my desk and take everything inside. Take EVERYTHING! I left a backpack for you. It's enchanted. It will protect you and Wildwood and help disguise the tools you'll need to continue our work.

The two of you must follow the map on the carriage house wall to the original courthouse's cellar. Everything Wildwood needs will be there, just as I have left this for you. She is the Maker, and the two of you will be a force. When you and I met, I'd just lost my Maker. Protect yours. Together you are in perfect balance. You are a powerful witch and will become so much more in time. I've tried to assemble as many volumes of our history as I could. It's written in the blood of a Sanquis Caeden, a class-three species, almost all but extinct. The Magick and the Maker can read anything written in Sanquis' blood. The scroll in the pocket of the backpack is the history of us. It is the origin of the Magick and the Maker.

No matter what comes, you must trust the Maker with your powers. Whether together or apart, cast a spell of protection over every place you call home, or you will never find rest.

By now, you know that I wrote most of my journals for the two of you. There is a spell I use. It will transform the blood of a Sanquis Caeden into ink. Follow the words, and always use this magick when you write about your demon work. Secure your journals and documents. Secrecy is imperative. Who we are, what we are, it must remain a guarded secret.

I have cared for you like a mother and wish I could be there to watch you come into your power. Only one Maker and Magick can exist in the world.

Don't mourn me, Shay. I have lived an extraordinary life. Now you live yours.

Benton"

Shay had tears in her eyes as she read the last words. "I didn't want to believe that she would hurt me."

"I know, love."

"Trust is never going to be easy." Shay wiped her tears with the back of her hand.

"I know, love." She was in my arms as she should have been when Mama Pierce died. I couldn't comfort her then, but I was here now. I whispered the words I knew she needed to hear. "It's okay to miss her."

I took Shay's hands in mine, leading us up the stairs and into our bedroom. When Shay surrendered to her emotions, I knew she would need to sleep. "Sit down, let me take care of you." Without resisting, I helped unlace her boots and set them next to the uniform stand in the corner. I pulled off her shirt and dropped it in the hamper. She unbuttoned her jeans and kicked them to the floor. I wrapped her in a nightshirt and helped her slide beneath the covers.

"Are you getting in too?" The tone of her voice was a fragile whisper.

The only place I wanted to be was beside her. "I am. Let me feed Dex, and I'll be right back."

"I'm so terrible. I can't believe I–."

"It's okay. Just rest."

I filled Dexter's bowl and carried it down the stairs, leaving it beside the dish of water. My favorite little dragon dog was where I thought he'd be, curled up in the center of the magick circle on my workshop floor. I crawled up beside him, resting against the warm fur of his body. "Hey, Dex." He rolled, pinning us together on the concrete slab. "You ready for some food?" He didn't answer, but I didn't expect that he would. I laid there looking at the workshop wall, combing my fingers through the thick German Shepherd's fur. I must have fallen asleep because the next thing I felt was a warm hand caressing my cheek.

"You look beautiful next to a sleeping dragon." She was wearing a t-shirt and shorts, and her hair hung untamed around her face.

"I didn't mean to fall asleep." My fingers slid along the bare skin of her leg.

She pushed it away. "Your hand is like ice."

"Your dragon isn't as warm as you are."

"I hope not." She reached her hand out to help me from the floor. As soon as all three of us were inside the sacred circle, Dexter's eyes opened wide, and he jumped up. "What is it, Dex?" He barked once as if she could understand him.

We turned simultaneously to see the map of Bannock lit up on the workshop wall. "Well, that's new." I looked for the candle holder, searching for the simple reason our room was turning blue.

"It's upstairs next to the bed," Shay whispered what I was thinking.

"How is this possible?" Ancient writing covered the carriage house walls from floor to ceiling, but there were additional marks this time. "Have you seen any of these before?" I pointed to the wall, usually covered by the sliding door of the office.

Shay stepped closer, and the room went dark. Standing in a shirt barely covering her upper body, she had nothing to use as a weapon, yet still, she moved closer to danger. "What is going on?" She turned on the light switch, blinding us as our eyes adjusted.

"Turn it off, come back." I waved for her to return.

Following my instructions, she tiptoed across the cold floor. "What are you thinking?"

"I can't believe you're *not* thinking." I grabbed her hand and tugged her inside the ring on the floor. The glow from the runes lit the room.

She turned to look at all four walls. "What did we do, Wil?"

"I have no idea, but it's freakin' cool." I held her in my arms. "Do you know what any of it says?"

"Not without some reference. I do see that weird maker's mark and what looks like maybe another."

"A third?" I asked.

Shay walked away again, leaving the ring, turning out the magick light show. "Give me a second." She ran up the stairs. I looked down at Dexter, who wandered off toward the food dish.

"Abandoned." Shay came back a minute later, wearing sweatpants and carrying the blue flame candle. "You just left me."

She set the light on the stand and walked back to the ring. Her arms scooped around my waist. "I'll never leave you, not for very long anyway." She smashed a quick kiss to my cheek.

"He left me too." I pointed at the dog across the room, crunching his food.

Shay ignored my pout and stepped back inside the circle. She handed me the scroll from her pocket. "Unroll that." She called her dog. "Dexter, come here, buddy." He finished crunching his dinner before running back to us. Shay patted his ribs. "Good boy."

The three of us were back inside the circle that was transforming into a sacred space. I wondered, not for the first time if this demon burial marker was something more. The walls of the workshop lit with a dazzling blue glow. "This is the craziest thing, and I've recently seen some shit," I said.

She was laughing. "Babe, roll the scroll open on the floor. Let's see what it says."

Benton left Shay a literal scroll, a seemingly endless stream of yellowed parchment wrapped around what could have been a bone? I dropped it to the floor. "Is that a freakin' bone?"

She sat down, rolling it open across the circle. "Looks like it, yes." She didn't cringe at the thought, making it clear that she had seen more shit than I. "The introduction is in Latin. That's weird."

"It kinda works in our favor, don't you think?" I leaned in against her for a closer look.

"For you and me, yes. But why would the history of the Maker and the Magick be in Latin?" She read the text letting it roll against the side of her hand.

"What's it say?"

"Give me a second. The last time I read a spell out loud, you came home seeing dragons and fairies." She turned to look at me. "It's mostly just the history of the people who came before us."

"Us, us?" I waved my hand between Shay and me. "You and I?"

She let the paper roll back on itself so she could answer. "Nope." She held it up so I could see. The parchment, read horizontally, was divided. "The top is the history of the Magick in Bannock. Well, it goes back before the town was here, but it's my line. And the bottom is the birthright of the Maker. That's you. According to this, the two move together, its synchronicity."

"Are these our family members?" I waved a finger over the letters.

She adjusted the parchment so I could see it. "They are, in spirit, but genetics aren't a factor."

"Being genetically connected would be a big problem for the two of us."

She touched my nose and my chin. It was evident from her skin's pale, freckled tone that a biological connection was a stretch. "Wil, I am about as pale as a human can be. I'm not sure about your ancestors, but I'm certain you and I did not come from the same gene pool." She held her arm next to my own.

"That's comforting." I grabbed her hand. "I don't want to think about a life without you in it." My lips touched hers, gentle at first. She opened her mouth, and my kiss was unapologetic and possessive. Shay's body relaxed, and the scroll fell to the floor.

She pressed her hand to my heart and pushed space between us. Her voice was low and breathy. "Stop distracting me." She brushed her thumb across my lips.

I kissed the tips of her fingers. "I can't help myself."

She stepped back and picked up the parchment. "Try, please."

"Focus, okay. I got this." I flicked the scroll with my finger. "Tell me what you think our history means?"

Shay picked up the athame and handed it to me. "Anchor the scroll down." She opened the parchment again, using her finger to trace the lines of the past. "This is the mid-1900's. Jacob Kota was the last maker, and when he died, a part of Benton and her powers went with him."

"Is that what happens?"

She turned the parchment on the bone, scrolling the timeline through the past. "It looks like the transitions happen every ninety to one hundred years."

I leaned closer. "Are you saying Benton was a hundred years old?"

Shay shook her head. "You saw her. That's not possible."

"Maybe not for a mortal human, but for a magick one?"

She wrapped the scroll back onto the bone. "It's just not…" In anger, she threw the parchment across the room. "Damn it! Why didn't she just tell me?"

My arms wrapped around her. "I don't know. Maybe she couldn't."

We sat together in the circle. Dexter was licking his paws, oblivious to the conversation around him. Shay tried to leave my embrace. "I want to finish looking at the scroll."

"Let me grab it." For the last four days, we'd managed to contain an overload of information. The transfer of power from Benton to Shay had skewed her sense of balance. I could feel the energy vibrating off her. I held the scroll behind me before stepping back inside our circle. "What do you know about the kind of magick that happened at the mill the other day?"

"Only the little scribbles Benton left. Why?"

"Have you considered what it means for you? For your practice?"

She reached around, trying to take the scroll from me. "Why? What are you thinking?"

"I wonder if the powers of the Maker hit me hard enough that I saw fairies, giants, and a dragon. Maybe your new magick is affecting you too."

"It is affecting me." She rubbed her hands together. "I can feel it."

"What do you mean you can feel it?" My shoulders tensed, and my hand clenched the scroll. "Why didn't you say anything?"

She closed her eyes and stepped away. "I was worried about you."

The scroll dropped to the table, and I reached to hold her hands. "You never told me what happened in the mill." I stepped backward, leading her to the apartment. She didn't respond as she climbed the stairs. "Shay?"

She walked across the kitchen, turning around to answer. "I'm not one hundred percent certain what happened in the mill." She opened the refrigerator and grabbed a beer. "You want one?" She held the bottle, giving it a quick tick-tock swing.

My arm stretched over the sink. "I think I need something stronger." The bottle of scotch was in the cabinet, and I poured two fingers more than I should. As I sat on the couch beside Shay, it was impossible to escape our new magick-infused demon hunting life together; the notes and sketches smothered the table.

"I was reading the spell on the wall. I remember watching you fall to the floor just as I said the last few words." She raised her feet on the padded stool in front of us. "I woke up..."

"Woke up?" I interrupted. "What do you mean you woke up?"

"*So mote it be*, can be a powerful request," Shay explained. She took a long sip of her beer. "After I said those four words, I felt a flood of power, a rush of force with incredible strength. It was hot and thick and so heavy. I felt dizzy and tried to steady myself, but I couldn't, and I guess I passed out. It could have been for a few seconds or a few minutes; I'm not sure." She sipped her beer. "When I came to, I wasn't thinking about myself. I was worried about you."

"Did you feel different?" I asked.

She shook her head. "A little. I picked you up and carried you outside." She took another sip of her drink. "I didn't want to leave without our gear or the candle holder."

"That seems to be an important tool." My wrist made tiny circles as I swirled my drink around the sides of the glass.

She nodded in agreement. "More than we knew when we made it, but the transfer of power from Benton to me... she had to know what was going to happen to her. That she was not going to survive."

"So that's how it works?" I interrupted.

Shay walked over to the table, pulling two sheets of paper from the stack and carrying her computer. She handed the papers to me. "From what I can tell, after reading more of her notes, Benton wanted me to come into power. She knew that someone was after you, and because of the poison, she could only help you by surrendering herself for me." Shay wiped the corner of her eye.

"I'm sorry I ever thought she would hurt you."

Shay's shoulders raised in a shrug. "I thought it too, and I knew her for ten years. I should have known better."

I took a sip of my drink and set it on the table. "What's our next move?"

Shay's fingers tapped the keyboard, and the screen opened on an image of a stone building. "Benton said that we need to go to the old courthouse. I think that's what we should do."

"And your powers?" I asked.

"I'm not sure yet." She ran her finger along the top of her computer screen.

"Tell me what happened in the field after we left the mill?"

She closed the computer. "I let loose magick I've never felt before."

I nodded. "I know that you did. I knew something was different." I reached for her hand, holding it in my lap. "What did you do, Shay?"

She rolled my hand over, running her finger along the faded scar in my palm. "I would do anything for you."

I felt tears fill the corners of my eyes. "Tell me." I choked out the words. The memory was overwhelming as she wiped my tears with the pad of her thumb.

"You didn't answer when I called your name." She touched my cheek. "You landed face down, and when I rolled you over, I thought you weren't breathing. I listened for your heartbeat, and I felt air coming from your nose, and then all I wanted to do was get you away from the energy."

"I remember being against the wall." I leaned into her touch. "I was outside. Tell me what happened in the field."

"It hurt." She confessed. "The thought of losing you felt like my own death. The silence was so empty."

I held her hands in my lap. "I wasn't dead."

Shay tried to pull away, but I squeezed her fingers. "I didn't know that at the time. I couldn't think. It felt like I didn't know anything at all."

"You carried me to the field. Why did you stop there?"

"I didn't have a choice. The power was so strong, and I had to remind the universe that you and I made a promise. I wasn't about to lose you after everything we've done to be together."

"You drew from the earth?"

She nodded. "I drew from all directions, from every deity, with all that I had. There was nothing else I could do. The power came. I felt it everywhere inside of me, and it was too much to hold. So I sent it through the goddess of the earth and back into you."

"You did that for me?"

"I did that for us." She raised my hand to her lips. "I love you more than anything."

My eyes closed, a slow, deliberate blink, as I let the significance of her words into my heart. "And what's the price for using that kind of magick?"

Glassy tear-filled eyes stared back at me as her voice broke. "I'm not sure."

"How will we know?"

Tears streamed down her cheeks and rolled off her chin. "I'm not sure of that either."

"That's enough for tonight." I finished my drink and stood up, taking her hand. "Why don't we do a balancing meditation and go to bed?"

"I'm exhausted, Wil." She walked to the kitchen sink, washed my glass, and turned it over to dry in the rack.

I stepped up behind her, wrapping my arms around her waist. I whispered in her ear. "I'll do all of the work tonight. You just let me take care of you for a change."

She surrendered, relaxing into my body. "That sounds kinda perfect."

I kissed her neck. "Why don't you clear a spot on the floor. I'll be right back." I grabbed a small bundle of sage from the tiny apothecary cabinet and a short brown taper from our bedroom closet.

"I think we should do the meditation here." Shay was right behind me.

"In the closet?" I smiled at her.

She took the candle and sage from my hands. "No, silly. In the bedroom. I think I'm going to be hard to move once we do the meditation." She placed the candle on a ceramic saucer, lighting it with a short stick match. Her voice was peaceful. "Offer of fire, take the flame, perform the act, my will be done." The sage bundle smoldered as she twisted it into the flame. "Energy to clear, for wisdom and purification." She sat down on the floor, raising a hand for me to sit with her. I crawled behind, circling her with my arms.

"Let me care for you tonight." I took the bundle of smoldering sage, waving it over her body. I fanned the ember until the smoke surrounded us. "How am I doing?"

She nodded. "So far, so good." Her breath was warm against my hand as she blew the tight wrap of herbs. The smoke drifted in a circle around us.

I whispered in her ear. "You can remind me when I'm getting it wrong." Her body relaxed against me.

"There is no wrong way, not between us."

It was my turn to ask her to be quiet. "Shh, I need to concentrate." Shay worked magick all of the time. It was instinctive for her to kiss a sacred stone or to dance in the cascades of moonlight. With her, there was never a doubt that everything was honored. I wanted her to feel that precious too. "I call upon the three; Maiden, Mother, and Crone." I couldn't see a smile, but I imagined one on Shay's face. "We are deified in this space, and I ask blessings for the Magick." She turned in my arms.

"You can't call me that."

I shook my head at her. "It's what you are, now. We need to balance you and the source of this power." Maybe it was saying the word out loud, in a sacred circle, or just the idea that she was stronger than she knew, but Shay was the Magick in Bannock. "Do you remember how it felt when we were girls?"

She turned just enough to look at me, nodding that she remembered who we had always been together. "Yes."

"That first time, you took in so much energy that you collapsed."

"I didn't know that I shouldn't."

"Exactly." I held her against me. "I knew how to help you then, and I know how to help you now."

"What if something…"

My hand came around, placing a single finger to her lips. "Shh, nothing will." She kissed my finger. "Trust me. I've got you this time."

It was not simple, the ability to trust, but she surrendered to me and to all of the enchantments she'd explained before. My right hand came around to cover her heart. "I am the light. She is the light. We are the light." My left hand reached out to the side. "Receive protection, give protection." Like a song between us, she started to repeat my words in a faint whisper.

Shay's hand came up to cover my own. "I love you."

We sat in the silence of our bedroom, lit only by the flicker of that flame. Her body rested against my own and the energy of the earth surrounding us. "I love you too, Shay."

CHAPTER VI

Supernatural

The five-thirty alarm was buzzing, but I held tight to the woman wrapped around my body. Her leg felt perfect, thrown over my hip, and her head rested on my chest. As I moved toward consciousness, I sensed the exchange of magick against my skin. Our grounding spell from the night before was exhausting and effectively super-dosed us to sleep. I felt rested, but as my eyes opened, I knew something was happening to the woman in my arms. I reached over to silence the clock, shifting away from her body.

Her hand clenched my hip. "Don't move, please."

I stretched a little farther. "But the alarm?"

"Wait, just for a second. I'm trying to balance myself."

"Without me?" I thought my comment was cute, but Shay didn't laugh. I looked at her limbs, tangled across my own.

"What the, you're freakin' glowing." The corporeal energy of the Magick was pouring off of Shay.

"I know." Her hand raised. "I've been laying here trying to figure out what the hell to do with this." Dashes of light outlined the edge of her scars like the sneaky gleam peeking through the cracks of a door. "Hold up your hand." She asked.

We placed our palms together, and I could feel the power shift from her body into my own. "Whoo, it's a lot." I felt the oscillation of magick travel through me.

She sat up, breaking the connection. "Come here. I've got an idea." We sat together on the bed face-to-face, palm to palm, legs crossed, knees touching. I nodded for her to continue. "I'm going to push energy from my right hand into your left. All you need to do is feel it and push it back."

"Is all of this from my Maker powers?" I asked.

"I think it is." Her fingers wriggled against my own. "Close your eyes." The sheets of the bed were tangled around us, making a tiny, rumpled ring. "I am the sister of all that is good." Her voice was quiet, hypnotic. "Choosing love and kindness as my source. Give as I receive and receive as is given." We repeated the rhythmic chant over and over until the six o'clock alarm sounded.

I looked at her hands still pressed against my own. "No more glowing."

"I think you and I might need to do that a lot." She stretched her arms over her head.

"You want me to hold your hands and transfer magick energies more often?"

She smiled at me. "Yes, I think I do."

"I'm all yours." I didn't try to hide my smile. "You don't have to ask me twice."

Shay's laugh was comforting as I watched her walk to the bathroom. I wondered about the power inside her. Was she built physically and emotionally to carry so much? The shower turned on the same time I heard the soft clicking of Dexter's paws on the hardwood floor.

"Hey, buddy." I climbed down to sit beside him. "How's my dragon?" He gave my face a sloppy swipe with his tongue. "One day, you're going to tell me, aren't you?" I didn't expect to hear anything as I reached for the crumpled shirt at the end of the bed. I ran my fingers through my hair, confident that I'd be at the forge after Shay left the house. "Come on, Dex. Let's go have some breakfast."

The apartment was dark, peaceful, as the beautiful dog followed me to the kitchen. I filled his dish with food and water and noticed the dangling latch on the greenhouse door. "Weird." I rolled the old barn door away to reveal the glass-lined A-frame structure. Shay's plants were taking hold in their new home. I walked through, thinking about Shay, our shared experience with Mama Pierce, and the gift of magick. I checked the lock on the door leading to the rooftop.

"What are you doing in here?" The sound of Shay's voice made me jump as strong arms wrapped up from behind. "Oh, sorry. I didn't mean to scare you."

I nuzzled against her. "It's fine. I just saw the unlatched door and thought it was weird."

"It was probably me." She held me closer.

"You?"

"I got up for a few things in the middle of the night." I nodded, waiting for more details. "You might find a small bundle of Horehound and Bay in the bed."

"I might?" I stepped out of her embrace to fill the watering can from the faucet. "Horehound and Bay for?" I was going to guess, but Shay was a brilliant teacher. I trickled water over the fresh cuts on the plants she used.

"Horehound to balance energy and ward off evil." She winked at me. "Just in case." Shay tucked her fingers into the towel to tighten it around her chest.

"And bay?" I asked as I placed the watering can back on the shelf.

"For purification and healing, but mostly, I like the way it soothes my soul. It's like a cool cloth against my forehead."

"And it helped?" It was my first chance to look at Shay and see that the shower washed away our morning energy work. Her cheeks were rosy, and her eyes looked bright.

"It did." She leaned against the frame of the door.

"You should have let me help you." I stepped closer, closing the space between us.

Shay looked away. "I didn't want to wake you up." She explained.

"Maybe you should have." My finger hooked the knot of her towel, and I tugged her closer.

She looked into my eyes. "Yes, I know that now, but in my defense, you used a lot of energy last night."

"I can handle it," I explained as I kissed her.

She smiled as she pulled away. "Yes, I know that too."

The oversized cotton wrap covered her body, and I pointed up and down from neck to knee. "You going to wear a towel to work today?"

Shay shook her head and turned to walk away. "Definitely not." I followed her into the bedroom. "Do you have plans for your day?" She asked as she opened the closet door.

"I thought I might try to forge a piece of the demon material from Benton." My shoulder fell against the doorway.

She stopped buttoning her pants. "You feel comfortable doing that without me?"

"Babe, I'm a blacksmith."

"No, you're the Maker, and we don't know what that means yet."

"I'll be fine. If something weird happens, I'll call you."

She tucked in her shirt. "I'll come by for lunch if I can." She sat down to put on her shoes.

"Perfect, I'll grill some sandwiches."

She dropped her foot to the floor. "In the kitchen, I hope." She looked up to smile and wink.

"Maybe."

The Velcro tore away just before Shay slipped the vest over her head. "Yum."

"Speaking of yum, you need breakfast?" I asked.

"Quick eggs would be amazing."

"I'm on it." I left her to finish dressing and passed Dexter on my way back to the kitchen. He heard the sound of her vest calling him to start his day. I made a simple scramble of fresh herbs and eggs, ready to go when she walked into the kitchen.

The pot of coffee wasn't quite half brewed, but Shay didn't wait to pour a cup. She leaned over my shoulder. "Smells good." She kissed my cheek.

"It'll taste better." I scooped the scramble into a toasted tortilla. "Quick eggs, just for you."

"Thanks, love." She took a bite.

"You home at three today?" I asked.

She nodded, finishing the mouthful of food. "Give or take. I'm not sure what the department is doing for Benton."

"You know where I'll be."

"I can't wait to see what you create." She snugged her hat in place. "I need to go."

She tried to get away with a quick kiss, but I tugged her collar, pulling us closer for a proper goodbye. "I love you."

"I love you, too." She walked to the edge of the stairs, looking back. "Come on, Dex." I heard the door close and lock. I stood in the doorway for a long moment dreading the silence of my empty house.

I cleaned up the kitchen before making the bed. A small bundle of herbs rolled out from under Shay's pillow, just as she'd warned. I wondered how many tiny Wiccan packages I would find until we figured out these new powers. "This is going to be a fun ride," I said to myself. Maybe I needed a familiar of my own.

The firebox of the forge looked ready for action, charged with Maker energy. I was distracted by thoughts of magick as I walked into the workshop. I wandered into the office, staring for a long minute at the pile of demon steel left behind for me—the new Maker. In Bannock blacksmithing history, I was next in line, tasked to create magickal armament, but I wasn't sure what for. I thought about Shay coming into her power at the same time and wondered what might be helpful for the strange challenges ahead.

I poured out the can of demon steel cutoffs I'd collected from the previous projects. I lined the five pieces on the anvil. "What if?" I said. What if I attempted to combine the cutoffs to form one solid mass? I clipped the apron around my neck, feeling the abrasive scorched leather scratch across my arm. I'd need to replace it if today's adventure was as fiery as before. I cleaned every piece on the grinder, steering clear of the flaming sparks. I welded the gatekeeper steel to the class-fours, sandwiching the fairy metal in between. Once together, I had a block of checker-patterned demon material attached to a two-foot-long pole of scrap. I'd use the scrap as a handle, making it more efficient to move from the forge to the anvil.

Tiny bits of scale from previous work peppered the floor of the workshop. If demon anvil dust had value, I was going to keep every single bit I made today. I swept the old mess into a pile, scooping it to the scrap bin. The floor was clean, and I was ready to spark the forge to life. The woosh of air sucking out as the igniter hit the propane was a sweet sound to my blacksmithing ears. I placed my steel into the fire, waiting for the grey metal to transform to bright white.

Forge welding temperature, on a combination demon experiment, didn't feel dangerous at all.

There is an abundance of standing and waiting in the art of blacksmithing, but today I noted every spark and flicker as the project transformed. I uncorked the bottle of flux, a key component in the forge welding process. The coarse white powder acted as a bonding agent, promoting a clean weld between different metals. Well, at least it did when I used it on non-demon steel. I hoped for the best, and I pushed the powder-covered pile back into the forge. I pulled the white-hot project from the fire, placing it on the anvil. I drew my arm over my head, hesitating at the memory of the sound my hammer made the first time it struck demon material.

My hammer dropped. I was surprised by a more familiar echo. The demon steel embraced the impact of my swing and the material moved. It didn't cry out but instead the spatter of liquid metal burst in the air like Fourth of July sparklers. This was unexpected and I had no explanation for the fantastic show.

Maybe the demon agony fell silent for the Maker and sparkled instead? Perhaps forging the ethereal steel without my power was the reason behind the echo of horror and the Maker powers were a celebration? I was about to forge my first project as the empowered Maker of Bannock, and the mystery behind that reality continued to grow.

I hammered the project for hours, heating, fluxing, folding, and turning until I had a thin plate of square-patterned demon armor. The configurations and markings of each demon cutoff crisscrossed like ancient textile. It looked beautiful, cooling atop the anvil.

The particles of scale on the floor were a hazy shade of blue, and I was careful to collect as much as I could, but it was impossible to get all of the fine powder. I looked up at the clock, surprised that it was after three. If my luck held, Shay would be home in time for me to shape the breastplate for a better fit.

My demon-forged project was ice cold on the anvil by the time she arrived. Shay was dressed in full uniform; her work gear slung over her shoulder in an overstuffed bag. Dexter looked happy if that was possible for a dragon-dog. I was trying to play it cool about my experiment, handing her the container of solid blue anvil dust I'd collected.

"Oh, is it demon scale?" She dropped her bag to the floor and leaned in for a quick kiss.

"100% pure dust of demons."

"Demons? Ssss as in many?" Her emphasis on the plural was adorable.

"Yes, I experimented today." I rubbed Dexter's head as I reached around to pull the Velcro of his K-9 vest. I wondered if our four-legged officer might need demon armor as well.

Shay was already unbuttoning her uniform shirt. "What kind of experiment?"

I noticed the stain on her sleeve. "What's that?" I stepped closer, tugging on the fabric.

"It's from a call." She brushed at the stain. "It's grass. I was chasing a guy on foot and had to tackle him."

"Human guy or demon guy?"

"As far as I could tell, human." She unbuttoned the cuff, removing her shirt. I could see the red chafing along her forearm.

"Full-on tackle?" I reached over to touch her swollen skin.

She grabbed my hand, stopping me. "Babe, it's fine. I'm fine. It's just a grass burn." She held it up for me to get a closer look.

"Just a scratch?"

She nodded. "Uh-huh."

I leaned in to kiss it. "I don't like it when you're hurt."

"This is nothing." She pulled me closer for a hug. "I showed you my day. Now, you show me yours."

I walked over to the anvil and grabbed the plate of demon armor. "I might have played around and mixed the cutoff pieces from the first five projects."

"Played around?" Her eyebrow raised, and her lips pinched into a straight line. She was not amused.

I held up the quarter-inch-thick plate in front of my chest. "It's armor."

"Why would you make armor?"

I looked down at her forearm as I gave her the plate. "You seriously have to ask?"

Shay held it in her hands. "It's super light."

"Yeah, weird, huh?"

"Is this for my vest?" She raised it in front of her chest, mirroring the body armor she was still wearing.

I nodded. "I was thinking about you and your magick and all of the non-human calls you get." I took the armor from her hands, holding it in place, matching what was under her nylon vest. "I have no idea how strong it is or even if you could wear it."

"Can it stop human weapons?"

I shrugged. "I have no idea. I haven't tested it."

Shay backed away and turned to run up to the apartment. She didn't say a word and left me holding the armor plate where her body had once been. I heard boots on the stairs and the pounding of her feet in the apartment. Her steps were softer on the way down, and she was talking on her phone when she set a steel box on the table.

"Yep, good. Probably in about twenty minutes." She was wearing jeans, a BPD t-shirt, and her hair was down around her face. Shay looked ready for a night at the bar as she reached to drop her duffle bag in my hand. "Put the plate in here. I've arranged some time to test it."

It was apparent that Shay was more excited about this demon experiment than I was. "Test? Where?"

"Dani has a piece of property, an old homestead just outside of town. She said we could use it to do a little shooting."

I was excited and frightened at the same time. "We are going to shoot at this?" Shay was checking the contents of her duffle; she held up two sets of earmuffs, safety glasses, and gloves. She flipped the latch on the steel box, and a ridiculous amount of ammunition was inside. "Planning for an apocalypse?" I tilted the box to get a better view.

She looked up, smiling. "We confiscated most of this, and some are . . . let's call them experimental."

"What does that mean, exactly?"

"It's a surprise." She flipped the cover and latched it tight. It wasn't hard to miss her excitement as we left the carriage house.

We drove past the city limits of Bannock, turning onto a winding gravel road. If I didn't trust Shay as my girlfriend and lover, I would have thought this was the perfect lead-in for a horror story execution. When we stopped, I could see the country-style shooting range; a pedestal of barn wood mounted to a metal post that looked like a table. Across the open field, I could see, every ten to twenty yards away, slatted lumber walls with paper target remnants peppering the edges. It was apparent Shay and Dani had come out here before. "This is scarier than the mill." I saw the slender trail of rocks leading to a small cabin.

Her laugh wasn't comforting. "It's okay. We shoot here all of the time." Dexter stayed in the back seat of the squad car, his paws crisscrossed under his head, the door open in case he wanted to wander. He seemed comfortable parked beneath the shade of a tree.

I have never held a gun in my life. I've never wanted to own one or shoot one. The fact that my girlfriend had more than a few was an adjustment. She laid out a shotgun, pumping it a few times until she was sure it was unloaded. She placed her service weapon beside it after removing the magazine and chambered round. I was surprised when she laid down her taser. The line-up of weaponry appeared to cover the human armament she planned to use. She unpacked her duffle bag, placing the ear protection and yellow-tinted glasses beside the firearms.

"A few quick things." She placed her hands on the table. "From this position, we are standing at the firing line. If anything, other than a target is in front of us, guns are down on the table. Got it?"

There was no confusion that this rule was absolute. "I got it."

"Good," Shay said. She pointed at the target structures in front of us. "Everything on the other side of the firing line is downrange." She looked at me before laying her hands on top of her service weapon. "When you take out a gun, it always points downrange. Always!"

The procedures were intimidating. "Okay." My hands were sweating.

"I'm going to put this downrange." Shay held up the breastplate, waving it in the air. "Let's start at fifteen yards."

I nodded; a bit overwhelmed by how she moved around the range with excitement in her voice. She set the demon plate on a target about fifteen yards away. Although I was hesitant about being here, she was entirely at home.

Shay walked me through firing at a range. "I'm not going to load anything until we are ready to shoot." She looked at me and, for the first time, noticed my apprehension. "Are you okay, Wil?"

I crammed my sweaty hands in my pockets. "I've just never shot a gun before."

She stepped away from the table. "Never?" she asked.

I shook my head. "Not ever."

Her hand raised to touch the back of my bicep. "I had no idea."

"It never really came up." I looked into her eyes.

"Are you afraid of them?" She asked as she steered my hands free from my pockets.

"I'm not afraid so much as I know the damage they can do."

"There's no denying what guns can do." She confessed. I had never watched my girlfriend perform this part of her job. She was fearless. "I'm going to teach you." She opened her duffle bag and pulled out a compact handgun. "This is a twenty-two." She held it in the palm of her hand. "It's smaller, lighter, and easier to handle. When you decide, I'll show you how to shoot." She flipped a lever by her thumb to check the safety and removed another clip of ammunition from the bag. "I think I'm ready. Are you okay?" I nodded. She flipped the power switch on her ear covers. "These will block the sound of the gunshot, but you'll still be able to hear me."

"Will it block the sound from the class-four metal?" I pointed to the cuff around her wrist.

"I guess we'll find out." She handed me a pair of safety glasses. "Keep your eyes safe too." She looked over at the car. Dexter was asleep with his head down on his paws, half hanging out the open door.

There were so many things to consider as Shay sighted the handgun on her target. How would demon steel react? What would the combination of demon do to a regular bullet? What if it ricocheted back at us?

"Firing!" She yelled in warning and I watched her finger squeeze the trigger. Her first shot hit dead center. She laid the gun down, and we walked out to take a look. Her fingers trailed over the face of the demon steel. "You saw me hit it, didn't you?"

"Looked like you got it right in the center." The plate was flawless; the shot didn't even scratch the surface. She propped it back in place.

Shay kicked through the rocks on the ground until she found the gnarled copper of the bullet. She picked it up and held it to me.

"It stopped a bullet."

Shay's fingers flexed around the lump of copper. "Let's try the shotgun." Her green eyes squinted as her smile rose with excitement. I followed her back to the table and stood beside her, watching her load the rifle. She tucked it tight against her shoulder, bracing for the recoil. "Firing." She warned again before taking a deep breath and letting it out before pulling the trigger. Even with the earmuffs on, I jumped when the gun went off. The plate launched off the target base, up into the air. It was a definite hit, and I was impressed. Shooting was just one more thing to add to the list of talents this woman possessed. We walked through the grass and stopped where the chest-plate landed. It was more than ten feet from the original position. "I know you hit it."

Shay pulled her ear covering down around her neck. "This isn't possible." It looked new, unblemished, fresh from the forge.

"Got any C4 in that bag of tricks?" I joked as I bumped her hip.

Her eyebrow raised. "What do you think I do for a living?"

"I don't know, but you're going to do it much better wearing this." I handed the armor plate to Shay. Her finger lingered over the edge. "Maybe you should make one for yourself?"

I shook my head. "I'm good. I'll just stay behind you."

"Human shield, huh?"

"Protected by demon armor, you'll be unstoppable." I looked down at her wrist. "Maybe you should take a shot at that fancy bracelet while we're here."

"That's an excellent idea." She slipped it from her arm, leaning it against the target. The cuff was much smaller, and I wondered if it would flip in the air like the breastplate. We settled behind the firing line and put on our earmuffs. Shay chambered a round in her service weapon. "Firing!" she yelled, and I watched her sight in on the cuff, take a deep breath and let loose a single shot. The cuff flipped up into the air, an apparent hit.

"Do you ever miss?"

She smiled as she clicked the safety. "I've trained very hard not to." She laid the gun on the table and jogged downrange to pick up the cuff. She waved it in the air as she walked back. "No damage at all." She brushed the cuff against her chest, knocking off the dirt from the ground. "Nothing, not even a scratch." She set it down for me to inspect.

"That's unbelievable!" I turned it over, wondering why demon steel stopped every shot. "Are demons bulletproof?" I asked.

"None that I've encountered, at least not yet." Shay tapped the handgun with the back of her knuckle. "You want to take a shot?"

My shoulders tensed, and I sidestepped the table. "I don't think I do."

Shay tucked the armor plate under her arm. "When you're ready."

"Guns scare me." I confessed as I took the demon armor from her hand and set it on the table.

"Bad experience?" Shay asked. She dropped to one knee and unzipped the duffle bag on the ground.

"Something like that." I leaned my elbows on the table and looked down range at the battered targets.

She unloaded each of the guns, securing them inside the duffle bag. "You're not a fan?"

I picked at the weather-worn knothole in the tabletop. "I guess I'm not."

"Care to tell me why?" Shay leaned against the table, resting her arm close to mine. I looked at the scars on her hands. Not so long ago, she had the courage to tell me about her own. Wounds on the inside, no matter their age, were easier to hide.

"I've seen some stuff." The vision of the boy on the ground flashed in my mind.

"Stuff?" Shay was patient, and I knew a part of the questioning came from concern, but I wondered if extracting information was also an unspoken side effect of the job.

"I never knew his name, and I don't know who shot him, but I found the body. He was blue when I started CPR."

"He died?" Shay asked.

My grip rubbed the splintered edge of the table as I leaned back to stretch my body. My head dropped against my bicep as I turned to look at Shay. "Yeah, it made an impression. Once I held him in my arms, I knew that kind of power over life and death . . . I knew I just didn't want the responsibility." I looked up at the cloudless sky. "I'm sorry I never told you."

"Don't apologize." She rested her arm against mine. "Remember when you came to town, and you pulled that knife." Shay rubbed the scar on the back of her hand. "I understand how hard it is to forget, and there's nothing wrong with the choice you've made."

"I'm comfortable forging any weapon you need." I flicked my finger against the plate of demon steel.

She kissed me. "That sounds perfect."

I slid the cuff back onto her wrist, looking over at the sleeping dog. "I wonder why Dexter didn't bark when you hit the armor or the cuff?"

"Just more questions to add to the list." She replied.

I kicked the leg of the tabletop. "The part that sucks is we're the only ones who can answer them."

Shay bumped my hip. "With you as the Maker ..." She tapped the center of my chest. "and me as the Magick." She poked her thumb to her chest. "We've totally got this."

"Just like that?" I was skeptical.

"I have faith that we will figure it out." She threaded her shoulder through the strap of the duffle bag.

"I sure hope so." I held her hand as we walked to the car.

"Do you think you can make the plate fit into my vest?" She asked

"When I was forging, I did my best to shape it, but now that you're off duty, I can lay this one next to your old one and make it a perfect mirror to what you've been wearing."

Shay dropped the duffle bag in the trunk before calling her dog. "Come on, Dex, have a little run." He jumped out of the back seat and ran around in the grass. We followed him to the clearing.

"What are your thoughts about our little test?" Shay asked.

"I guess we know it'll stop a bullet. What else do you think the combination of demon steel will do?"

Her hand trailed down my arm and our fingers tangled together. "I can't be sure. The stopping power probably came from the gatekeeper."

I raised our joined hands. "Or the class four that gave us this." I tapped the cuff on her wrist.

"Perhaps," she said.

"I wonder if your vest will burn blue."

She dropped my hand and crisscrossed over her chest. "I hope not. Can you imagine trying to explain that?"

"Don't the other cops know?"

"Yes, they do, but knowing and seeing are two very different things plus—" She pointed at her chest, "glowing boobs?"

"I'd like to see that."

"I bet you would." She grabbed me around the waist.

I pushed the hat from her head and kissed her square on the lips. "Thanks for being so patient with me out there."

"We each have our reservations. Maybe in time, you'll be more comfortable." She set me down on the ground.

I tugged her hat onto my head. "Maybe."

We watched Dexter run as we wandered on the property. I got a better look at the tiny stone path leading to a shed-sized log cabin. The trails cut through the tall grass were clear signs that someone visited often. "How is it that Dani owns this place?"

"Her family has ties to the first settlers," Shay explained. "It's part of the mine."

"Mine?" I pushed the hat back so I could get a better look at Shay. "Are you saying a gold mine?" My brow lifted, and my eyes went wide with curiosity.

Shay waved her hands, quick to respond. "Yes, but there was never much of a boom here for Bannock."

"Oh." I kicked at the stones buried in the grass.

"Don't be so disappointed," Shay tugged my back pocket and pulled me closer.

"I suppose if there were a boom, this wouldn't be a ghost town, and I probably wouldn't be here."

"Exactly." Her arm hooked around my back, and I leaned into her.

We walked along the pebbled trail and noticed the rubble of blasted stone and sand. "Dani's really into rocks. Is it because of the mine?" I asked.

"It is." Shay leaned over, picking up a stone from the ground. "I guess it's in her blood. From what she's said, she grew up playing in the abandoned tunnels." Shay threw the stone, and we watched it sail out of sight.

"Sounds dangerous."

She ran her hand over her hair and pulled it loose from the elastic. "Kinda like enchanted blacksmithing?"

I shrugged, downplaying the danger. "Not even close." I sat in the grass and tugged Shay to sit between my legs. "Can we go up there some time?"

She twisted to look at me. "To the mine? Seriously?"

"Why not?"

"I never thought about going in. I can ask Dani if you're interested. I'm sure she'd make time to show us."

I twirled the tall blades of grass around my finger. "She seems like a great person." I knew there was nothing romantic between the two but there was a close bond I wanted to understand.

"She is."

"What was it like for you before I moved to town?" I was fishing for anything Shay might share about her life before me.

Shay leaned into my body. "Here in Bannock?"

"Yes." I'm not sure why I asked, but she rarely talked about her life before I took ownership of the carriage house.

She was quiet for a moment, picking at the smudge on her boot. "I guess I worked a lot." She pulled her knees in and wrapped her arms around them.

"What does that mean?"

She rested her cheek on her knee and adjusted to look at me. "I wanted to be more than a good cop. I wanted to be on top of my game. So when I had the opportunity, I worked."

"And for fun?" I brushed a hair from her cheek.

"You're gonna laugh." She gave me an intimidating stare. "Don't laugh at me."

I slapped my hand to my heart. "I wouldn't."

She shuffled her boot over the rocks, knocking them loose. "I studied magick."

I pulled my knees in and wrapped my arms around, mirroring her position. "For fun?"

"Yep, and because I wanted to know as much as I could."

I thought about the loaded shelves in her studio. "So, you've actually read all the books in your house?"

"Every single tome, at least once."

"And socializing?"

She looked down at her scarred hands. "I felt safer alone, I guess. No questions to answer." She held her palm to me. "It was enough to explain these. The rest of my body was impossible to talk about."

"I guess you were holding out for the right person." I reached to take her hand. My fingers traveled across the scars on her palm.

"I didn't want to push *you* away." She closed her eyes. "Holding back, I know I made it very hard for you."

I shook my head. "Shay, you did what you had to do to survive. I have a lot of respect for that, for you."

"Life is very different for me now." Her hand covered my own. "Being with you. Having Dex. I feel like a family; all of us together is something I've always wanted."

My head dropped to her shoulder. "Yes, we are a family, and I wanted it too."

Like a menacing child, the dog came running out from the tall grass as if on cue, his fur drenched with water from the river. When he was a few feet away, he gave a heedless shake of his entire body, spraying the two of us. Shay jumped to her feet. "Dexter!"

As his butt hit the ground, a tiny burst of smoke puffed from his nose. I looked at Shay for a reaction and noticed the disbelief. "I told you!"

She shook her head. "That was smoke!"

I couldn't stop myself. "Your... dog... is... a... dragon!" I pointed at the discoloration on Shay's shirt, a mix of water and whatever else covered Dexter. "What is that? Is that blood?"

She wiped a hand across her arm. "I don't know what it is." She dropped to one knee to examine Dex, running her fingers over the soggy animal. "What have you gotten yourself into?" She looked up at me. "Someone's been out catching wild animals. I think we need to take a walk and make sure he doesn't stick his nose where it shouldn't be."

I offered my hand to help her up. "Lead the way."

We made a quick stop at the car. Shay loaded her gun, tucking it into a holster along with a taser and flashlight clipped onto a makeshift belt. Blue jeans and a half-loaded duty belt run a perfect second to her in full uniform. She caught me watching, and the smile of satisfaction she gave in response was all the encouragement I needed. Leash in hand, she called out. "Dexter, *ostende mihi*, show me." The dog took off full speed, and Shay was quick behind him.

Running was not a thing that I did, but I kept pace as long as I could. When I broke through the tall grass, I saw them standing over a pile of something dark, gooey, and completely void of life.

"What is it?" I asked. Dexter was licking between the pads of his paws, cleaning off the evidence of his kill. "Should he be eating it?"

Shay walked around the remains, tapping the pile with the toe of her boot. "I have no idea what class this was." Shay picked up a stick and poked at the leathery skin. "Dex has already taken care of half of the flesh. You see that saw-toothed bone?" She touched it with the stick. "It's part of a spine. It's a demon for sure."

"How the heck did he find a demon?"

She pointed at her K-9, who had moved on to licking other parts of his body. "He's not very forthcoming with answers." Shay unbuttoned the pocket of her pants to remove her phone.

"What do you think?" I asked as I stepped back. This was closer to a demon than I wanted to be, even if it was dead.

"He must have felt threatened." Shay was taking pictures with the camera on her phone.

"But this thing is massive." I stepped out of her way as she circled the remains.

Shay wasn't just taking pictures; she was thinking, working the scene. "Let's take Dex to the river and wash him off." She clipped a leash to his collar, and we walked through the field. She noticed the blood on her hand as she thumbed through the pictures. "This is . . . he's a mess."

The river water was running fast, breaking hard over the boulders, and I was hesitant to enter until Shay led us to a stone and sand-covered launch. I stepped close enough to cup my hands and scoop up water to pour over the dog's furry face. "Damn, that's so cold." The dog sniffed the air around us before jumping over the rocks and splashing himself. As he paddled, the river washed away the stain of demon blood. I looked at Shay, staring off deep in thought. "I can see your mind is going a mile a minute. Talk to me."

"Dexter shredded that demon like it was yesterday's newspaper."

"Darlin', your dog is a dragon. Maybe he eats demons?"

"There's no research."

I turned my head, looking back and forth from Shay to Dexter. "For dragons?"

She sat down on a massive wet rock. "For any of this." Her eyes followed the frolicking K-9 as he landed on the opposite side of the river.

I swished my arms through the water, washing the demon spatter off of my skin. "Maybe we should stop asking why and just see what comes." I wiped my hands on my pants.

"I'm not sure about that." Shay followed my lead and washed her bloodied arms in the flowing river water. She looked up at the same time Dexter stopped moving. His growl started low in the gut and turned from a howl into a throaty huff. I felt the heat of Dexter's fiery breath just before Shay threw herself over me, taking us both into the deep flow of the river. We popped up at the same time to see Dexter transform into a creature of disbelief.

His paws feathered out with claws greater than my hand and wrapped around the rocks of the riverbank—his hind legs reflected with beveled carapace, turtle-like armor plates. My eyes blinked hard, trying to focus on the animal transforming in front of our eyes. Dexter's face no longer fluffed with fur but thick flexible iridescent scales. He was a full force dragon about to unleash on whatever was bending the trees in front of him.

The heat of Dexter's breath filled the air as he lurched toward the demon breaking through the grass and brush. I didn't move, not because I couldn't but because I didn't want to miss a second of what was coming. The demon stood twice the average person's height, and the savage glow in its eyes was the first clue that it didn't come in peace.

Shay was yelling at me, but the soul-splitting sound of the fight stole my attention. "Take a deep breath." It was all I heard as her arm pulled me into the stream, and we both fell under the water. I fought to float back to the surface, but Shay held tight to keep us beneath the action. The water above was on fire. She dragged me with her across the river and away from Dexter and the demon. Soaked from head to toe, she pulled us up the riverbank. "Wil?" She crawled over the top of me. "Are you okay?"

I rolled to my side, spitting and coughing up a mouthful of water. "Holy Dragons! Did you see that?" Her body pressed against me again, forcing us hard to the ground. I felt the splattering of rock and branches just before Shay went limp.

I rolled us over, trying to prevent her unconscious body from slamming against the rocks of the shore. I heard Dexter's huff of fire and watched the demon leap over the river full-on aflame. Before I could say a word, the dragon shredded the burning monster, scattering pieces through the air. When the threat was over, I watched Dexter sway and stagger until he transformed back into the furry German Shepherd, we called our dog. Everything after was a blur. Did he fly or jump over the river to land beside Shay? I couldn't be sure. While I tried to figure it out, he was trying to revive the unconscious redhead.

"Come here, Dex." I reached for his collar. He was sticky and wet with the same demon sludge that brought us to the river's edge. His dog tongue smothered Shay's cheek as he dropped down beside her, waiting.

I crawled over the top of her. "Shay?"

Her hand came up to the side of her head. "What the hell hit me?"

Her eyes were closed tight. "It was a rock or maybe a piece of that demon?" There was no way to know. "Can you open your eyes?"

Her left eye squinted to take a quick peek at daylight before closing. "Oh, uhh." She turned over, vomiting against the rocks. "Nope, it's all kinda dizzy and fuzzy."

My first thought was a concussion. "Here, rest against me for a minute." I held her in my arms.

"What just happened?" She asked. I looked at the furry dog, sitting at attention, waiting for Shay to reward him for his victory.

"I'm pretty sure that Dexter just killed another demon, and I saw him full-on transform into a freakin' dragon."

Shay jerked, trying to open her eyes and sit forward. The motion was too much, and she heaved on the rocks again. I held her hips, preventing her from falling back in the water.

"Hon, you need to be still for a little bit."

"I don't think I have a choice." She laid between my legs. "Dexter." The dog's ears perked as he crawled closer. "Come here, buddy." His nose pushed into the palm of Shay's hand. "What kind of trouble did you make?"

I expected to hear an answer, but the dog whimpered before collapsing against his partner. I held my hand over Shay's face, covering it in shadow. "Let me look at your eyes? I need to see if I should call for help." I was worried the puking would start again, but when she peeked at me, I could see the fluctuation of her pupils. "They react the way they should. I think you'll be okay, but maybe you should let me drive home."

"I'm not even sure I can walk."

"It's okay. We'll take it slow." I put my arm around her waist and helped her stand. Shay squeezed her eyes closed. "I'm just glad we don't have to cross that river." She leaned hard against my shoulder and the belt around her waist dug deep into my hip. "You doing okay?"

Dexter was close to her side, cautious not to trip us. "My eyes are still closed."

Progress was slow, and as we broke through the grass to the open field, I saw the old truck in the gravel. "Did you know Dani was coming out here?"

"She wasn't sure if she could make it, but she was going to try." Shay's foot started to drag, so she shifted more of her weight against me.

"How much does she know?"

"Hey, dead eye!" Our new arrival yelled out, at the same time recognizing Shay was leaning against me for help. She started running toward us.

"Dani knows almost everything." She struggled to open her eyes.

"Almost?" We'd run out of time to sort out the unknown as Dani approached us.

Her hand came up under Shay's swinging arm. "Pierce?" Dani wrinkled her nose when the remnants of the demon swiped over her arm.

"Hey, D." Shay was trying to downplay her injury.

Dani looked between the two of us and down at the bloodied dog. "What the hell did all of this?"

"We aren't sure." Shay squinted, trying not to look up at the sunlight. "Wildwood was the only one who saw it before Dexter got involved."

I let Dani help, and together we walked Shay to the car. I grabbed the sunglasses from the visor and covered Shay's eyes.

"It was a demon. I haven't seen many, but that was something from hell." My voice was loud and maybe a bit enthusiastic.

"Probably not hell. Most likely, it came from the mine." Dani propped Shay on the patrol car, leaving her against the fender.

Shay slid down the side of the car, resting against the tire for support. "You want to explain that?"

"Here's the thing, Pierce." She hesitated, looking between the two of us. "How much does your girlfriend here know?"

Shay laughed, finally able to open her eyes beneath the sunglasses. "Maybe she should be asking you the same question?"

Dani shrugged. "Maybe she should." She pointed toward the tiny cabin. "You think you can make it inside?"

"Yes." Shay held up a hand. Before I could react, their wrists slapped together, and Dani had Shay on her feet. "You carrying?" Shay asked.

Dani slapped her left hip. "Yes, I sure am."

"Good." Shay squeezed the buckle on her belt. "Take these and grab the shotgun from the trunk."

I looked back as Dani threw Shay's belt over a shoulder. "Are you expecting more trouble?" I asked.

They answered in unison as if responding to a morning roll call.

"Always."

"Always."

I shook my head, trying to figure out how so many cops had become such an essential part of my life. Shay was slow walking to Dani's cabin, even with my help, giving Dani time to open the door for us. It looked hundreds of years old from the outside and looking inside; my estimate was reasonably accurate. The weathered building was a single-room cabin with a loft above the door. I assumed a bed was in it because the only space for us to sit was at the knotty pine table. I helped Shay to the chair.

"Was this a homestead?" I asked.

Dani latched the door behind us. "This was the first cabin built in this part of the country." She plunged the handle on the well pump. Water gurgled into a small, battered washbasin. "My great-great-grandfather built this with his wife." She reached for a towel on the shelf above the copper sink and dropped it in the water. She set it in front of Shay. "This will help to clean off the blood. The water is pretty cold. You got an icepack in the cruiser?"

Shay swished the towel in the water. "Yes, in the first aid kit." Without another sound, Dani was out the door.

I took the towel from Shay's hand and twisted out the excess water. "Are you okay?" I stood behind her, washing the blood from her head and looking for a wound.

"I wasn't expecting demons on the firing range." She winced as I touched the tender skin.

"I figured that, but I'm more concerned about the blow to your head." I picked out the tiny rocks and bits of demon flesh from her hair.

Shay poked them with her finger. "Did you see Dexter?"

"You mean, did I see him turn into a freakin' dragon?" Shay's hair tangled in the towel, and I pulled too hard.

She winced, and her hand came up to touch her head. "Don't make me laugh. It hurts when I laugh."

"Sorry, love." I combed my fingers through her hair until I was satisfied all of the debris was gone. "You've got a nasty cut and a solid bump back here. Nothing that needs stitches, but we should get it washed out. I can't imagine demon blood is germ-free."

"Oh, and Dexter had one for breakfast and lunch," Shay added.

"You won't need to feed him for days." We turned, staring at the dog lying on the floor. "How do you think he transforms?" I wondered out loud.

Shay reached back, running her fingers over the lump on her head. "It's hard to believe he's a dog on the outside and a giant dragon on the inside."

"Does Dani know about Dexter?"

"Do I know what about Dexter?" She was standing in the cabin doorway, shaking the chemical ice pack to mix the ingredients inside.

Shay turned to look at her friend. "I seem to have inherited a familiar."

"Really?" She closed the cabin door. "When did this happen?" Dani dropped the ice pack on the table.

"Um . . ." I was hesitant to say anything. I looked to Shay for some guidance.

"That's a lot to cover," Shay explained as she touched the ice pack to her wound. "Maybe we should head back to the carriage house, and Wildwood and I can show you what's been going on."

Dani picked up the basin of water. "I'd love to hear this story, but do you think you can drive?" She poured the water down the drain and pumped more onto the dirty towel, pouring bleach over the top.

I raised my hand. "There's no way I'm letting her get behind the wheel."

"Dani, why don't you take my patrol car, and Wildwood can drive your truck." Even with a head wound, Shay was still taking charge.

"Department regs and all, that makes sense," Dani twisted the water out of the towel and draped it over the sink. "What about Dexter? Will he stay in the bed of the truck?"

"I've never tried." Shay looked at her K-9 partner. "Just put him in the back seat of my cruiser. I can wipe it down later."

I leaned against the cabin wall. "Probably not the first time there's been a smear of a demon in that car?"

"Never a demon-soaked dog. I'm certain of that." Shay pushed on the table to stand. "Give me a hand, sweetheart." I helped Shay out the door, and Dani closed it behind us.

"What are we going to do about the crime scene over there?" I pointed my thumb toward the piles of demon guts Dexter left all over the property.

"I'll have a look. Take some samples and pictures. Go through the motions, and when the scene is secure, I'll bring the car to the carriage house." Dani's offer was generous, even if she was the owner of the property.

"Why don't we just take Dexter in the truck." Shay clipped the leash to his collar. "He'll stay if I tell him to."

"Are you sure?" Dani asked. She held Shay's elbow until we were next to the truck.

"With everything that he just did. I want to keep him close." Shay pressed the ice to the back of her head.

"Sounds good." Dani opened the trunk of Shay's car and dropped the bag of weapons in before lifting out an evidence kit.

"Is the trunk of your squad car enchanted too?" I asked, only partially joking.

She laughed. "Not quite. Shay carries all of the extras." It didn't take any imagination to understand what Dani meant. I'd already experienced some of Shay's tricks.

Our walk to the truck's passenger door was slow, and I took my time navigating the bumpy road. Shay's shoulder was pressed against the glass of the door, one hand pinning the ice pack to the back of her head and the other white-knuckled to the ceiling's handle. I could tell that she was fighting her nausea with each passing mile. "We're here, hon."

"Oh, thank the goddess." She yanked up the door release and fell out to the ground.

I jammed the truck into park, running around to the side. She was hands and knees on the ground, heaving what remained inside her stomach, her fingers gouging the gravel. She pushed to stand, swaying. My arms caught her around the waist. "I've got you."

"Woo, that was not fun at all." The dog's paws were up over the bed of the truck. "Come on, Dex." He jumped out and met us at the workshop entrance.

"Do you want to go upstairs?" I pushed the door wide, and the dog ran a straight line to the circle on the floor. He barked at Shay.

"Quiet, Dex." He barked again. This time in a way that made Shay pause.

"I think he wants us in the circle," I said.

"No, I think he wants us to use magick." I sidestepped the forge, but Shay gripped the face of the anvil to catch her balance, dropping the ice pack to the floor. "Why am I so weak?"

I turned to look at her. "It could be that you body-slammed us onto a pile of rocks, or maybe because you got sprayed with demon guts." I paused, adding one last observation. "It could also be that huge bloody bump on the back of your head." I held tight as I helped her sit down beside the dog.

"Can you light the…" She noticed my move to strike the Dagger of Doom across the demon candle holder.

"I got it."

Shay's hand pressed against the back of her head. "I'm going to need that ice."

I picked it up from the floor. "It's covered in anvil dust."

"That's fine. I'll take a shower and wash in a minute. Just come sit with me." The request was easy to fulfill. I dusted off the pack and pressed it against Shay's wound. I felt the rise of magick as the three of us sat together inside the ring. The room turned blue from the light of the runes on the walls.

"What can I do?" I watched the ice pack fall away as Shay's hand rubbed against the wound on her head.

"It's burning?"

We sat, the three of us lit by the glow of magick. "What do you mean, it's burning?" I pulled her hair aside and watched the gape of her wound bubble and seal together.

"I mean, it feels like my skin is burning."

"Um . . . Shay. That's because your cut is closing." I grabbed her hand, touching the flakes of blue scale stuck to her fingertips. "It's healing you."

"What's healing me?"

I looked over at the bottle on the table. "The demon dust from the anvil. It's all over your hands. It's on the ice pack."

"Wil, it's kinda all over the place."

"If you could see this, you'd understand. The cut on your head is just a tiny little ripple. No blood, no wound, and no lump."

She reached up to feel the back of her head. "It's gone." She closed her eyes.

"That must have been what Benton meant." I left her sitting beside Dexter. I sifted through the files on my table, looking for the note about Jacob Kota. "Benton talked about being powerful together. When she lost her maker, she also lost her source for anvil dust."

"So, this is what?" Shay held up her hand, showing me the scale on her fingertips.

"Magick healing powder," I suggested.

She shook her head and scrunched her brow. "That's a terrible name for it."

"Unless you've got a better suggestion, I'm going with that." I picked up the jar of dust I'd collected. Giving it a shake, I handed it to Shay. "Maybe you should keep this locked up?"

"As long as the anvil dust is inside this building, it's safe."

"Kinda like the three of us inside this circle." I sat down beside her, watching the show of light against the workshop walls. "That's just never going to get old."

She pulled me closer. "I totally agree." Dexter jumped to his feet a few seconds before the knock on the door. He charged toward the sound as if he knew we needed to break the circle.

"It's probably Dani."

"So, you're saying it'd be a good idea if I let her in?" I didn't want to leave Shay.

"Yes, love, it would."

I swished my hand toward the chair. "Maybe you should get up off the floor."

"Right."

I helped her stand and watched to see how she moved through the room. "How do you feel?"

"It's funny, but I feel steady."

"It's that magick healing powder I made for you."

She sat down in the chair. "We aren't calling it that." Her hand moved to touch the back of her head.

"We'll see." I opened the door, and Dani was standing on the other side. A duffle bag over her shoulder and a piece of demon armor in her hand.

"Hey, Wildwood. How's Pierce?"

Shay yelled across the shop. "Why don't you come in and see for yourself?"

Dani set the bag on the table and slid our latest forge project across to Shay. "Is this what you were using for target practice?"

Shay's hand slapped on top of the armor plate before it went off the edge of the table. I looked at Shay, wondering what she was going to say. "Yes, why?"

Dani pointed at me. "Is this forged from demon material?"

"Yes, it is."

"Then, I think I figured out why the demons attacked."

"Am I going to need a beer for this?" I asked.

Dani was right behind me. "Yes, I think you will."

Shay took her time on the stairs. Although the dust from the anvil had closed her wound, she wasn't taking any chances. Her surrender into the chair wasn't graceful, but I was glad to see her acting more like herself.

We sat around the kitchen table, staring at the plate of demon armor in the middle. I still wasn't sure how much Dani knew about Shay being the Magick and about my transformation into the Maker, so I let her do all of the talking.

"You want to tell me about that, Pierce?" Dani tapped the metal.

"First, why don't you tell me why you think it initiated the demon attack?"

Dani pulled out her cell, opening up the photographs she'd taken from the scene. "This is a class-one demon. Or at least this is what's left of one."

Shay picked up the phone. "And?" She spread her fingers to zoom in on the details of the monster's remains. Shay tilted the phone as I leaned over her shoulder to get a better look.

"I'm guessing you forged that armor from the same creature?" It sounded like Dani already knew the answer to her question.

"Part of it is, yes," Shay confirmed as she passed the phone back to Dani.

"Part of it?" Dani's posture changed as she looked at the picture again.

I interrupted before she could ask another question. "I made that from a combination of five different demons."

Dani slid the phone into her shirt pocket and took a sip of her drink. "That explains a lot."

I held up my hand. "Wait, just wait one second." It was evident that officer Dannielle Forrest knew more than she let on about demons, blacksmithing, and how the two came together. "Who are you?"

CHAPTER VII

Sacrifices

The silence in our apartment was crushing. Neither Shay nor Dani wanted to tell me what the other knew. Perhaps they were protecting the secrets of this town, or maybe they were each protecting Regina Benton.

"Wil, you know that the police department is also responsible for investigating demon activity." I nodded. "If you think my skills are badass, you'll be happy to know that Dani is my backup ninety percent of the time."

"Another damn superhero?"

Dani laughed. "That's cute."

Shay held up a hand to silence her friend. "Please don't encourage her."

"Look…" Dani hesitated, picking up a piece of paper from the table. "Reg told me things after the attack at the bar."

Shay rolled the glass back and forth in her hands, her following words a whisper. "She knew she was dying the entire time?"

"Yes, she did."

"What did she say, D?"

The records of Regina Benton's life lay scattered across the table in the room. Dani picked up a notebook. "You have to understand that it's different for the founding families. Trying to protect the secrets. Holding tight to this myth of a *Ghost Town* is a logistical nightmare."

"I've been a cop in Bannock for almost ten years. I understand the secrecy."

"No, Shay, honestly, you don't." She pushed at a stack of papers, uncovering the file folder Andrea Peters had given to us. "Damn it, Andrea." Dani held up the file. "Have you read this yet?"

Shay and I looked at one another. Shay answered. "Open it, D. It's a joke. She gave me a redacted file."

Dani hesitated, and whatever thoughts she had, she decided to share. "That's because you haven't been to the old courthouse." Officer Dannielle Forrest was like finding a secret decoder ring and having no idea what you wanted to reveal.

"We've been a little busy."

"I figured Andrea had done this when we were at the bar. It takes a lot to set you off."

Shay shook her head. "When she said Benton called her to the hospital. . . "

"She was baiting you." Dani dropped the file on the table. "Don't let her do that anymore."

I interrupted. I couldn't stand all of the unanswered questions and speaking in code. "Will you please tell us what the hell is going on?" My voice was louder than I'd intended, but I was tired of the people of Bannock keeping their secrets.

Shay's arm came around, pulling me closer to her. "It's okay. We'll get the answers."

The tone in her voice was intended to comfort me, but it had the reverse effect. "Don't cop me right now."

Dani smiled as she leaned back in her chair. "That's cute."

Shay held up a single finger. "Dani, don't."

I crossed my arms and rested them on the table. "Why don't you start from the beginning, Officer Forrest?"

She looked at Shay. Shay nodded consent and I thought I was finally going to understand all of the secrets of Bannock.

"You know me as Dannielle Forrest, but that's not my birth name." She pushed the file on the table and picked up the copy of Shay's library book. She turned it over and touched her finger to the author's photo on the back cover. "Jacob Kota was my father." She looked up at us for a response. I admit my mouth was open, but Shay sat there, no reaction evident on her face. "He was…" Dani's voice trailed off, struggling for a word, "complicated."

Thoughts ran through my mind: What did she mean by complicated? Why was her last name Forrest? How could Jacob Kota be her father? I interrupted. "From our best guess, Jacob was a hundred and thirty-six years old." Shay nodded, confirming my number. "How is that even possible?"

Shay stared into Dani's eyes. "The Magick."

"Of course." I took a drink of my beer and got up from the table.

"My dad was a confusing guy."

This woman was frustrating. "I get the feeling, Dani, that understating information is an art form for you."

135

"I'm sorry that I have to summarize the history of my life at the same time I have to explain yours."

The history of my life was a trigger, and maybe my reaction was harsh. "You see, that's just it." I hit my hand on my chest. "I don't have a history. I don't know who or what or when. You say complicated and confusing, but I have nothing. I don't know where I come from, I don't know why I was left behind, and I don't know where I belong." Shay grabbed my hand and gave it a loving squeeze.

"That's okay, Wildwood, because I do."

I was almost thirty years old. I have recollections from as far back as when I was six. They are vivid, but they never included this tiny town or the old man on the back cover of that book. "Tell me what you know."

"I'm sorry to say that I don't know who your blood kin are. I want to be very clear if dad knew anything about you, that truth died with him, but the important part of who you are is what I know."

Shay was quiet up until this moment, understanding why the subject cut to the core she got up from the table and put her arm around my shoulder. "Are you okay?"

I couldn't answer so Shay turned to talk to Dani. "D, Wildwood grew up like me. You cannot try to tell us what's important. All we've ever had are questions. We never get any answers."

"I'm just trying to be honest, Pierce."

I walked out of the room trying to hide from the truth: that I would never find an answer to the one question I'd always ask. I could hear Shay and Dani talking, but I didn't let the words into my head. Bannock was part of my origin story, and that was an incredible piece of my puzzling life. I needed a break to let it settle into my soul again. I opened the trunk in the bedroom closet and removed a dark blue candle. I lit it, placing it on the floor in front of me. My head fell back against the edge of the bed and I stared up at the ceiling.

All of the confusion needed to stop.

The last thing I expected was a wet nose under my arm and a giant paw covering my thigh. "Hello, dragon dog." My fingers combed through the scruff on his head. My hand traveled down to his collar and found the remnants of his afternoon fight. "I think you need a wash, buddy." Candle in hand, I led Dexter to the giant tub. I'd never tried to bathe him, but he was eager to get into the claw-foot basin. I turned on the sprayer trailing it over his head and down his back. "Does that feel good?" It only took a few minutes to scrub and rinse away the blood and stink of his afternoon. He was motionless until the towel wrapped around his body. Hearing footsteps down the hallway, he tried to jump from the tub. I heard Shay come into the room.

"Good choice."

The dog was beside me on the floor, and I continued rubbing the fur of Dexter's face. "Yes, he was a little gross."

"Oh, I didn't mean the bath." She held up the candle.

"Blue to help balance." I turned away and wiped the corner of my eye on my shoulder and sleeve. If I looked into her eyes, there was no way I'd ever stop the tears. "Shay."

"Yes, love." I could hear the understanding in her tone.

My hands stopped moving as I stared at Dexter's head. "I just don't want my history to be a trigger anymore. I thought searching for my family – I just thought I was – I can't do it anymore." Silence. I turned to look at her.

Shay tucked her hair behind her ears and took the towel from my hand to finish drying Dexter. "I wish there was something I could do."

"Me too." For the first time, I looked at the remnants inside the tub. "That's pretty gross."

Shay turned on the tap, rinsing the tiny bits of rock and demon down the drain. "I'll pour some moon water over this. Say a little cleansing spell."

"Better safe than sorry?"

"Something like that." Shay opened the towel and dropped it by our feet.

"Did Dani leave?" I asked.

Shay shook her head. "No, I asked her to stay. I think we need to hear what she has to say." She held her hand to me, helping me from the floor. "Will you come back out?" I nodded. "Good."

She set the candle inside the tub near the drain. Her hand moved over the porcelain surface, and she whispered. "Blessed be to the spirit of all that is good." I watched in silence, leaning against the sink as she opened the container of protection salts and poured a handful in her palm. She sprinkled it on the porcelain surface and closed her eyes. "Release." She removed the cork from the bottle. The water was sacred, blessed by the powerful energies of a full moon. Shay poured it over and around the drain. "So mote it be." I thought about the firing range, and the river. The flash of fire and our real-life dragon. Shay's body knocking me down, covering me like a human shield. The light in the room reflected against the flush of her cheeks. Her smile was an elixir for my soul. "Goddess, you're beautiful."

She turned away to put the containers on the shelf behind her. "Am I?"

I crossed my arms. "Not knowing, makes you a thousand times more."

She tugged my forearms. "Come on, Blackstone, let's get some answers." She took a few steps and I saw the tangles in her hair.

"How's your head?"

Her hand came up to touch it. "Nothing, it's like it never happened." I pinched her just above the elbow and she jerked away. "Ouch, what was that for."

"Just making sure this isn't a dream."

She was rubbing the back of her arm. "Aren't you supposed to pinch yourself?"

"Oh, no way. That hurts."

Dani was sitting at the dining table, sliding papers from one pile to another. Talking to the picture on the back cover of the book. "I got this, you stubborn ass."

"Who are you talking to?"

"Right now, I'm talking to the dead guy on the back of this book." She flipped it over.

"Your father?" I asked.

She nodded. "Jacob was responsible for my conception and was tolerant, but we had a falling out."

"I'm sorry to hear that," I said.

She touched the photograph. "It wasn't my choice."

I could see that the story wasn't a happy one. "You don't have to…"

She held up a hand. "It's fine. My baggage can stay packed for tonight. I'm sure you want to know how we are all connected more than you want to swing from the branches of the Kota family tree."

"That would be helpful," I said. Shay stood behind me, her arm around my waist. I was aware of her presence, but it also felt like it was my turn to investigate.

"Reggie and my dad, they were cohorts and protectors much like the two of you, but the last few years, dad was alive..." Dani took a deep breath.

"Is this the complicated part?"

"It is." She looked up, perhaps to revisit a memory and I wondered what was so terrible that a father would reject their child.

I sat down at the table, looking at the book Jacob Kota had written. "Did they stop fighting demons together?"

"It was much more than that. Reggie and dad stopped speaking, and they had no idea it would break the Maker / Magick bond."

"Jacob was a blacksmith?" I asked.

"He was, among many other things." Dani pointed at the notes on the table.

"Did you ever work with him?"

Dani's solemn nod was confirmation that she had. "He was a very talented man, but no-one needs a blacksmith in an empty town."

Shay walked away, going down the stairs, returning a few moments later with the demon tools we'd forged. One by one, she laid them across the table. I pulled the dagger of doom from its sheath, laying it beside its matching punch dagger.

Dani turned them over, inspecting each one. "These are beautiful. You're very talented, Wildwood."

"Yes, she is." The smile on Shay's face was more than agreement. It was pride. Our love was everything, and I thought in the moment that the way she loved me was worth fighting for.

The leatherbound notebook caught my attention and I touched the cover. "Tell us what you know about the relationship between the Maker and the Magick?"

"I know that you're bound. I know for Benton, that commitment, after dad was gone, it was a curse."

I felt every muscle in my body tighten. I didn't want to be bound to my lover by a curse. Shay sat beside me. Her fingers squeezed around my fist. "We'll be okay."

"Yes, we will." My palm opened and I held tight to Shay. "Tell us what happened."

Dani flipped through the pages of her father's book. "It was because of me, their separation; it started when I wouldn't deny who I am."

"Why do you say that?" I asked.

"My father and I had a disagreement, and Benton took my side. Dad wouldn't forgive her or me, and eventually it killed them both."

"How is it possible that all of this happened, and I didn't know?" Shay asked.

"It happened long before you got here, Shay. I was a kid myself."

For the first time, I took a long look at Dani. If I compared her to Shay, she was almost a head taller, just over six feet. Her shoulders were broad, but I attributed it to the fitness lifestyle of law enforcement. I noticed the ring on her finger. Perhaps it explained the surname differences. "You're married?"

She nodded, playing with the gold band. "We've been together for almost twenty years now. Married for three. We had to wait for it to become legal."

"You're gay too?"

Dani nodded and smiled as she looked at her ring finger. "Well, my wife is for sure." Shay shook her head at Dani, an obvious inside joke.

My questions continued. "You and a girl . . . that was the disagreement that came between Benton and Jacob?"

"It was part of it."

"So he was a big giant phobe?" I said through clenched teeth. Shay pulled my hand into her lap and held tight to the bond between us.

Dani shook her head. "As I said, it was complicated." We sat there for a long moment; Dani staring at the photo of her father and Shay and I watching, waiting.

Shay's questions broke the silence. "How much do you know about what happened to us? About how we come into our powers?"

"I know enough to be helpful, but Benton left everything in the journals." Dani picked up the notebook and handed it to Shay.

"We started going through them, but answers just lead to more questions." Shay fanned the pages, showing us that the information had doubled since the secondary ink was revealed. Dani couldn't see any of it.

"Go through the journals, Pierce."

"That's it?" I asked.

"As far as your powers go, yes. That's the best I can do." Dani picked up the armor plate, flicking her finger against it. "Can we talk about this instead?"

"What do you want to know?" My tone was defensive, maybe a bit harsh but Dani's change of subject was intentional.

"Is it bulletproof?"

I swiped my hand over the top of the body armor. "See any marks?"

She inspected the demon steel. "I don't."

Shay interrupted, excited to share the results of our firing range adventure. "I hit it dead center with a nine-mil round and a black magic."

"You shot a bear round at this?" Dani turned the armor over, rubbing her hand across the material.

"It didn't even leave a scuff mark." I added. I was proud of my creation, even if it was experimental.

Dani looked at Shay. "Your girlfriend is very bold. I don't think dad ever mixed demons like this."

"Really?" The idea that a blacksmith wouldn't attempt to combine different grades of demon metal seemed like a wasted opportunity.

"I can't be positive, but his work was pretty straightforward."

"That's too bad," I said.

"It was." She dropped the plate on the table, picking up the dagger of doom and its matching blade. "Tell me about these."

"They were my very first demon project."

Shay took her dagger from Dani. "You want to talk about experimental? Wil found the metal in her forge and used it before she knew anything about Bannock's history."

Dani passed the Dagger of Doom to me. I twirled the point of the blade against my fingertip. "I knew a little. I just had a hard time believing it."

Dani lined up the rest of my creations, surveying my work. "You've made some great weapons." She touched the circle stamped into the metal. "And your maker's mark. Did you know about it?"

I looked at Shay, and she shook her head. "We don't know much of anything, Dani."

"Benton was sure you'd have figured it out."

Talking to this woman was frustrating. "How? That doesn't even make sense." She was holding back, and if I could see it, I knew that Shay could too.

"Reggie wanted to tell you, but she was worried that you wouldn't go to the mill if you knew it would end her life, that coming into your powers as the Magick would essentially kill her."

Shay stood up from the table and dropped her dagger on top of Benton's journal. "She's right. I wouldn't have done any of it."

"Bannock needs you." She pointed back and forth between my girlfriend and me. "It won't survive without the two of you."

"Why the sudden desperation?" I asked.

"That's just it. The desperation isn't sudden." Dani held up the sketches we'd made based on the map written in demon blood. "This symbol here. It was my father's maker's mark." Shay's gentle nod of the head confirmed what we suspected. "Without a maker, Reggie struggled to balance her power."

I interrupted before she finished, worried about my fate. "And your father?"

"I'm sure you read the coroner's report?"

Shay opened a folder, looking for her printout from the internet search. "I found this." She handed the document to Dani. "I'm guessing it wasn't a horse that killed him?"

"Such a stubborn ass." She dropped the page. "It was a class one attack. He never had a chance, not without the protection of Reggie's magick."

Shay leaned against the kitchen cabinet. "I'm so sorry, Dani."

"It was his choice." She pushed at the pile of paper on the table until a building sketch moved into view.

I touched the picture before Dani could cover it. "What's at the old courthouse?" I poked it with my finger.

Dani laid the map of Bannock beside the sketch, pointing at a location not far from the carriage house. "This building was the original courthouse. Everything moved to the jail a few years after." She looked up at the ceiling, thinking. "What year was the carriage house built?"

I held up a hand, pointing back and forth. "The two of you should know this answer. You've lived here longer than I have." They didn't respond. "The 1830's."

"Right, well, the original courthouse was built around the same time." She opened her father's book. "There was a murder in that building. They never found the killer, but they wouldn't have."

Shay tilted her head in thought. "I read the newspaper story. Jacob's book didn't mention the crime, but he went on and on about the building's history. He loved it."

"He did. Probably more than anything."

"So what's the real story?" I felt drawn to Jacob in a way I'd never felt before. He wasn't blood, but he was my chance to feel connected to someone.

"The murder was a demon attack." Dani explained. "It was gruesome. I've seen the crime scene photos."

Shay interrupted. "You've seen the file?"

"My father was obsessed. Reggie gave him anything he wanted."

"Why?"

Dani looked at the author's image on the back of her father's book. "My mother was the victim."

Shay closed her eyes. "How? How's it possible that I've never heard this before?"

"Bannock is a place with a lot of secrets."

I knocked on top of the table. "You do like your mysteries, that's for sure."

Shay pushed away from the cabinet. "It seems like mysteries and secrets follow us around." She put her hand on Dani's shoulder. "I'm sorry about your mother."

"To be honest, I hardly knew her."

"Did she have powers? Was she a practitioner?"

Dani stood from her seat, walking around the kitchen. It was apparent the subject was complex. "Dad was enigmatic, and I never got the impression that my mother had any powers. I was only two years old." She buried her hand deep in her pockets. She shrugged the last words. "I don't have any memories that are my own."

"I don't have any memories." Shay put her arm around her co-worker. "I am so sorry to bring all of this up, D."

"It's okay." She looked over at me. "I want to help you. The way that Reg couldn't."

Shay sat down beside me. "Why couldn't she?"

Dani poured a glass of water from the sink. She turned around, facing our curious expressions. "You already said that you wouldn't have gone to the mill if you'd known."

"Never, I would never."

"That's why she was silent."

I thought about my future. Would I live frozen as a twenty-eight-year-old? "Are we immortal?" I asked.

Dani finished the water in her glass. "Did Reg look like she was over one hundred?"

"She didn't look a day over fifty."

"She wasn't immortal so much as the power of the Magick slows down aging."

I held up a hand, hoping they would stop. "This is too much. I can't take any more." I walked to the stairs, dropping down two at a time to the workshop below. I stood in the center of the room, staring at the walls. "This is impossible."

Shay's arms came around me. "It feels that way, doesn't it?"

"I don't want to lose you." I clenched her hands and pulled her closer.

"Oh, love. I'm here."

I was beginning to trust that there was strength in a show of emotions, especially with Shay. Today's adventure in the world of demon-fighting was just the beginning, and now that my powers were active, there was no turning back. "What if I don't want to be the Maker?"

"I don't think there's an alternate choice for a replacement."

I turned in her arms and found a hint of optimism in the beautiful eyes staring back at me. "Being the Magick doesn't scare you?"

Her forehead touched my own. "It scares the shit out of me, but that's just because I don't know enough. Once we finish the transfer of power, it'll be okay."

"Okay?"

"I'm afraid that's the best I've got for now." She kissed me, and that was the dose of reality I needed, rooted by the power of her magick.

"For now," I agreed.

We turned toward the sound of a cough and a noticeable clearing of her throat. Dani was standing at the bottom of the stairs looking at the two of us. Her arms were loaded with our demon forged treasures. "Before I go, would you mind showing me how your weapons work?"

My arms dropped as Shay stepped toward the table. "Bring them over here." Shay gripped her punch dagger, scraping it against the Dagger of Doom. They sparked a showy flame, and she threw it at the candle holder. The flaring transition from yellow to blue was an exquisite light show. She thrust her dagger-filled fist toward a piece of scrap metal, slicing it from top to bottom.

"Intuitive reflection?"

I looked at Dani, questioning. "You know what that is?"

"I've heard about it."

I thrust my hand out toward her. "Welcome to the team."

She shook my hand. "Thanks, I guess." The wall behind us lit up from the glow of the candle. Dani turned to see the map of Bannock written in demon blood. "Holy shit!"

I didn't try to hide my smile. "Yep, pretty amazing, isn't it?"

She didn't respond, drawn instead to the illuminated pattern on the map. Her fingers traced the shape. "Dad." The glowing symbol was the mark of Jacob Kota.

"This is your father's mark." I already knew the answer.

"It was."

"There's something else you need to see." Shay dipped the top on our blue flame candle in the quench bucket beside the forge, and the room went dim. She led us to the circle on the workshop floor, calling the dog to join us. "Dexter." His paws slapped against the ground until he flopped to the floor in the center of the ring.

Dani's eyes were wide, and her mouth fell open in amazement. "You are the ones."

Shay interrupted. "It's crazy, isn't it?"

I watched Dani's fingers glide across the wall, landing on the third maker's mark. "Sabine Althora. This was her mark."

I looked at Shay. "Ever heard the name?"

"I haven't."

"It's in the scroll. You have the scroll from Reggie's desk, don't you?" Dani asked.

Shay left the circle, turning on the lights inside the workshop. "We looked at it, yes, but we haven't had a chance to translate them."

"What language is it in?" Dani asked.

"Latin," I answered. "I guess it's good that one of us is fluent."

Shay picked up the scroll, rolling a short section out. "It seems odd. Reg didn't know the language at all."

Dani held up a hand. "It's not odd. It's intuitive."

"Of course, it is." I reached for the scroll. "The blood of Sanquis Caeden is more than disappearing ink."

"That's why Reg and my dad used it."

I held the scroll in my hand, unwinding the parchment to the first section. "It's in English."

"Basically . . . whoever holds this, acts as the translator?" Shay tapped her fingers against the aged parchment.

Dani shrugged her shoulders. "Yes, but for me and for the rest of the world, it's just a gross old bone wrapped in parchment."

Shay held up a hand. "Wait, just wait. How do you know all of this, Dani?"

"That's on Reggie." She walked away. "She was where you are right now. She and dad had to figure all of this out, and it put them in a lot of danger. Dad lost my mother in all of the confusion. Reg didn't want a lack of knowledge to hurt either of you."

Shay reached for my hand. "I wanted to believe that she wouldn't hurt me... us."

"Reggie loved you, Shay. She did everything she could to protect you." Dani said without hesitation.

"I see that now."

Dani shuffled the forged projects across the table. "The daggers are pretty cool. The candle will come in handy, I'm sure. What about this?" She flipped the axe head until the handle was in her palm.

I answered. "The axe appears to be just an axe. Nothing special so far."

Shay threw an arm around Dani's shoulder. "Have you seen weapons like ours?"

"I have." Dani nodded.

"Are you prepared to be a part of this too?" I asked.

"I don't think any of us ever had a choice."

CHAPTER VIII

Union

I could hear Shay's voice outside the carriage house door saying goodnight to Dani. I was sorting the never-ending pile of notes and files back into the box when Shay's arms wrapped around me. "Dani said she would stop by after work tomorrow."

"Good, we can pick her brain some more."

"She also told me to turn off my alarm and sleep in because she's covering my shift."

I turned in her arms. "Why would she do that?"

Shay stepped away, reaching in her back pocket for a business card. "She gave me this number. Said I should talk to a doctor at this clinic."

"Clinic where?" I took the business card from Shay's hand. "Have you ever heard of this place?"

She squeezed her arms, giving me a tiny hug. "I trust Dani, and if today was any indication, I think I might need someone who knows about me. About us."

"I guess we should prepare for anything." I picked up the demon metal armor plate on the table. "Let's finish this tonight."

Shay looked at her watch. "It's almost midnight."

"Do demons keep track of time? They're going to come for you even after midnight."

"Yes, but not here." Shay shook her head. "A little dramatic, don't you think?"

I picked up the jar of anvil dust. "You might have a different opinion if it wasn't for this." I put the bottle in Shay's hand as I walked away. "Can you go get your vest, please?" She was already up the stairs before I could turn around. I sparked the fire in the forge, giving it time to heat up. I heard the Velcro tear away as she walked back into the room.

"You want me to pull out my plate?"

"Yep." She removed the regulation Kevlar, holding the pocket open while I slipped my demon armor inside. "That's not bad."

"Let me put it on." She slipped it over her shoulder like she'd done countless times before. "It's super light." She lifted her arms, moving her torso in every direction to test the fit.

"Where does it feel tight or restrict movement?" I asked.

She rotated her arms in small circles. "Right shoulder needs a gap here." She gripped the vest by her armpit with her thumb. "My gun hand needs full mobility."

"That's easy. How about here?" I grabbed near her ribcage. In the blink of an eye, her hands shot out in a tactical maneuver catching me off guard, forcing us against the workshop table.

My breath hitched, and my heart was racing at the speed of her action.

"Holy shit," Shay shouted, backing away from me with her arms in the air.

"Holy shit is right. I didn't even see you move."

She stood motionless. "I didn't. I mean, I did, but I didn't."

"This is crazy. Is it possible the armor enhances your reaction time?" I asked, wondering if the inquiry was ridiculous.

"I think it might." She stepped back. "Maybe while I'm wearing the armor plate, you should keep your hands to yourself?"

"Baby, that is the last damn thing I want to do when you're in uniform."

She laughed. "I'm very aware of that." Her left arm came up. "It's rubbing the scar here."

I didn't touch her. "Take it off, and I'll make the adjustments. It won't take much time."

"Did the body armor sense you as a threat?" Shay asked as she set the plate on the anvil and pulled up a chair to watch me work.

"I'm not sure." I used my tongs to set the project inside the white-hot forge. "It could be that this combination of demon material doesn't mix well."

"I need to be able to touch you."

"You bet your ass you do." I set to work tweaking my creation, heating and reheating, tapping the edges to make a perfect silhouette of Shay's chest. I laid my tools on the anvil, heating the plate one more time to hammer in my finishing touch. I flipped over the demon metal, striking my mark so it would rest over Shay's heart.

"It's going to need a few minutes to cool before we can recheck it," I explained.

"That's good. I've got an idea how to kill some time." She reached for the strap holding the apron on my shoulder and pulled me in for a kiss.

"Be careful. Everything's hot in here."

"You're very perceptive, my love." Her fingers combed through my hair, tugging it free from the elastic tie. Her kiss was gentle until it wasn't, and I longed for every touch. She released the clip holding the apron around my neck.

"You better keep your pants on in here, woman." I swatted her hands away.

"It wasn't my pants I was concentrating on."

I grabbed her wrists. "If you think I'm getting naked next to a two-thousand-degree forge, you're out of your gorgeous mind."

Her pout was adorable, even if it was phony. "What if you just kiss me?"

I planted a quick kiss on her cheek. "What if while we wait for this to cool, we do a cleansing and get it ready for action?"

"You're all work and no play tonight." She crossed her arms and followed me as I picked up the armor with the forging tongs. I carried it to the center of the circle on the floor.

"I watched you get knocked around by a demon today. I just want to do whatever I can to protect you." I laid the project on the floor.

She acquiesced. "I'll get the supplies we need."

I worried that my choice to do magick instead of fooling around upset her. It wasn't that I didn't want her hands all over me, I just wanted to keep her safe, and that was my single-sighted priority. She came down the stairs with her arms full of supplies. I wasn't sure if she intended to distract me by untying her hair, but it did. She set candles at North and South compass positions after making a ring of salt on the floor.

"Are you ready?" She asked, holding a hand out for me. We sat face to face.

"Shay?"

She set the athame on the floor before looking up at me. "Mm, hmm?"

"I love you."

She didn't say a word. She just smiled. Her voice broke as she began. "Energies of the universe, we call you here to cleanse this armor with virtue to purify the demon blood from which it was born."

She held her hands above the metal plate, sprinkling salt over the top. "Spirit of earth and air, bring strength and truth. Release the negative, defuse the fragmented forces that shaped this armor." She waved the athame in front of her body.

"Forged from fire and called to be and do my will, I cast away all that is evil." She waved the tiny knife through the candle's flame and touched it to the hot demon armor. "My obeisance to truth and the boundaries of love and nature, for good to ward out evil."

She poured a measure of water over the plate and a burst of steam engulfed it as she began reciting, "Blessed by the goddess to be true, washed by the tears of the earth, in love and in honor, dispelling evil. In peace and in trust and in my faith." She looked at me as she said the final words, encouraging me to repeat them. "So mote it be."

"So mote it be." I whispered and looked at Shay. "I love it when you do magick." I said.

"I know. I feel the same about watching you work." She held her hand to me, and our palms came together.

"Shay, please don't think for a single minute that I don't want to make love to you."

"It's silly." She tugged my hand.

I squeezed my fingers so she would look into my eyes. "Your feelings aren't silly."

She let go of me, waving the back of her hand to test the heat coming off of our project. "I think it's cool enough. Can we test it again?"

"Grab your vest."

She opened the pocket, and I fed the new plate inside. "Is it too snug?"

"No, it's good. I don't want it to shift around when I'm running." Her explanation was matter-of-fact, practical. I tried not to think about why she'd be running in her uniform, although I knew it would involve danger. I watched her repeat the movements she'd made earlier, imitating drawing her service weapon. "This is so perfect."

Without thinking, I threw my arms around her and caught her off balance. "Good, that's very good."

She pushed against my shoulders, instantly aware that the armor didn't deflect me. "You're hugging me."

I smiled. "Yes, I am."

"No, I mean you're holding me."

I realized what she meant. "Oh, is it a fluke?"

"Fluke?"

I corrected myself. "I mean, the armor didn't defend you as it did before."

"Try something more aggressive."

"Shay." My eyes said, no, as I glared at her.

"Don't think, just move."

I took a deep breath, turning around as if I didn't want to do it. If I was going to hit the floor, I might as well give this a real test. I lunged at Shay's shoulders, using the full force of my weight. I expected to hit a wall of protection. Instead, I hit my lover, knocking us both against the door.

"Hello there." She said. "I guess you fixed it?"

"Did I?"

Her lips crushed against my own. "As long as you can touch me in uniform, that's progress."

"I think the real key is if it's going to protect you when you're working."

Her arms tightened around my hips, drawing us closer together. "If it makes you happy, I'll ask Dani to take a swing at me when I go back to work."

"No! That will not make me happy at all." I patted the top of her shoulder. "Will you be serious for a minute so we can figure this out?"

She loosened her hold, but she didn't let me go. "What's different? What did you change in the last hour? Let's talk it through."

"Nothing. I heated it and rounded some edges." I turned in her arms, looking at the anvil and my tools. "I didn't even polish it." I held her wrist cuff.

"We blessed it. Maybe that's the difference?" Her hand moved to the side of my neck, pushing the hair away to reveal my shoulder. Her kiss was tender against my skin.

"Please take it off," I said.

"Your shirt?" She tugged at my collar.

I shook my head. "No, you perv, your vest." I rubbed the skin where her kiss had just been. "I can't think when your lips are on me."

"That's not going to help us."

I stepped out of her embrace, holding up a hand to keep her in her place. "Take off the vest."

"Yes, ma'am." The Velcro ripped away, and she pulled the armor over her head.

"Thank you." I opened the inner pocket to remove the plate. I checked the edges where I'd made the adjustments, turning it over and spinning it around.

"We keep doing this," Shay said. "I can't believe we keep doing this." She smacked her forehead.

"Doing what?" I was confused.

"This." She pointed to the maker's mark. "Your mark is the difference."

"It always comes back to the mark of the Maker." I said

"Your gifts and my magick. When the two of us put our work together, we are more powerful. Benton said something like that in the letter."

"So, you protect me, and I protect you." I collected the tiny bits of anvil dust I'd just created. "And this?" I held my hand out to her.

"Benton's letter said something about feeding the lodestone."

"What does that even mean?"

"I think it has to do with the anvil dust. I'm adding it to the list of unknowns."

"List? It's more like a catalog."

She laughed. "I'm hoping that Dani can help us answer some of the big questions."

"Yes, Dani." I took Shay's hand, leading her toward the apartment stairs. "What's the deal with her anyway?"

"Twenty-four hours ago, I would have said she's super into rocks. Now I think that's the least interesting thing I know about her."

I covered my mouth with a yawn. "This just gets better and better." I stopped at the top of the stairs, watching Dexter curl up in a ball on the floor. "And what about your K-9 partner over there?"

"I'm not sure." She walked toward the bedroom. "You ever read anything about dragons?" She asked.

"Do graphic novels count?"

She stopped at the foot of the bed, looking at me, considering the idea. "Maybe?" She stripped out of her clothes, dropping them in the laundry basket. "They can't hurt." She walked out of the room.

The water turned on in the shower. I picked up Shay's shirt and touched the stain of blood around the collar. The memory of helplessness, of carrying Shay away from the river. The sound of shredding demon flesh. It was all haunting. The transformation from dog to dragon kept playing in my mind. I was beginning to understand the importance of Dani and any detail of Bannock's history she could share.

I carried the shirt to the sink, running water and spot remover over the bloodstains. I scrubbed away most of the remnants of our afternoon, wondering what else was coming. I looked at my reflection in the mirror, shaking my head at the combination of blood and dirt smeared on my face. "Dexter's a dragon." I heard the shower turn off and the curtain pull away.

"What did you say?" Shay stepped over the ledge of the tub. I dropped her shirt in the sink and moved closer to hand Shay a clean towel. I draped it around her shoulders.

"I said, my girlfriend is gorgeous."

She cinched the towel around her arms. "Is she?" Shay stretched to wrap around me.

"Wait, I'm still gross with demon. I'd hate for you to have to shower again." I turned toward the bath, adjusting the water temperature for myself.

"I'll risk it."

I pulled the shirt over my head. Before I could do anything, her lips were against my own.

"What was that for?" I asked.

"Because I love you and because I can't believe he's a dragon either."

I stepped into the hot spray of water, watching as the remains of our demon fight rinsed through my hair and onto the bathtub basin. "This is disgusting."

"Keep washing. You'll be amazed at the places that demon squished into."

I lathered shampoo into my hair, opening my eyes to see the streaks of red run down my torso. Shay was right. I washed a few more times until all that remained was the white spiraling foam in the drain. It felt good to be clean. I wasn't surprised to see Shay waiting with my towel in her hand. "Do you think I'll have to wash demon guts out of my hair often?"

She laced the towel around my shoulders, pulling my naked body against her own. "From my experience, yes."

"I think I'm going to build a shower in the workshop." She rubbed the towel against my back.

"Really?" Her curious expression made me smile.

"It'll be a thousand times easier to hose down our dragon dog without this giant tub around him." Shay draped the towel over my head.

"I didn't even consider that."

"I can't stop thinking about it. There are a thousand things that we just don't know."

"We know one thing about him." She said.

"Oh yea, what's that?" I asked

"He likes the taste of demons."

CHAPTER IX

Boundary

There's something utterly perfect about rolling over at the break of dawn to feel your lover sleeping beside you. To see someone you admire, someone who seems more significant than the skin they are in, at rest. It didn't often happen, not with this woman next to me.

Her arms lay tucked up under the pillow, and I could barely see the profile of her face through the tangles of her hair. Wanting to touch her, to reveal my desire, was second to my wish to respect what she needed most, rest.

Her body was still. I wondered if she was taking in breath until I saw the slow rise of her back and the leading edge of the scar on her ribs. I rolled to my side, adjusting just enough to get close without touching. I knew the moment I yielded, those dazzling eyes would open, and she'd charge back to the table filled with the history of her magick and my own. I thought about my past and wondered what pieces to the puzzle of my life she might finally discover. After Dani's visit and her revelation about Jacob Kota, it was impossible not to have hope.

I heard the scratch and pit-pat of paws in the hallway and rolled off the edge of the bed. I tugged on a pair of sweatpants and a shirt before intercepting the giant German Shepherd in the hallway. "Hey, Dex," I whispered. "Need to go outside?" He didn't answer, but I didn't expect that he would.

I clipped the leash to his collar and led him down the stairs and out the door. I noticed the full moon setting to the west and remembered how powerful the Earth would be for the next few days. We took our usual route, stopping at Shay's to check the mailbox on her front porch. Today, tucked between the leaflets and advertisements, was a letter addressed to Shay Pierce and Wildwood Blackstone. I folded the envelope in half, tucked it into my pocket, and dropped the junk mail into the recycle bin on the porch.

The final stretch of our walk led us to Slammed. I'm sure Dexter was trying to figure out where his snack friend had gone. I stopped to read the flyer taped on the door. It was an announcement notifying the town of Benton's funeral service. I thought about my girlfriend sleeping in our bed and how this news might affect the rest of our day.

We circled once around the park, and Dex took a drink from the river before returning to the carriage house. I passed the old Courthouse building and wondered what secrets we would find. The root of Shay's power as the Magick of Bannock was somewhere inside. I shook the handle on the front door, peeking through the slats across the window. It was empty and looked more ominous than the old grist mill. Dexter pawed at the boards by the door. It felt like a warning, and I followed him away from the building and back toward home. I wasn't going to ignore the tiny dragon ever again.

It was almost 8 am when we walked into the apartment. I expected to see my girlfriend sitting at the table drinking coffee and reading a dusty ancient text. The kitchen was empty, and the lights were off. I unclipped Dexter and followed him down the hallway into the bedroom.

Shay's body lay sprawled on the bed, almost as I'd left her, except for the blanket drawn over her body. The dog dropped to the floor beside her. I took off my clothes and edged into my spot beside Shay. I tried hard to let her sleep, but I could feel the rise of magick energy coming from her. I curled closer, slipping my arm under her pillow to hold her. Shay's hand was hot to the touch. I bent the corner of the pillow to see if her scars were glowing.

"Honey?" I gave her a little shake. "Shay, Honey." My fingers curled around her shoulder as I rolled her onto her back. Her face was pale. I shook her again, and her eyes popped open.

"What?" Her voice was heavy, like her throat was dry, and I could see the scars on her chest take on the same glimmering as her palms.

"You're glowing."

Her hands came up in front of her mouth. "I feel so sick."

"What can I do?" I asked.

Before Shay could answer, she rolled off the bed, stumbling over Dexter as she ran to the bathroom. I could hear her vomiting, and I stood in the doorway. "What can I do?"

"Horehound and Bay. Bundle them." She paused to throw up again. I ran to our tiny greenhouse hidden behind the sliding barn-wood door. I plucked off leaves from both plants and tied them into a tight bundle with a braid of sweetgrass. Shay was leaning against the side of the bathtub, striking a match, trying to light a candle. Dexter spread his body on the floor, his paws pressing hard enough to leave huge fleshy prints against Shay's thigh.

"I got it," I said and took the matches from her shaking hands. With a quick strike, the flame flickered on the skinny white taper. I tipped the candle to pool wax on the floor so it would stand on its own, desperate to take care of her. I rolled the green leaves through the flame, and the herbs crackled and burst into a flash of fire. I blew on the bundle, and the sweetgrass puffed a dense lingering smoke.

Tiny beads of sweat covered Shay's face, and her voice lacked the usual passion for spellcasting. "I am sister to all that is good, choosing love and light as my source. Give as I receive and receive as is given." Shay grasped my hands. "Keep saying it." It was impossible to miss the desperation in her voice.

I helped her sit so we could place our palms together. I needed to take some of the magick she couldn't contain. "I am the sister of good. Choosing love and light as my source. Give as I receive and receive as is given." I didn't stop. I chanted over and over until my mouth went dry. The force of her powers passed between us like lightning arcing across the sky. I lost track of everything, but the breath Shay was taking and the change of color to her cheeks.

"I am sister . . ." She started to say it with me. I could feel the cycling energy move in and out of our hands. The candle was halfway to the floor, which meant we'd been repeating the chant for more than thirty minutes.

Her eyes opened, and she drew her shoulder up to wipe her forehead.

"How do you feel?"

She turned her palm over, resting it in mine. "Like I've been binge drinking all night."

"What do you need?"

"Water, that would be good." She looked at the floor in front of her. "That wax is going to be a real pain to clean up."

"Are you honestly worried about the floor right now?" I handed her a glass of water. "After all of this?" She didn't answer. Instead, she gulped until the glass was empty. "More?" I asked.

"Yes, please." She stayed in her place on the floor, and Dexter inched his scruffy head into her lap. "Hey, big boy." He licked Shay's hands.

"You feel like you can make it back to the bed?" I asked.

"You'll have to lift me." She gripped the rim of the bathtub. "Can you help me brush my teeth first?"

"Of course I can." I stood behind her naked body. Shay was holding the sink for support as I squeezed the paste on her brush. Her body weight shifted, leaning against me to steady herself. It was awkward but effective, and a few minutes later, we stumbled across the room to our bed. Shay collapsed to the mattress, but I could feel the moisture of sweat on the sheets. "You can't lay here, love."

She wriggled over to my side of the bed.

"I guess that works for now." I covered her with the top sheet.

"Make another bundle of herbs, will you? I think we'll need to use them again."

"In a minute. I want to hold you first."

My heart was racing. I hadn't realized until Shay's body laid across my own.

"I can feel your heart." She stretched, looking up at me. Her hand rested between my breasts, and I knew her in a way I never had before. "*Vulnerasti cor meum in domum suam.*" The words were a whisper against my shoulder.

My hand came up to cover hers. "Oh, wow. What was that?"

"It was me entrusting you with my love."

"What does the Latin mean?" I asked, wondering how a few whispered words could invigorate me.

"I said that you were my heart and my home."

I pulled her on top of me. "You're my heart and my home too."

Her lips crushed against mine, and there was nothing left to say. Her hand drifted over my shoulder and across my chest, and her lips followed. I was content to surrender to every touch. Shay had me, and I was happier for it.

~~~~~~~~~~

A few hours later, I opened my eyes. The bed was empty beside me, and I was disappointed that I wouldn't get to watch Shay sleeping. I could hear her voice in the kitchen, and I giggled, thinking about the conversation she was having with Dexter. The clock read 11 am, and I wondered why Shay left me in bed to sleep for so long. I threw a t-shirt over my naked body. It was just long enough to cover all the vital bits. I thought about getting a kiss and a cup of coffee as I walked into the kitchen.

"Good morning, sleepyhead."

I was rubbing my eyes. "Someone rocked me right back to sleep."

I heard the sound of a third person clearing their throat and looked over to see Dani leaning against the wall.

"Hey, Wildwood." I could hear the squawk of her lapel mic as she raised her coffee cup in a makeshift wave.

"Oh, hey." There was no hesitation. I spun around to walk back into the bedroom to put on my sweatpants. When I returned, Shay was pouring me a cup of coffee.

"Sorry, Wildwood. I stopped by to check on Pierce." Dani explained.

"Not a problem. I just thought she was talking to the dog." We all looked at the sleeping ball of fur in the corner. "Obviously not."

Shay interrupted. "I was just telling Dani about the problem I've been having in the morning."

"The surges." Dani gave them a name and continued with the explanation. "They're going to keep happening until you do the second ritual."

"You mean we have to repeat what happened at the mill?" I asked. My nose lingered over the hot cup of coffee.

"Yes, you came into your power through that incantation. Shay has to do the same."

"And you know this, how?" I asked a little louder than necessary.

Dani hesitated.

Shay stared at me and back at Dani before scolding us. "Look, you two, I love you both, but you need to trust me when I tell you to trust each other. We are all on the same team here."

"Base to Forrest." The radio squawk made me jump.

Dani pushed the button on her shoulder "Forrest, go." She walked down the stairs giving me a little time to talk to Shay.

"Are you going to tell her everything?" For the first time since I entered the room, I noticed the spread of firearms on the table. Shay had pieces of her service weapon separated, and she was jamming an old toothbrush into the cracks to clean it.

"I need her help." Shay wiped the excess oil from the barrel and reassembled the parts back into a gun. "She's got more experience in the department, and her family history might just make coming into power easier."

"Easier, how?" I asked.

"The truth is, what happened this morning, my magick has never been so out of control." She punched the clip into the butt of her gun and fit the loaded weapon into the holster on her duty belt.

I didn't know what to say. My abilities as a blacksmith and the Maker didn't seem to cause an imbalance in me. "Do you think some of that magick should be mine?"

"I wish I knew." She set down the gun belt and opened one of Benton's journals. "This entry references the Maker and the Magick." She dropped the book on the table and picked up another. "So does this one, but it also says that balance is essential."

"Are you physically able to go through what you did just a few hours ago? Can you do that again?" I asked, a little louder than I meant to. I was scared, and I didn't understand why Shay wasn't.

"Maybe, I don't know. That's what Dani and I were talking about." Shay unzipped the leather pouch and dropped the gun oil and towels inside.

I set my cup of coffee down on the table and picked up the book Shay was just reading. I thumbed through, stopping on a sketch. "What about the lodestone? Did you figure that out?"

"Do you know what it is?" Dani asked as she walked back into the kitchen.

"You're just everywhere today." I knew my tone was edgy and that she didn't deserve it, but every time we answered a question, it only created more.

"Sweetheart, please. We need help." Shay looked at Dani. "I don't know anything about a lodestone, but something tells me that I should."

"How about a conjuring stone? Lodysshe?" Dani carried her coffee cup to the sink. "Magnetite?" It was clear that no matter how many ways Dani named this rock, I had no idea what it was.

"Magnetite is what travelers used for compass points, right?" Shay asked.

"Yes, early civilizations used a lodestone to magnetize compass needles so they would point north. Before that, they had to rely on the stars."

"What does that have to do with becoming the Magick and the Maker?" I interrupted.

"As far as using a compass, nothing, but if the two of you want to balance your powers, you'll need to feed your lodestone."

"And find our true north," Shay said in a whisper.

"Do you have any magnetite?" I asked Dani. "You're the rock expert. What do we do?"

"My suggestion, honestly? Go finish the ritual, and that might help with the surges."

"And the stone?" Shay asked.

"I'll see what I can find." Dani started walking toward the stairs. "I gotta get out of here. There's an accident out at the city limits. Call me if you need anything else."

I watched Dani leave, wondering if we were going to take her advice. "Well, how do you feel about that?" I asked Shay.

"I feel like this morning was rough, and this afternoon is about to get worse, but she's right. I can't live like this, and if these surges get any stronger, I don't know if I can control them."

I reached around her, the chair pinned between us, and rested my head on her shoulder. "I'm scared for you," I whispered in her ear.

"A little fear is good. It'll keep us sharp."

I pushed off the chair. "I don't want to be sharp."

Shay stood up from the table. "Let's put some gear together and head over to the old courthouse."

"I don't like it." I fanned through the piles of research. I didn't want to watch Shay suffer through another ritual.

"I know, love."

"What if I make a mistake?" I asked.

"We'll take care of each other."

I considered my latest demon metal creation. "You'll wear the body armor?"

"I will." She snapped her fingers. "And don't forget about our dragon. We've got a demon-eating weapon that we didn't have last time." I looked at Dexter, who was grooming his paws with his tongue.

"I wish I found that comforting." I pat the dog on his head. I turned around, and Shay was loading her backpack. I handed her a notebook and a few pencils. "You have salt and candles in there?"

She nodded. "And the athame, some moon water, the cup, and a few other tools. I'm planning to set up an altar and create a sacred space before I translate anything."

"I'll follow your lead."

"Maybe," she tugged the drawstring on her backpack, "you should put on some pants?"

I pushed my hands in the pockets of my sweats and felt the crease of our folded letter. I pulled it out. "Oh, I almost forgot about this." I held it out for Shay.

"What's this?"

"The letter was in your mailbox." I unfolded the envelope so she could see the front. "It's addressed to the both of us."

"You could have opened it." She flipped the plain envelope looking for a return address.

"I thought we should be together, just in case," I explained.

"Good idea. It's funny; there's no return address, and there's no cancelation mark on the stamp." She tore the flap of the envelope, opening the folds. She turned it over and dumped the contents on the table.

A tiny pile of ash fell out. "What the hell is it?" I took a step back, and Shay leaned in for a closer look.

"I have no idea." Shay walked away and returned with a tiny test tube. She used the edge of the envelope to scoop all of the fragments of powder into the container. "The test kit is in my car. I need to run down and get it." She pushed the tube into her pocket.

"Someone mailed us demon powder?"

"I don't have any idea what it is, and they didn't mail it; our secret admirer dropped it off."

"Another mysterious helper?"

Shay put on her shoes and synched the laces. She looked up at me. "Or a saboteur."

I rubbed my hands over my face. "Do you think we could get just one day of non-demon action?"

172

"Maybe." She walked to the stairs and turned to look at me over her shoulder. "But probably not today."

I held the envelope, and I followed her down to the workshop. She went out to her car and returned with the battered metal case. As she unpacked the kit, I cleared a spot on the worktable. She dropped a bit of the powder into each tube of the kit. The class-two vile lit up with a purple glow.

"Have you ever seen that color?"

She nodded.

I hesitated to ask for fear of the answer. "What's it mean?"

"Fairy Folk. Powerful concentrated magick. No one should have this." She shook the container. "Who the hell left us fae dust?"

I'm sure she was talking to herself, but I answered. "I don't recognize the handwriting." I gave her the envelope.

"I don't either." She set it on the table. "I think we should go to the old courthouse and see what's there."

"Are you sure you're up for it?" I asked.

She walked to the corner and poured the contents of the test kit into another bottle. "No, I'm not, but I need more answers." She waved her hand over the pool of liquid. "Rest now, sweet fairy folk." She turned a cap on the bottle and put it on the shelf. "I'll worry about you later." She was speaking to the contents as if they would reply. I was curious to know why. "What are you going to do with that?" I pointed to the shelf.

"I'll hold on to it just in case."

"In case what?" Magick was such a curious experience.

"In case I need to identify the mischief behind our little gift." Shay looked at me. "You going to go out like that?"

I rubbed my hands up and down my legs. "I'm going to put on some pants and maybe some sleeves."

She clicked the test kit back in the box. "Good idea. I think we're going to drive this time, just in case."

"Throw everything in the truck, and hey…" I hesitated until she looked at me. "Put on your vest."

"Roger that." She gave me a little salute before pulling her hair into a ponytail. I leaped up the stairs, two at a time. What should I wear to a Magick acquisition? I pulled on a pair of jeans and a t-shirt and snugged the dagger of doom to my hip. I didn't have much more to carry, considering that Shay was our best weapon. I laced my workbooks and looked at the uniform hanging in the corner. I was almost certain that after today nothing would ever be the same.

CHAPTER X

Augur

By the time I dressed, Shay was waiting in the passenger seat of my truck, trying to fasten her seatbelt. Dexter barked at me from the open bed before flopping down for the ride.

"Do you think he understands what's about to happen?" I asked as I slid into the driver's seat.

Shay leaned against the door and looked at me. "I wish I knew."

I tapped a knuckle against the center of Shay's chest and felt the solid demon armor protecting her heart. "Are you sure we're ready for this?" I asked.

"As ready as we're ever going to be." She slid the demon axe from her lap and tucked it between the seats.

"Just in case?" I asked.

"Always expect demons, love."

"Right, I remember." I started the truck and checked all the mirrors before backing into the street. The traffic in Bannock was light for a weekday which made the drive to the deserted building effortless. I pulled into a parking lot littered with years of candy wrappers, plastic straws, and cigarette butts. The combination of trash, gravel, and crumbling concrete confirmed that very few people frequented the building.

"I'm a little anxious," Shay whispered as I shifted the truck into park.

"That's okay. Remember that we are supposed to be here, and that Benton went through this once too."

"Yeah . . . Benton." She looked out the windshield— silent for a long moment. "The funeral is on Friday." She said.

My hands clenched the steering wheel, and I closed my eyes. I knew if I looked at Shay, I would see the pain of grief that was impossible for her to hide. "I saw the announcement on the door at Slammed."

"Will you come with me?" The tone of her voice was quiet, fragile.

I rested my forearms over the steering wheel, leaning closer to the dashboard, and turned to look at Shay. I saw a lifetime of broken promises reflected in her eyes. "If that's what you want, I'll be wherever you need me."

She reached for my hand. "I'll always want you by my side."

"Good." I squeezed her fingers.

She took a deep breath and released it slowly through her lips. "I guess we need to do this."

"I guess we do." I left the key dangling from the ignition. "Let's go get you some magick."

I heard the crush of rocks and crumbled concrete under her feet as she climbed out of my truck. Dexter jumped over the well of the tire and landed beside Shay who led us to a reinforced steel entrance in the alley between the buildings. The service door looked new compared to the rest of the crumbling brickwork surrounding it. I thought it was odd, but then most of this town was. She had a key, and I wondered why they kept it secure. "That's different."

"What?" She turned the key in the lock.

"Walking in without a pry bar."

She pushed the door giving it an extra shove with her shoulder. "There are a few historical artifacts in here. We do regular building checks. Dani dropped off the key this morning."

I followed her inside. "Oh, what kind of artifacts?"

"That." She pointed at the immense sculptured carving on the wall, extending over our heads and across the ceiling.

My eyes traveled up and over, following the twisted pattern above my head. "It's stunning."

"Isn't it." Shay stopped in front of the intricate artwork. If I touched the carving, I could sink my fingers into the bark of the patterned tree.

"It's a willow tree. That's very curious," I said.

"It is?" Shay closed the door, locking the three of us inside the building. "Tell me why you would say that?"

"Give me a minute." I had an overwhelming need to sit down in front of the tree. There was a message on the wall that only my heart could see. I closed my eyes, and visions dashed like a spiraling kaleidoscope. The tree trunk stretched down into the darkness of mystic soil, tendrils grasping deep, drinking from the life-water of the Earth's energies. I saw the massive tree come to life, swelling and shrinking like a heaving chest, breathing in and out with the winds of change. I watched as the limber spindly branches twisted into a symbol I didn't recognize. The willow switches fell to the ground, weaving into the silhouette of a woman's form. I could feel Shay behind me. She was patient. I don't know how long I meditated, but the artwork's spirit had a lot to say. When I opened my eyes, Shay was smiling.

"Tell me." The excitement in her voice was energizing.

"At first glance, it's a complex carving of a beautiful tree," I explained.

Her eyebrow arched with curiosity. "I can see that much, but what did it tell you?" She asked.

I laid my hand on the floor. "The base . . . the roots are deep. The Earth's energies feed it." I dropped on one knee to get closer. "If I'm looking for a direction or roadmap, everything suggests that we start right here and follow the lines from the ground up." I tapped the tree where it touched the floor.

"Do you realize what wall we are standing in front of?"

"It's the north wall." I turned around to look at her.

"It's our north wall." Shay was digging in the backpack, removing our traveling altar from inside. She flipped her purple cloth in the air, floating it down to the floor. "Keep going." She encouraged.

I dragged my hand over the carving. I could feel the pulse of the Earth. "Whoo, this is something." I waved her over. "Come here."

"What is it?"

"Just come here. I think you need to feel it." Shay stopped beside me. I reached for her hand. I flexed her index finger with my own and pressed them to the carved lines of the massive willow. "You feel it don't you."

I watched Shay close her eyes. "Whoo, is right."

I moved our hands away. "No more touching. Let's read the rest of the wall."

"Okay, love. Tell me what you know." Shay stepped back.

"I know that . . . I feel like I've been here before." I walked away from the carving so I could see the entire wall. "The shape of the trunk, it looks like a body."

"Really?" Shay squinted her eyes, trying to adjust her view.

"You don't see it?" I pointed at the outline.

Her lips parted, letting out a muffled huff. "Maybe it's a Maker thing?"

I smiled. "Maybe it is." I continued. "The largest limbs, running horizontal to the floor, are outstretched arms, and the hands are holding the sun and the moon."

"Hon, I see the sun and the moon, but I don't see hands."

"Are you serious right now?"

"I am." She finished laying out the athame and the tiny bowl. She scraped the edge of our candle holder, sparking the blue flame to life. "Come over here." She opened a miniature bottle of moon water and poured it into the bowl.

"See any runes?" I asked.

"I don't. Do you?"

"I see a stunning goddess." I looked at my girlfriend and back up at the wall. "You honestly don't see any of it, do you?"

"I wish that I did."

"Tell me what you *do* see," I said. "Let's try that."

"I see a spectacular willow tree. That's what I assumed everyone saw, until just now."

"Is there anything special about the tree?" It was interesting that our view of the carving was so different.

"Aside from the fact that it stretches over your head and onto the ceiling?"

"Yes."

"No, not really."

"Is there a lower level to this building?" I asked, confident that we'd find more answers beneath our feet.

"There is, but we have to move the boards by the front door to access it." Shay picked up a notebook and pencil and rolled them into her back pocket. She walked toward the building's main entrance. A shadow followed her across the floor.

"Stop," I yelled. Shay froze in place and turned to look at me. The shadow kept moving until it disappeared beneath her.

"What is it?" Shay asked.

I could feel a force slice through the cracks on the weathered floor. It was cold, and I wrapped my arms around myself to shake the chill. "Death," I said. "Can't you feel it?" I steadied myself against the wall.

"It must be Dani's mother," Shay explained. "The murder happened in here, and I don't want to think about the terrible crime scene."

"I'm sorry, Shay."

"It's alright. I just need to remember to stay sharp." She looked over her shoulder at the dog lying beside me. "Dex, watch over us."

He barked once before walking to Shay. "Good boy." She patted his side. I waited as Shay pulled back the locking bar hidden by the landing. One by one, she flipped the weathered floorboards over to reveal a staircase.

"This feels like the part of the story where we should run away from danger."

Shay looked over her shoulder at me. "You're kidding, right?"

I pinched my fingers to make a tiny gap. "Only a little."

Shay reached for the flashlight in her pocket. "Bring the blue flame." She disappeared down the steps, followed by Dexter and a hesitant me. I was cautious on every step, waving the candle back and forth between the walls and support posts. In every direction, I saw rocks, but on the north wall, beneath the carving, I could see the continuation of the artwork above us. I was hoping the spell we needed would be simple to find, but I was disappointed when my foot landed in the dirt. I couldn't see my girlfriend, but the beam of light from her hand gave me her location. She was fearless, and for a moment, it felt reckless.

"Hon, maybe you should let me light the room with the blue flame?" My hand traveled over the rough foundation stones as I followed the wall around.

"Good idea." The flashlight clicked off, and the only thing between us and the mystery of this creepy basement was the steady blue glow of candlelight. "What do you see, Wil?"

I turned to look at Shay. "Holy crap!"

"What?"

"Look at your hands." I brought the flame closer to reveal delicate spiraling lines covering Shay's fingers. They were more than the runes on the carriage house walls. "Roll up your sleeves." She slipped out of her shirt instead, revealing symbols that wrapped the length of her arms. "Can you read them?" I asked.

"They aren't runes. They're like blacklight tattoos."

"Do you have blacklight tattoos?" I asked. "I didn't know you had tattoos at all."

She rotated her arms. "I didn't, until just now."

"Give me your notebook. Let me draw what I see." I set the candle on the pillar base, a rippled ledge of fieldstones supporting the upstairs floor. It held the light between us, and I did my best to copy each of the symbols I could see. "How do you feel about taking off the rest of your clothes?"

"How do you think I feel?" She turned to follow the sound of Dexter as he explored every inch of the lower level.

"Dumb question, I know, but I can see there are more under your shirt."

I heard Velcro tear away and watched as she and her K-9 partner communicated the complexity of the situation with their eyes. Shay's undershirt whipped over her head as she kicked off her shoes. She unzipped her pants and dropped them to the ground. The glow of the flame reflected off the new images on her body.

"Wow." I couldn't stop myself from reacting to the symbols peppered all over her skin.

"Wow, as in good?" She pushed the top of the notebook, trying to see my sketch.

I drew one of Shay's markings, an image of three spirals joined in the center and held the page up for her to see. Her finger trailed across it. "It's a triskele. The Celtic symbol for fire, water, and Earth. We use all three to do magick."

"I saw this upstairs, in my meditation, when I was reading the wall."

"You did?"

"Yes. Do you think this is part of a spell?" I asked. "Is it telling us how to end the surges you've been having?"

"Maybe it is. I can't be sure. What else do you see?"

I placed my hand on her shoulder, tilting her body toward the light of our candle. "A pentacle, but it's got a bunch of lines through it."

"It's another reference but for all five elements."

"Does it mean something if it's upside down?" I asked.

"Only when the intention is for protection." Shay tapped the notebook in my hand. "Can I do something really quick?" She flipped to a blank page and sketched two silhouettes of the human body. "Number each symbol and put that number right where you find it on my body."

"Good thinking." I took the notebook from her hands and pointed my finger toward the ground, making a twirling motion. "Spin around and let me see your back." She didn't hesitate and turned to reveal the rest of her body. The paper and pencil dropped from my hands.

Shay heard my gasp and watched my expression. "What?"

"It's a damn dragon. You've got a massive freakin' dragon from your shoulders to the bottom of your thighs."

"Did you say a dragon?" She asked, stretching and twisting her head, trying to see that part of her body with her own eyes.

I nodded—the shock of seeing the image of her familiar leaving me speechless.

"Can you take a picture?"

I didn't respond. I was trying to think why and how, but the answers didn't make sense.

"Wildwood!" She clapped her hands to snap me out of my thoughts. "Can you take a picture? Please."

"Where's your phone?"

Shay dug through her pile of clothes. "Here." She adjusted the camera for darkness.

"I've never seen anything like this," I said. The flash didn't flicker, but the camera caught the light blue glow of Shay's body. "Look." I held the phone in front of me.

She covered my hands with her own, holding the image closer. "Wow, that's on *my* back?"

"What do you think it means?"

She looked at her dog and back up at me. "Take off your shirt."

"Do what?" I wasn't expecting her request.

"Take off your shirt. I want to see if you've got markings too."

It made sense, but it also struck me that we were stripping down naked in a hundred and fifty-year-old basement. I took off my shirt and closed my eyes, afraid of what symbols would appear on my skin. "What do you see?" My arms stretched out as I made a slow turn.

Shay's hand stopped me. "There's just one symbol on you."

"Where? What is it?" I twisted side to side in an attempt to see where it might be on my body.

Her hand pressed to my left breast and rested over my heart. "It's your Maker's mark. I swear this is the most out-of-this-world out-of-my-body experience I've ever had."

I looked at Shay. "This means we are in the right place." I wasn't asking her a question.

"Yes, I think it does," she said. I tugged my shirt over my head as she picked up the notebook and pencil, handing them back to me. "Finish sketching my markings, and then let's look at the north wall." Shay made a slow shuffling turn so I could note the last few images.

"Just to be clear." I didn't look up from the paper. "I am very aware that you are completely naked in front of me."

"Good to know." I didn't have to see her face to understand that my confession was what she needed to hear. In a different time and another place, she would have covered the scars that dashed her body, but she no longer carried the burden of shame, not with me. She trusted my love, and that made the two of us stronger. I finished my last sketch. "I count six different symbols that are repeating."

Shay was jumping back into her pants. "Do you know what all of them are?" Her hands punched through the sleeves of her shirt, and her head popped out of the collar.

I admit I was distracted, watching her silhouette disappear beneath her shirt and pants.

Her voice was louder, demanding. "Babe?"

"Sorry, you're just—" I couldn't find the words to express how beautiful Shay was without making it about her outward appearance. "I love you."

Her hand came up to touch my cheek. "I love you too."

Putting together the puzzle that was my life, Shay's love was an essential part, and having it, being touched by it, brought peace. It was a feeling I only dreamed possible. I heard the rip of Velcro and watched as the vest fastened back across Shay's chest.

She pressed herself against my hip. "Okay, lover, show me what we got."

I handed the notebook to her. "This is it." We stepped closer to the light as she studied my scribbles and sketches to decode what she could.

"All of the symbols on my body are telling. The upside-down pentacle is a warning of danger. The triskeles suggests we should focus on earth, water, and fire. The spiral which I counted most on this silhouette is a call to spirit."

"What you're saying is that *you* are the spell. And now that we've figured that out, all we need to do is flip your switch."

"That's a massive oversimplification, but yes."

"How do we do it?"

She pointed to the rest of the symbols. "That's where these come into play. Are you familiar with these three?"

"They're Egyptian, right?"

She nodded. "Yes, this one here." She pointed to what looked like a cross with a handle. "This is the ankh. It represents many things, but in this situation, for our spell, I think we should call the mother goddess Isis. It's super important because she's the bringer of magick. Not just in the ancient world but in the pagan world also."

"And the eye?" I asked.

"The son of Isis." Shay traced the drawing with her fingertip. "It's always represented by the left eye."

"I'm not sure what you mean."

"See this swoop? If it loops to the right, it depicts the eye of Horus. If it loops to the left, it's the eye of Ra."

"What's the significance?" I asked.

"It is the difference between night and day. It is the literal moon and the sun."

"And if Horus is the moon, then we need to do the spell at night?" I guessed.

"Not quite at night, but more-so under the power of a full moon." She explained. "Which happens to be occurring today."

"So, you really are the Magick." I touched her cheek.

"It's never been more clear." Shay picked up the candle holder and walked toward the north wall carving. "Tell me what you see."

"It's a wild tangle of roots, earth, and stones." I turned to look at my girlfriend. "Why would this be here where no one would see it?"

"It's here for us. It has to be the genesis, the source of our power."

"Maybe we should do the magick here," I suggested.

"I'll go up and get the backpack and our altar." There was no question it was the right thing to do. Shay's flashlight flicked on, and she climbed the stairs to the first floor. My fingers traced through the intricate carving until everything I touched felt alive. The Earth's energy moving through the ground was intense. The magick inside of me could hear the call of the sacred element. I sat in the dirt, placing both palms so I could feel the ground between my fingers. My left hand moved to the carving on the wall. I opened my eyes, and Shay was there. The backpack dropped to the floor right before she collapsed.

"Shay!" My voice sounded loud as it echoed off the walls. Dexter jumped toward Shay's body on the floor, sniffing her face and torso.

"Lay down, Dex," I yelled. He listened to my command and stretched against the length of Shay to protect her. I opened the backpack and placed the athame in the dirt, followed by our candle and a tiny dish. It was a sloppy altar at best as I trailed a ring of salt around Shay's body. Dexter didn't move.

I made everything up as I tried to recall all of the spells Shay and I had executed together. I lit a white candle with our blue flame feeling a sense of urgency as Shay lay motionless in front of me. I drew a pentagram in the dirt, hoping everything I was about to do would stabilize her power and bring her back to me.

"Fire, light from the darkness be in my circle." I set the candle on one point of the star. "Water, wash away the past, and summon the new." I poured moon water from the little bottle onto the second point of the star. I was thinking about the spiral on Shay's body, so I moved clockwise in that direction. "Air, source of life, breathe into the Magick unity with those before us." I didn't know how to represent air, so I blew a handful of dust across the dirt drawing so it would land on the star's third point. "Earth, the place we call home, mountain to cave, the rock in our solid foundation. I call you to this circle. I call you to the Magick." I held out my hand, and a stone appeared in my palm. I had no idea where it came from, but I set it on my star's fourth point.

Shay didn't move.

"Isis, mother goddess, bringer of magick, please be here in our circle. Lay your power upon her. Fill her, kindle balance as I call the elements to life." I didn't know what else to say. I thought about all of the symbols hiding beneath Shay's covered body. I counted them off on my fingers: pentacle, triskeles, spiral, Isis, triangles, and Horus. I'd forgotten Horus.

"Son of the mother, Horus. Bring the light. Fill the magick with what only your eye can see. I am the light. She is the light. We are the light." I chanted it three times before saying. "So mote it be."

I had no idea what else I should do, so I surrendered. I let the spirit of this dark space guide me. I crawled beside Shay and Dexter, waiting for either of them to move. I held my hand beneath her nose, feeling the air escape from her exhale. "Shay."

She was absolutely still, and her shallow breath scared me. I thought about the transfer of power in the grist mill and tried to remember what happened when the Maker's source-power came to me. I laid a hand on Dexter. Whatever bond was between them held fast. "Dex." The dog didn't respond either.

The minutes that passed felt like a lifetime, and the absence of the two of them was haunting. I sat up, looking at the candle I'd lit for the spell. It was less than half-burned, which meant it was time to chant. I went back to my spot on the floor. I picked up the new stone and held it in my hand. It had to be the key to something.

Like a voice in the wind, it came to me. *"Feed the lodestone."*

I wasn't a geologist like Dani, but I'd bet my life that this rock was the conjuring stone Shay needed. We should have spent more time learning about its power. I thought about all the symbols I'd drawn on the floor, and then I remembered the two tiny bottles inside the backpack, fairy powder and anvil dust. They had to be the key. I sprinkled the two in the tiny saucer. I used the last of the moon water to make a slurry and drew the eye of Horus on one side of the stone and the symbol of the goddess Isis on the other.

I was risking her life that this combination was the answer, but I'd run out of ideas. I sat beside Shay, holding the painted rock in my hand, calling on every bit of power that I could.

Waiting was unbearable. I saw the sketch pad on the floor, catching a glimpse of the tiny numbers I'd written on the penciled representation of Shay's body. I saw the void in the center of her chest and followed an idea. I ripped away the Velcro of her vest to reveal the t-shirt underneath. I remembered waking up with a rock on my chest after the Maker power entered me. I pulled on the collar of Shay's shirt and slid the symbolled stone over her heart.

This assembly of magick was the best that I had. I gripped the shoulder of Shay's vest and heaved her limp body into my lap. I held her as if nothing in this world mattered because it didn't. "Come back to me, Shay. You're my heart and my home." I said it over and over until the echo of my words became a song. I closed my eyes and hoped that everything I said, mixed with my magick, would be enough.

I don't know when I started to cry, but fear began to settle in. I rocked her in my arms and waited for those beautiful eyes to open.

I felt a furry paw brush against me, and then a wet-nosed dog face pushed Shay's cheek. Dexter was awake. I shook my girlfriend. "Shay."

Her arm came up to grab her chest. "It's cold." She said. Her voice was a whisper.

"What?"

Her fingers scooped into the front of her shirt, and she pulled out the stone. "What is this? It feels like a piece of ice. It's so cold."

I reached to take it. "I'm pretty sure it's . . . hot as hell." I dropped the stone to the ground. "Holy shit." I blew on my hand to cool it.

"Wildwood?"

I froze at the sound of her voice calling my name. "Hi," I said.

"Hi." She tried to sit up, and I cradled her with my arms. "What happened?" She asked. Her voice was faint.

I was more excited to see her eyes open and to hear her speak. "I believe I used my magic to help you get yours."

She picked up the rock. "What is this?"

"A conjuring stone . . . I think."

"You think?"

"It came to me when I called the Earth element to my circle."

She held it closer to the candle flame. "Came to you?"

"It just appeared in my hand."

She turned the stone over, inspecting every side. "And it's a conjuring stone?"

"I don't have a clue, honestly, but I fed it."

Shay's lips turned up with a smile. "And these?" She pointed to the symbols I'd made on the stone.

"Isis and Horus. I asked for their magicks to become your own."

"That's a big order."

"How are you holding that in your hand?"

She gave it to me. "It's a rock. How do you hold a rock in your hand?"

"That's not funny. Just two seconds ago, it nearly burned my skin." It was still warm to the touch but certainly not ice cold.

"You had it on my chest. It felt like you put a chunk of ice right over my heart."

"I didn't know what else to do."

Her hand came up to my cheek. "You did great. I'm okay." She kissed me. "Do you think we can get up off the ground?"

"I think I'd like to get the heck out of here," I said. Shay used my shoulders to push up from my lap.

"Where's Dexter?"

"He was right here. He never left your side."

"Well, he's not here now. Dexter!" She yelled.

Our white candle flame was still burning, and I picked it up from the ground. I waved it in the air, hoping it might shine a light on the location of our dragon dog. There was no sign of him in the room.

"Dexter. *Nunc autem venit!*" She shuffled through the dirt, commanding him to come now. The blue light of our demon forged candle flickered as if a holiday sparkler replaced the wick. I watched her sway toward the rooted carving on the wall. She was trying to disguise that she was standing on unsteady feet.

I reached my arm around to help balance her. "Take it easy. We'll find him."

The blue flame sparked off the end of our candle, and we looked in unison to see the massive face of our dragon pinched between the splintered joists of the boards above us.

"What's wrong with him?" I asked.

"Hey, buddy." Shay's hand stretched toward the animal. "Nothing's wrong with him." His face slipped out of the shadows.

"Why is he in— why's he a dragon?"

"I . . . have . . . no . . . idea." Shay's words lingered in amazement as he dropped down in front of us. It was the closest we'd ever been to him in dragon form. Shay's hand was steady as her fingers reached to touch the rippled snout on his face. His snort was loud, and for a moment, I forgot that this was our sweet furry dog.

But Shay didn't. "Hi, Dex."

His head shoved against her hand. I wondered if they were speaking through telepathy or the default communication between a cop and her partner. Shay was unwavering as the dragon tail swooped around and pounded the dirt. He was stunning with the blue flame reflecting the iridescent shimmer of his chest-plate scales. I resisted the temptation to touch him.

"Is he talking to you?"

"I guess he is, sort of." Shay answered.

"What's he saying?"

"I think he's scared." Dexter pushed his nose against Shay's hand. The moment they touched, the light of the blue flame doubled in size, and the dog appeared in front of us. There wasn't a crazy melting transformation. It was like a switch flipped, and Shay was the connection. His hairy body lunged forward, knocking Shay to the ground. They were an adorable pile of fur and hugs, rolling together.

"Hey, boy." She grabbed the sides of his face, scrunching his ears until she was satisfied her K-9 companion had returned.

"Is he okay?" I hesitated to ask.

She looked at me. "I think so."

"You think we did it?"

"I don't know how to tell."

"Do you feel different? More powerful or something?"

"No, not really."

"See any fairies . . . or giants?" I shook my head, trying to reconcile the question I just asked. "Because you know I saw some shit when I got the Maker abilities."

"Yes. I remember every second of that experience."

"This kinda feels anti-climactic."

She lifted her shoulders in a shrug. "I admit I'm a little disappointed."

I leaned over the pentacle I'd drawn in the dirt. "I guess we should clean this up. Get out of here and figure out what comes next." She didn't respond. "Shay?" I turned around, and the two of them were gone. "What the hell!" I carried the candle around the basement, looking from floor to ceiling for a sign of either of them. "Shay!"

I kicked the flashlight lying on the ground. I picked it up and turned it on, shining the beam of light everywhere, still unable to find them. I collected each of the magick tools spread out on the ground and put them inside our bag. I threw the backpack over both shoulders and clipped it snug across my chest. I had no idea what was coming. I studied the pentacle on the ground and picked up Shay's stone. *This has to mean something.* The thought bounced around in my head as I put the rock in my pocket.

I moved the white candle away from the tangled root mural and left it to burn. I placed my hands against the wall. "Where are you, Shay." The vibration was strong, almost like a heartbeat, in the palm of my hands. "Show me where you are, Shay." The sensation transformed to sound, reminding me that listening, and hearing were different things. I closed my eyes. "Come on, baby, I got you." The beat turned into a flutter, and I felt the temperature change just before my hands filled with the sensation of ice-cold water. "The river." The sound of my voice echoed through the hollow of the space. My shoes pounded up the stairs, and I didn't think about anything but Shay. I threw the backpack onto the seat of the truck. She had to be there. It was the only place. I could drive to Dani's property in less than ten minutes if I pushed it.

I pushed it, hard.

The dust kicked up from the tires of my truck, leaving a cloud of smoke behind me. I had no idea if I obeyed a single traffic sign, but it didn't matter. I was where I hoped Shay would be. The truck slid across the gravel when I slammed the gear shift into park. Everything was in motion when I jumped from the driver's side door. My actions were reckless, and if I'd been right-minded, I might have remembered the consequences of our last visit. I heard the crunching of rock under my feet and felt the thistle and briar tear at the weave of my jeans. Nothing slowed me from getting to the river's edge. I heard the water before I saw it, and my eyes fought to focus on the creature running at me. It wasn't Shay, and it definitely wasn't Dexter in either form.

My feet slipped out from under me as I tried to reverse my momentum. I fell back against the grassy path and focused on two razor-sharp taloned paws and a face with flesh-ripping teeth. I had nothing but the Dagger of Doom as a weapon for defense, and I wasn't excited about the prospect of getting close enough to use it. I tried to get up, maybe make a run for the truck, but my shoes slipped across the grass. I rolled over to my knees and heard two things: The sound of an animal panting and the voice of my girlfriend, Shay.

"Stay down, Wil!" She yelled.

I didn't have time to turn around before the face of an axe flew by. It landed square in the center of my attacker's chest, and seconds later, a transforming dog-dragon tore onto the downed demon. My heart was thundering as I watched the carnage unfold. Dexter ripped the beast from throat to belly, and when he carried his prize off in the grass, the axe was lying in a pool of demon remains.

"Holy hell, Shay. What was that?"

Her hand fell out in front of me. I reached up, and she tugged me to my feet. "It was Dex."

"I got that much. I mean, what just happened to us?" I slapped my hands across my legs and shirt, knocking the debris from my body.

"That's what I meant. Dexter brought me here."

"How?"

"I'm not one hundred percent sure, but my best guess is some kind of teleportation."

"Shut—the—hell—up!" I bent down to grab the axe and walked away from the bloody scene. I held up a hand in surrender. "Nope! I'm rejecting all of this. Dragons, teleportation, magick infusion in girlfriends, this is like some crazy fantasy B-movie shit." I looked at the bloodstains on my beautiful hatchet and bent down to rub it through the grass.

"Honey, I think you're in shock."

"You think?" I walked toward the sound of the river. "This is more than shock. What's more than shock—traumatized . . . stupefied . . . befuddled? That's it. I'm befuddled."

She put her left hand under my elbow and her right hand over my bicep. I had no idea how she did it, but she led me to sit on a giant rock along the river's shore. Dexter was already there, splashing his bloody paws in the water.

"Look at me, Wildwood." The sound of her voice was like a caress, and at this moment, it pissed me off even more.

"You disappeared!" I yelled.

"I didn't do anything. Dexter must have sensed the demon and brought us here."

"You left me."

"No."

I put my hand up to cover her mouth. "Please don't. I was in that damn basement, and when I turned around, you were gone, and I was there in the dark, alone."

She pulled my hand from her face, clinging to my cold fingers. "I didn't know. I don't have any control over the dragon side of my dog."

"That's going to be a problem, don't you think?"

"For right now, maybe." She touched my chin. "Look at me." I closed my eyes. "Wildwood, look at me."

When I opened my eyes, I could see the courage Shay possessed in intense situations. She trained to be the voice of reason in a storm, and right now, I was a raging hurricane.

"Your magick didn't come, did it?"

Shay took the axe from my hand and set it on the rocks beside us. She tugged on my wrists until I was standing in front of her. She turned me toward the river and wrapped her arm over my hip. Her right palm turned up in front of us, and a glow of blue light poured from her scars.

"I've seen that before."

"*Ignis.*" The word came from her lips, tickling my ear. The light flared into a flame burning in the palm of her hand.

"Okay, maybe I haven't."

Shay kissed my cheek. "You did it. I can feel the swell of magick like I've never felt it before."

CHAPTER XI

Fire

The sound of the river was all I could hear as Shay held a blue flame in the palm of her hand. After today anything would be possible.

Shay's right hand was flat against my abdomen as she snuggled our bodies closer together. She whispered in my ear. "Please don't be afraid." I wasn't. In fact, I had no emotions at all. I was numb and silent. "Sweetheart, talk to me."

I hesitated before touching her hand. I swished my pointer finger back and forth through her flame. "You're not very hot."

"I think I should be offended by that." She said as she pushed against me.

I closed my eyes as the raspy tone of her voice ignited intimate places. "Funny, that's not what I meant." I bumped myself against her. "I mean, your flame doesn't burn my skin."

"I think that's because you and I are bound."

"You *are* the Magick."

She placed my whole hand over the flame in her palm. She turned our hands over and lifted her own from mine. "And *you* are the Maker." When her hand moved away, I was holding the flame.

"Holy crap!" Everything was going to be different between us.

"I'd say we found our balance." She brushed the hair from my neck and kissed behind my ear.

The whisper-light touch of her lips sent shivers through my body. "How did you do that?"

"It's intuitive, my love." Her fingers trailed along my bicep and across my forearm until they stretched alongside my own. "Give it back to me." Her right palm hovered over my flame.

"I don't know how."

"Yes, you do. Believe. Feel it in here." Her left hand rested against my heart.

I hesitated.

"Believe that we are bound by more than magick." The whisper of her words took my breath away. My chest heaved with excitement. Trusting the tiny strands tangling us together, I focused on two being one. I threaded my fingers between hers and rotated my hand. When I pulled away, Shay possessed a blazing orange flame in the palm of her hand. "I did it."

"You absolutely did."

"What does it mean that my flame isn't blue?" I turned in her arms and placed my hand over her lips. "No, don't say that you don't know. Please. I just want to have a minute without thinking about research or books or whatever mystery surrounds our life."

She kissed the tips of my fingers. "How about I say that I love you."

"That's perfect, for now." I turned to look at Shay's hand. She rolled her fingers into a fist, and the flame went out. "Amazing."

Shay sat down on the boulder at the river's edge and tugged my arm to sit beside her. "Have you seen Dexter?"

I shook my head. "I don't want to imagine what he's doing to that creature."

"Demon, it's a massive creature, and I'm pretty sure Dex could sense it. I think that's why he brought me here."

"So, he can talk to you?"

"It's not talking, actually. It was just an image, a visual thought." She rubbed her eyes, frustrated. "I don't know how to explain it."

"But he just took you?" I watched the water pour over the river rocks near the toe of my shoe. Her hand was on my knee, and without thinking, I made tiny circles over her scars.

"It's his job to lead me toward trouble."

"Like this?" I looked at Shay, recognizing for the first time that she was covered in dirt and maybe the blood of a demon. "Holy hell, look at you."

Her head turned left and right, surveying the damage to her body and clothes. "The landing was a bit rough." She unfastened her vest and tossed it in the grass.

"Did you fly on a dragon?"

She smiled. "It wasn't flying. We disappeared and just reappeared. Now you see us, and now you land in a pile of dirt, rocks, and demon."

"And you're okay with that?"

She started to untie her shoes. "I guess I have to be. I don't have a lot of choices, do I?" She tugged off her socks and pulled up the leg of her pants. She dipped her toes into the river and inched her legs until the water touched her knees. "Woo, that's cold."

"You're going to get your clothes we—" Her t-shirt landed on top of the vest, and her pants followed. "You're going to get naked. Really?"

Her breath hitched as she waded into the shallow. "I need to get this off my skin." Her head disappeared beneath the surface.

"Are you serious?" I was talking to the tremble of the river. I heard Dexter barking behind me and turned just in time to see him launch his sticky wet body into the water. I had no desire to swim with either of them. Shay's head popped up right beside our dragon-dog.

"You should come in. It feels so good."

I scanned the edge of the river, looking for the next unknown. "I'll take a shower when we get home."

She fanned a massive wave of water at me. "Get in here, Wil."

"We just got attacked by a demon, and you want to go skinny dipping?"

She walked through the water until she was standing at my feet. She grabbed my ankle. "Just come in. Dex will protect us."

I watched the animal paddle himself to shore. Before I could make a move, he shook his head, and the rest of his body followed until dog-scented river water smothered us all.

"Really?" I shook the sleeves of my shirt. "Damn it, Dexter."

"You should have come in."

I should have, and I did but not before draping my wet shirt on the limb of the tree. The water was like ice, so I took my time inching in, letting my legs adjust first. Shay was impatient, and her warm body wrapped around me from behind.

"Now, that feels much better." She whispered in my ear.

"For you." I relaxed against her body. "Gosh, you're so warm."

"Uh-huh." We floated together until we came to rest against the face of a huge boulder.

"Do you think this is smart?" I floated between her legs. "It feels a little reckless."

"I promise you. If something comes, Dexter is prepared." Her chin touched my shoulder.

"You promise? How can you know that?"

"I'm not sure how to explain it." She said.

I rested my head, looking up at the clouds in the sky. "Try."

"Can you just trust me on this?"

She was the one person who earned my trust. "Yes."

"Good, now can we do a little sacred wash here. My body has just been through something."

I couldn't stop myself from laughing, "Darlin', you have quite the ability to understate the ridiculous levels of danger we find ourselves in."

"And you find that trait attractive, right?" There was confidence in the question like she knew I felt safe in her arms.

"Sexy as hell."

"That was my plan all along."

"Can we talk—" her hand cupped my breast.

"No more questions. We need to share some of this magick."

"No more, yes . . . more of your hands."

Her palm slid over my heart. "Energies of the Earth—love from the mother. Isis, divine being of power and balance of virtue—spread this magick."

Love is baffling. Her love mixed with the levels of energy flowing between us was intimate. I could feel her inside of me like never before. I wondered if this connection was because of the Magick and Maker bond or if it was more. I didn't dare break the energy work that was happening at the moment. I felt drunk and sober, high and mellow, but what hit me most was that I wanted to feel this way forever.

"Is this okay?" she asked.

"Yes." The sound of that single word felt foreign in my ears.

Shay shifted her body so she could see my face. "Wildwood, you're so pale."

I closed my eyes and tried to concentrate on her words. "I'm a little dizzy. Maybe too much magic."

Shay climbed over to lift me out of the water. I could feel my heels slide from the rock to the soil of the shoreline. My fingers flexed into the earth, digging to balance the source of my Maker power. I felt the energy flow through and out to the ground around us. Water and earth elements might complement one another, but I wasn't strong enough to contain both.

Her naked body hovered above my own. "Tell me you're okay?"

"I will be. I just need a second." My breath was shallow and quick, and I felt the chill against my skin. Shay draped her shirt over me and felt around in the grass for the rest of her clothes.

"Give me a second. I'll make a fire."

I laid my palm up toward her. "*Ignis.*" I stuttered the word through chattering teeth, and an orange flame appeared in my hand.

She stopped. "You are so amazing." She tugged her pants on over wet skin and covered her chest with my shirt. "Let me grab some firewood."

She was gone before I could say another word as Dexter pawed through the tall grass. I could feel the heat from his fur as he lay down beside me. He was not much drier than I, but he was warm. I pulled Shay's shirt over my head and put the rest of my clothes on. Shay dropped a few pieces of wood near my feet and used the axe to cut kindling small enough for a fire on the bank of the river.

"You want to do the honors?" She held my hand toward the kindling.

"*Ignis.*" I started the tiny shavings on fire.

"This is going to take some getting used to," she said.

"It's so damn cool. How is this my life?" I slid closer to the heat of the flames.

She was staring into my eyes. "I think that all of the time."

"Why don't you bring that magick over here and make me warm?"

"So bossy." She stepped around the little fire. "We have some things to talk about."

"I know," I said as I rubbed the length of my arms. "Can it be something easy for right now?"

"Easy like what?" She asked.

"Maybe we can talk about some food. I'm starving."

"What do you have in that?" She hitched her thumb to point at my truck.

"Did I leave it running?" I heard the purr of the engine.

"I think you did," Shay answered as she pushed off the ground.

I wrapped my arms around my body to stay warm and followed her to the cab of the truck. "It's got to be almost out of gas. It's been running for over an hour."

"Do you think we can make it back to town?"

I rubbed my hand across the dashboard. "Sure, it's not that far."

"Let me go grab the rest of our stuff. Dex!" She yelled for the dog before pushing her pointer and pinky fingers in the corner of her mouth and letting out a loud whistle. The beautiful animal came racing toward the truck.

"What about the demon?" I turned off the engine. "Don't you think we should clean it up?"

"We have to find it first, and we need to go back to the old courthouse and secure the building."

"You're a little off your game today, superhero."

"I think I should get a pass, don't you?" She kicked her foot onto the tread of the tire and fixed the laces of her boot.

"Just this once." I tugged her pocket as I circled the truck.

Shay followed the trail through the grass, retracing where Dexter had dragged the demon remains. When we found them, there wasn't much left to conceal.

"I can't believe he ate all of that." I kicked at the pile of bones and flesh.

"Looks like everything but the leg bones, ribcage, maybe an arm, and the head."

"That's pretty gross."

"Can you help me? We can throw it in the fire and burn it all." She picked up the gristle joint of what looked like a knee or maybe an elbow.

"You want me to carry demon guts?" I tried not to gag as a slime slathered chunk slapped across my palm. "This is not part of the job description."

Shay had the rest of the demon stacked in her arms. "It is now. The Magick and the Maker are bound together. That means we clean up the guts together, too."

"Gloves. I want gloves next time and maybe a plastic bag."

"Next time, we can take the patrol car. I've got everything we need for cleaning up a scene like this."

"Of course, you do."

I dropped my remnant on the ground beside the fire. Shay placed each of the pieces she was carrying into the flame. They popped and crackled as the liquid in the flesh boiled and charred. The fire wasn't hot enough to transform the remains into forgeable material. "How long does it take before you can't recognize it?"

"Bones don't melt. It'll take a while."

"What about our firepower. Do you think we can heat this faster?"

"What, you don't like sitting with me by the fire?"

"I do, but not with the aroma of roasted demon in the air."

Inspired by the disgusting smell, I summoned my fire. "*Ignis.*" My palm flashed with a bright orange flame, and I directed it at the pile of burning demon and smoldering logs.

"Impressive." Shay held her hand up in front of her body. "*Ignis.*" The white-hot flame she held flickered before turning blue. We stood shoulder to shoulder, directing our lights until they crossed paths. Everything inside the ring of fire burst into something beyond the tempered heat of the tiny campfire.

"Now that's impressive." I couldn't stop the words from coming out of my mouth. We watched the fire burn until a pile of ash and embers remained. It could have been romantic if it wasn't for the wet dog and roasted demon.

"Splash some water on the embers. I'll grab the rest of our gear. It'll be dark soon."

I did my best to shuffle handfuls of river water up to the fire along the shoreline. It was not an easy task, but I was stirring the slurry of ash a few minutes later. "This looks like a regular old campfire pit. I don't see anything that resembles a demon in here."

"Perfect." Shay kicked at the pile.

"You ready to go?" I asked.

She held up her vest. "Whenever you are." Her hand stretched out to me.

"Leave nothing behind, right." I kicked through the grass along the path. "You double-checked?"

"I didn't come here with much."

"Don't remind me." I opened the driver's side door and climbed into the cab. Shay dropped the tailgate, and Dexter jumped in the bed.

"Good boy." When he laid down, she patted his torso, pushed the tailgate closed, and came around to her door. "How much gas is in the tank?"

I turned the key and checked the fuel gauge. "Under a quarter tank. We'll make it to town."

She climbed in beside me. "Good. Stop at the old courthouse and let me close things up."

"Are you sure you're okay to go back inside tonight?" Going back into that building was the last thing I wanted to do.

"Not much choice, love. I opened the can of worms. I need to close it up."

I pointed at the pile on the floor by her feet. "Put your vest on, please."

"Yes, ma'am." She slid it over her head before locking her seat belt over her hip. "Let's hit it."

I shifted into reverse. "Don't say that when I'm driving."

"I trust you." She reached across the back of the seat and held my shoulder.

"After everything that's happened in the last few hours, let's not tempt the fates."

"Good idea." She patted the dashboard of the car. "Thanks for rescuing me."

"Are you talking to my truck?" Shay was adorable, rubbing the contoured ridge of the glove box and falling back in her seat.

"Not just the truck." Shay turned to look at me. "You too."

"Well, I may have violated a few traffic laws to get to you." She laughed. "Just a few?"

"In my defense, I'm not sure how many there are, but I'd break every single one to save your life."

"My life wasn't in danger." Shay said.

I pointed to the handle sticking out of the backpack. "You threw our axe at a demon. How were you not in danger?"

"I threw it to protect you, remember that?" She pulled it from the bag and held it up to the light.

I thought about stumbling to the ground as the giant monster came toward me, "Yes, how could I forget."

"Dexter was there. I was safe." She said as she wiped the blade across the leg of her pants.

"I'm pretty sure the image of him shredding that demon is etched in my memories forever."

"You know that won't be the last time, right?"

"I'm aware." I noticed the gas station sign a few miles from town. "I'm stopping to fill the tank. I don't want to risk running out of gas."

"Sounds good." Shay plucked her thumb against the honed edge of the axe. "There's still not a scratch on this." She held it up so I could see.

"Demon material is still such a mystery. I wish Benton were here to answer—" I stopped, when I realized what I'd said. I hesitated before looking at Shay, scared to see sadness in her eyes, smacking myself for being so insensitive.

"It's okay." She reached for my hand and gave it a reassuring squeeze. "I wish she was here too. For a million different reasons."

"I'm so sorry." I smacked myself mentally.

"Don't be sorry, Wil." Shay looked out the window. "We will figure out what we don't know."

I pulled into the gas station. "When?" I shifted the car into park. "I just want to understand what we are up against."

"Demons, mostly." She said with no hint of humor in her tone.

I flopped my arms over the steering wheel and turned to look at her. "I love you, Shay."

"But?"

"There is no but. I just love you, and I wanted you to know."

"You came for me. More than once. I will never doubt your love."

"Good." I opened the door and adjusted the pump to fill my truck with gas. Dexter was standing with his head hanging close to my shoulder. His dog breath was heavy beside my ear. "Hey, buddy." I clicked the handle of the pump so it would continue while I gave the K-9 my attention. "You flew away with my girl." I shuffled the fur around his ears.

"We didn't fly." She leaned against the side of my truck.

"Whatever you did . . ." I stared into his dog eyes. "No flying away with my girlfriend." Dexter barked as if responding to my request. "Good, I'm glad we understand each other." I heard the gas nozzle click off and returned it to the pump.

"Are you corrupting my partner?"

I turned around to look at her. "As if I could."

Our next stop was the old courthouse, and I wasn't as excited to enter it this second time. Shay reached for the door handle and noticed the door wasn't closed. "You didn't lock it?" She pivoted her arm across my chest, pushing me against the wall.

"I was in a hurry. There are a lot of things I didn't do."

"I know, but wait." She pushed hard on my chest. "Stay here." Dexter's body sat rigid as Shay ran back to the truck. Seconds later, she returned with a belt around her waist. She pulled the straps on her vest to draw it tight. "Dexter, *ante*." She waved him into the building and turned back to me. "Stay close, please."

My immediate thought was, *duh!* "I was planning to."

Shay drew her weapon and followed the K-9 inside. The beam of her flashlight waved in a zig-zag pattern casting light around the open space. Dexter was sniffing everything as we traced his steps. I'd never felt so safe and terrified at the same time. My second experience in the old building wasn't anything like the first. I could feel a wave of magick energy sweeping through the room, and I knew that was why my companions were stepping lightly. They could feel it too.

"I don't see anything."

I jumped. The sound of her voice startled me. "Shit, woman. Give a signal, would you please?"

She looked over her shoulder at me. "I'll try to remember for next time." She pointed to the stairs. "You want to come down with us?"

I was conflicted. "I'm not sure if I should."

She wriggled her fingers for me to come closer. "You can do this."

I reached to hold her hand at the same time Dexter started barking. Shay pulled away to grip her gun, and she stepped down into the basement. Her flashlight reflected off Dexter's eyes as the flashlight beam swept over the floor. "What'd you find, Dex?" His teeth raised in a snarl as Shay focused her light on his target. She paused on a shimmer bouncing against the carved timber wall.

"What is it?" I asked.

"You don't recognize them?" She looked back at me.

We stepped closer until I could believe what I was seeing. "Are they fairies?"

"Pretty amazing, don't you think?" She held out her hand. "Dexter, soft!" The German Shepherd crawled down into a sphinx position.

"I don't understand," I said.

Shay holstered her gun and dropped to one knee beside the wall. She spoke to the tiny fairy in a language I didn't understand. I watched, fascinated by the exchange and enchanted by the woman I loved. Dexter's head tilted as if he knew what they were saying. The creature responded to the sounds Shay was making with her lips and tongue. I had to guess they were words, but it was a language I didn't recognize. The beam of her flashlight turned off, and I heard her whisper a single word. "*Ignis.*" The flame flashed in the palm of her hand, and I stepped closer to watch the exchange between them.

"Come here." She waved me over until I could see the tiny being perched on her fingertip.

"What are you?" Every idea I ever had about the supernatural world was in question, again. Three inches of glistening fairy flittered in front of me.

"It's okay." Shay put an arm around my shoulder.

It was impossible to think that seeing fairies was ever going to be okay. "Are you sure about this?"

"Come and meet her. She's quite charming."

There was something incredible and unbelievable about Shay talking to the delicate fairy on her fingertip. "What language are you speaking?"

"It's Gaelic."

I could feel my brow and forehead wrinkle with questions. The most obvious, "You know Gaelic?"

Her smile, lit by the flame in her palm, was almost an answer. "I know a bit. I've got a few books, and Benton spoke it."

"Yes, Benton would, wouldn't she." It was a statement more than a question, but the talent buried deep in the history of Bannock was a constant evolution. "Why are the fairies here now?"

"That's what I was asking. She explained that the folk of the forest watch over this sacred carving. It holds powers revered for the earth element."

"Okay." I couldn't argue with that; I'd felt it myself.

Shay continued. "The fairy said she's here because of our spell, the surge of magick was so compelling, it called to her, and when she arrived, she could feel that we'd come into power, but the building was empty."

I pinched my arm just to check if all of this was real. I felt the sting and finally believed that this was my life. "You're saying she came to see us?"

The tiny sprite sprang from Shay's fingertip and flew across the room to where Dexter lay. Shay clenched a fist, extinguishing the flame, leaving us standing in the dark; again. The flashlight clicked on, and I heard her chuckle. "She also wanted to see the dragon." The beam of light stopped on Dexter, who was snorting at the fairy resting on his nose.

"I can understand that." I couldn't hide my smile as I watched the tiny drafts of smoke puffing the fairy up in the air. "When was the last time she saw a dragon?"

Shay spoke a few words, asking the fairy my question. "She says she's never seen a dragon in her lifetime." Their conversation continued, and as much as I wished I knew what they were saying, I was captivated by the language coming from my girlfriend's mouth. It sounded easy and coarse at the same time, and I didn't want her to stop.

Shay laughed, and the little being zipped away. I could hear the flitting hum of wings whistling in the air. It was a familiar sound, but I didn't understand why. "We aren't the only Bannock residents who haven't seen a dragon before?"

Shay stood and wiped the dust from her pants. "I guess not."

Dexter brushed against my leg. "Hey, buddy. You're making a lot of friends." He didn't respond, but I kept trying, hoping one day he would speak his first words.

The beam of Shay's flashlight passed over the artwork on the wall. "There is so much energy pouring out of the carving."

She placed her palm against the artwork. "Come and put your hand on it."

I didn't have to touch it to know. The Earth was awake in the basement of this old building, and Shay and I were responsible for it. "Would you call me a chicken if I told you that I'm afraid to touch this with you at the same time?"

"Afraid I'll disappear?"

"Actually, yes."

The flashlight clicked off, and I could hear Shay stepping closer, closing the space between us. Her arms came around my waist, and she pulled our bodies together. "I'm sorry."

I relaxed in her embrace. The two of us had an unspoken agreement about forgiveness. "I didn't mean it like that," I explained, "and honestly, you don't have anything to be sorry for."

Her hands slipped up my back, and I could feel the balance of energy between us. "We need to be patient with our powers."

"I couldn't agree more." I brushed the hair from her eyes and tucked it behind her ear.

"Dexter is a big part of my power, though."

"I understand that too."

She leaned in closer. "Good, now would you please just kiss me so we can finish what we came to do."

"Yes, ma'am." I touched my lips to hers. I wasn't about to let the moment pass. I opened my eyes when she pulled away. Her forehead touched my own, and I truly believed in magick. Not just the spellcasting and *Ignis* flames, but in the heart-thumping, body-tingling that only mutual respect could create.

"We should finish." I felt her breath on my lips.

"Yes, we should." I tucked my thumbs in the loop of her belt, tugging her hips closer to mine.

"You have to let me go." Her lips said go, but her body didn't move away.

I kissed her again, and when I pulled back, I felt her sway. "I can let you go, for now." I gave her hips a little shove, just enough to break the contact between us. "Woman, what you do to me."

"What I do to you?" She pointed at her chest with a slick smile.

"Focus."

She pulled her hand through her hair and tied it in a ponytail. "I'm good. I got this."

I ran my fingertip over my lips. "You are a good superhero. Very, very good."

Shay started kicking the dirt on the floor, shuffling the star I'd made, and concealing any components of the spell I recited. I pointed the flashlight, confirming there wasn't a trace of us in the basement. We climbed to the first floor, and I helped Shay roll the floorboards back into position and lock them in place.

I stared at the carving on the wall, lit by the setting sun.

"I can't get over the artwork. I would like to know more about who created it."

Shay threw her arm over my shoulder. "I'm sure we could find some more details at the library."

I draped an arm over her hip. "You've been in this town for ten years. Haven't you ever been curious?

"Maybe, but not enough. I was focused on my day job and magick."

"You've been really focused." I bumped her hip.

"I'm starting to rethink that decision."

"Are you planning to tell me about the conversation you had downstairs?"

"It wasn't a big deal. The fairy was very curious about Dexter. I told her to come to the house some time, and we would let her talk with him."

"Talk to the dog?"

"Talk to our dragon dog."

I held up my hand to stop her from saying anything more. "Don't try to explain it." I swept the floor with my foot, wiping away our shoe prints. "I'm so curious that I don't even care that you can communicate with the fairy folk and never told me."

"There are a lot of things I haven't told you." Shay clapped her hands together, wiping off the dirt.

"A lot?" I asked.

"More than I can count." I followed her to the door, and she opened it so I could step outside. Dexter barked as Shay removed the key from her pocket and locked the deadbolt. "What's up, buddy?" His butt slumped to the ground, and he settled once the key was back inside her pocket.

"What was that about?"

"I haven't got a clue." Shay dropped the tailgate of my truck, and the K-9 jumped up into the bed.

"I wish he could talk," I leaned over the wheel-well. "I'll bet he has a lot to say."

"He's had a few weird days." She said as she walked around to the passenger side. "I can't even imagine how his dog mind works."

"And his dragon mind too." I opened the driver's door and sat behind the steering wheel. She was beside me and looked behind at the enormous German Shepherd who was licking his hind leg.

"It's crazy." She leaned over to pinch my arm.

"Ow, what was that for?" The mischief in the gleam of her eyes was almost enough to ease my pain.

"I just wanted to make sure this is my life."

I thought about the last time I pinched her for the same reason. "Damn, woman. You've got a fierce pinch. That's going to leave a mark." I rubbed the back of my bicep.

"I think you'll survive."

"Maybe." I rolled my shoulder, trying to view the back of my arm. "Look, I think I can see it already."

Shay threw her head against the back of her seat. "Will you please take me home?"

"Your place or mine?" I turned to look at her, serious about my question. Shay felt like home to me, and I wanted to be anywhere she was.

I could see the exhaustion in her eyes when she turned to answer. "The carriage house feels more like *our* place."

I didn't try to hide the smile on my face. "The carriage house it is." There was a conversation in our future, and it would involve a blending of our lives. I wanted Shay to live with me forever, but I wasn't sure she'd ever give up the little house with the bright orange door.

CHAPTER XII

Farewell

I stepped out of the shower and wrapped a towel around my chest. I dried my hair and put on a simple collared shirt. It was dark grey and the nicest one I owned. As my fingers pushed the tiny buttons through the holes, I thought about the women I loved and lost; Mrs. Adleman, the teacher who helped me pass the fifth grade. Gran, the woman who gave me the gift of magick and self-confidence, and Mama Pierce, the woman who let me call her mother even though I was a stranger.

It still felt impossible that they were dead even after all of these years. I draped my towel over the hook and swiped my hand across the mirror, making a clean view on the steamed glass. I stared for a long time at my reflection. Today was not going to be easy. I walked into the living room to find Shay.

Leaning against the hallway corner, I watched as she ran a hot iron across the crease of her dress-uniform pants. Her coat was hanging on the door. She'd spent a half-hour pinning commendation bars to the left breast of her dress uniform jacket. Her badge was in place with a black elastic ribbon stretched around. The attention to detail was as much about saying goodbye as it was a testament to the seriousness of Shay's profession. The mood was solemn as I expected the entire day would be.

Shay and I were experts at saying goodbye, but we weren't great at moving on.

"You doing okay?" I asked, concern evident in my tone.

She lifted the iron and looked up at me. "No, not really." Grief is a solitary experience. We all do it in different ways, but her honest response made me fiercely protective.

"I can tell. You've been pressing the same line of that pant leg for the last few minutes."

Her lips crushed together, and she closed her eyes. "I was thinking about my first year on the department. Learning about Bannock." She looked at me.

"Was it hard to believe that demons were real?" I asked.

She forced a smile and shook her head. "I was thinking. . ."

"What, sweetheart?" I wondered why she would pause.

"You probably won't believe me, but it was more about the reality of becoming a police officer."

"Not demons?" I sat down at the table.

"Sometimes demons are easier." She turned the dial off on the iron and unplugged it from the wall.

"I'm not sure I understand."

Shay clipped the cuff of her pants to a hanger and hooked them on the door beside her jacket. "We hunt demons like wild animals. There's no question about why because they're hunting us. People aren't quite as easy."

"Humanity is sketchy sometimes." I added.

"Not all of it, but there are moments when good guys look like bad guys."

I hesitated before saying her name. "Benton?"

"I thought she betrayed me . . . us. I still feel guilty about it."

"You were following the facts. That's all you could do."

Shay opened the cabinet and removed a mug. She filled the cup from the fresh pot of coffee, and steam drifted as she lifted it to her lips. She blew across the top before taking a sip. "Reg was a good cop. She was a great teacher and mentor, but she was always my friend."

"But she was more." I stood up to walk closer to her.

"Yes, she was. She was family, and I didn't know it."

I took the mug from Shay's hand and set it on the counter. I saw the glassy tears hanging in the corners of her eyes. "You knew, deep down. More important, Benton knew." I held her face in my hands, wiping her tears with the pad of my thumb.

"Do you think so?"

"She loved you like you were her own. She even said so in the letter. Everything that's happened since the attack, she did it all because she loved you."

"I wanted to tell her." Shay turned away, trying to hide the tears that were impossible to stop.

"I know, my love." I pulled her into my arms as if the armor of my embrace could ease her suffering. She shuddered against my chest. Abandonment left scars, and I understood the price of vulnerability attached to sorrow. I held tight, without thought of time or space, as the love of my life released years of suffering. It was Shay and me, as it always should have been.

"We're going to be late." She reached for a tissue and wiped her cheeks.

"I doubt that's possible." I pretended to check the watch I wasn't wearing.

She pushed my shoulder with a playful smile. "I should get dressed."

"I probably should finish, too." My fingers held tight against the small of her back. Her head fell to my shoulder.

"I need one more minute, just like this." I felt her hands clasp behind me.

"I think I do too."

It was longer than a minute. I carried Shay's uniform to our bedroom and watched her dress. This time the protective layer of her demon-Kevlar vest stayed on the hook. Dexter pushed by and flopped in his spot on the workshop floor as we walked down the stairs. Shay looked perfect. I didn't have much for formal occasions, but I owned clothing for goodbyes. As I said, Shay and I were experts at leaving people behind.

"I'll drive." I folded a few tissues and put them in my pocket.

"That's probably a good idea."

The drive to the service was quiet and the cemetery was a few miles west of the Carriage house. Shay was unusually distant as we sat in the car once we arrived at the cemetery. I watched her brush the stray dog hairs from her uniform pants. She was organizing herself, and I was patient until she was ready. She took two deep, huffing breaths like she was preparing to lift a thousand pounds over her head.

"Okay," she looked at me. "I can do this." She slipped the bright white gloves over her hands.

I jumped out of my seat and ran around to open her door. Shay clutched my hand and held tight as we walked together through the grass. The morning dew was beading across the tips of her polished boots. I wondered about Dexter and her decision to leave him at the carriage house, but I didn't share those thoughts. Shay was thinking about Shay, which was something she rarely did.

Officer Forrest was waiting with a woman I guessed was her wife. The stranger's dark hair was twisted in a tight braid, hanging down her back. She was shorter than Dani by almost a foot, and the size difference was flattering to the pair. Her skin was a rich tanned color like my own, which complemented her long blue dress. The lace around the bottom was touching the grass, and I could see water stains from the morning dew. She was a beautiful woman, and I was curious to know more about her.

"Hey, Dani." Shay held out a hand.

"Hey yourself." Dani pulled her in for a hug and whispered. "You doing okay?"

Shay answered with the same soft voice, "Not really."

"Me either." They separated. The woman cleared her throat as if reminding the two police officers that we were present. "Oh, shit. Sorry. Uh, Amelia, this is Wildwood. Wildwood, this is my wife, Amelia."

"Nice to meet you." I stretched a hand. "Weird circumstances but *nice* just the same."

I noticed a cane in her right palm so her left raised up to shake mine. I looked into jet black eyes so much like my own.

"I've heard a lot about you, Wildwood. It's great to put a face with the name." I nodded. It was always weird to meet someone for the first time at an occasion like this.

Dani interrupted. "We should find a place to sit."

"Yes." Shay led us to the graveside canopy. She stopped in front of the funeral attendant.

"Officer Pierce?" He asked.

"Yes." I felt the corded trim on Shay's glove squeeze against my bare hand.

"Please come sit in front. We have a place for you and your family." Four vacant folding chairs sat marked in front of the gravesite. The names Forrest and Pierce were side by side. The center space near Benton's relatives was confirmation that Shay was considered family. We made a solemn line as we took our seats.

Funerals are never pleasant. They're a reminder of mortality and unfulfilled dreams. People in uniform surrounded me, an endless stream of faces I'd never seen before and would probably never see again. Shay squeezed my hand and held it in her lap as we listened to the service.

The minister spoke of honor and commitment and a life well-lived. They were predictable words delivered to comfort the living. "If anyone would like to share, please come forward." He said.

Shay squeezed my hand and let it go. She stood and turned to face the crowd. When she looked up at the people in the group, the rims of her eyes were red.

"Regina Benton was a complicated woman." Shay pressed her lips together, fighting back her tears. "She knew how to make a friend, but she also knew how to be one. That's not an easy way to live. I was barely nineteen when I started at the department; a baby really, and I was fortunate, no, I was blessed to be her rookie." Shay pulled a tissue from her pocket, and her gloved hand came up to wipe her eyes. "Reg didn't hold back.

Damn, she was tough. She called out every mistake. Always emphasizing if you couldn't work together, you shouldn't work alone. She had high expectations for me, so I had them for myself. I respected her for that." Shay paused, looking over at the casket. "She taught me to be a better police officer, an honest one, and that putting on this uniform meant something. I can never repay her for that." Shay closed her eyes, and the tears flooded through. "Reg, wherever you are, I'll miss you forever, and I'll never forget what you've given me." Shay reached out over the flag-draped casket, resting her white-gloved hand on the flag's blood-red stripe.

She returned to her chair, and I leaned to whisper in her ear. "That was beautiful."

"Thank you." She smothered my hand with her own. "You doing okay?"

I forced a smile and whispered back. "I'm fine."

I didn't bother to ask because I knew Shay wasn't okay and that it was all she could do to stifle the tears. The resonance of a solitary bugler made me jump as the echo of TAPS filled the cemetery. The gunshots sounded, seven rifles firing three times. I wept, uncertain why that display of respect for ultimate sacrifice tore at my heart.

The American flag draped over the coffin was raised by young officers in uniforms groomed to perfection. I watched their confident hands slide across each crease as they buried the flag's red stripes inside the folds. A precise sacred triangle of blue covered in white stars was the final result. The tallest officer's steps were purposeful as he made his way toward the family. I expected the flag to rise into Benton's older cousin's hands, but the officer walked by him and stopped in front of Shay.

He lifted the folded flag before turning it around, so the triangle point faced his heart. His voice was deep as it broke through the silence. "On behalf of the Bannock Police Department, please accept this flag as a symbol of our appreciation for your family member's honorable and faithful service."

Shay's cheeks were streaked with tears as her hands took hold of the flag. She stared at the last physical connection to her friend. I didn't know what to do as I sat and watched strangers pass in front of the coffin; some dropped handfuls of dirt on the casket while others set flowers or small polished stones. We sat together until most of the attendants were gone. Dani dropped to one knee in front of us, and I was grateful for her help.

"Hey, Pierce. You want to say goodbye?"

Shay looked up, fragile and shaken. "Uh, sure. I mean, yes."

I slipped my hand under her arm to help her to her feet. Shay held the flag over her heart as the four of us walked to stand at the grave. She passed the folded cloth to me and tugged each glove from her hand. She removed a small bag from her jacket pocket.

Shay's voice was a private whisper as she forced the words. "May the sweet wings of Rhiannon's birds carry you on your next journey. May your soul find rest, my beautiful friend." She opened the small bag, pinching the herbs between her fingers. She rubbed the tiny leaves into dust and sprinkled them across the open grave. "I'll miss you, always." She clutched the bag in her hand.

We stood together. A solemn line of strong women saying goodbye to the most impressive person to walk among us. I didn't know her well, but I knew that much was true.

"Will you please take me home?" Shay's eyes were glassy with tears.

"Yes, love." I held my hand to her.

"You're not coming to the bar?" Dani asked.

"Maybe later." Shay turned and hugged her and stepped closer to hug Amelia. "Pour one for me, just in case."

"I'll pour one for both of you." Amelia reached a hand out to shake mine.

"Maybe the two of you could stop by the carriage house later instead." I suggested.

"Maybe we will." Dani held an open elbow to her wife, and I watched as they crossed the cemetery lawn, but Shay didn't make a move to follow. We were the last of the attendants, and I could tell the funeral directors were waiting to lower the casket until we were gone. Shay wasn't ready to leave.

"Talk to me, love." I put my arm around her waist.

She clutched the flag to her chest. "I didn't expect this."

"The flag?" I asked.

"Yes. It should have gone to her cousin."

"I'm guessing that's not what Benton wanted."

She wiped the tears with her finger and the pad of her thumb. "I don't know how to do this."

"So far, you're doing okay." I held her tighter. "I'll stand here all night if that's what you need."

"I know that you would. That's why I love you so damn much." Her head fell against my shoulder. "Wildwood, I don't want to be apart."

"We won't. You can come back to my place today."

Her head turned toward me. "That's not what I meant."

"What, honey?"

The tone in her words, the vulnerability in her voice, it left no question. "I want us to live together. I want to be with you."

"I thought that's what we were doing," I said.

"I want to sell my place. I want us to live together at the carriage house."

"Are you sure about that?"

Nodding, she turned in my arms. The flag fell away to her hip. "I don't want to waste a single moment."

"We won't."

She stepped away from my embrace and knelt in the dirt, taking a small handful of soil. She sifted it into the tiny bag, drew the strings tight, and tucked it in the fold of the flag. I didn't know why but I was sure there was a particular reason, and she would explain when the time was right.

"I'm ready now."

"Are you sure?"

She forced a smile. "Not really, but I can't stay here forever. Benton is already so far away."

"Yes, she is."

It felt ridiculous to drive the short distance from the carriage house to the cemetery but returning home would have made for a lengthy walk. I was responsible for directing Shay from the graveyard to the truck and from the truck to our bedroom in the carriage house. Dexter followed us up the stairs and waited beside the bed as I helped her undress. I wondered if the tear stains would fade into the heavy woolen jacket. Shay crawled across the bed and collapsed in a cocoon of pillows and blankets.

We all say goodbye in very different ways. Shay and I were experts at it, but we weren't great at moving on.

CHAPTER XIII

Diversion

It was the middle of the afternoon, but I still had mixed feelings about leaving Shay alone in bed. As much as she wanted to sleep, I couldn't shake the restlessness inside me. Everything about today felt out of balance. Grief propelled my best friend and lover toward a personal darkness I understood. Sometimes it was easier to be alone than to let people in and watch them go.

I changed out of my shirt and pants. They weren't as impressive as the dress uniform hanging on the door, but they were my best, and that was enough. I felt like a compass arrow spinning without direction. I hardly knew Benton, but her absence from Shay's life was difficult to witness.

I sat down in the kitchen to lace my boots. Distraction is good for the soul, and maybe a few hours of pounding hot steel would help me cope. The kitchen table was clear except for the flag resting on the edge. I had no idea what to do with something so sacred.

The hefty thump of my boots on the stairs was the only sound in the carriage house, and the echo was like the ballad of grief. I stood in the workshop staring at the hammer resting on the anvil. The forge was cold, and the room felt very much the same. I loved the process of transformation, of turning a rusted piece of metal into a life-saving tool. I ran my finger across the face of the anvil; I wasn't going to blacksmith today.

The beast of a dragon-dog lay curled in his circle on the floor. Dexter looked up as I approached, and I had so many unanswered questions as I dropped to one knee in front of him. "Hey, buddy. You want to go for a walk?"

His giant paws stretched out, and I wondered what it was like inside his head. I grabbed the leash from the bottom of the stairs, and when I turned around, his wet nose was bumping my hand. He definitely wanted to take a walk.

The town of Bannock isn't big enough if you're hoping to disappear into obscurity. After opening the carriage house, I knew enough people to say hey and offer a friendly nod. Dexter and I walked to Shay's house, and I thought about her desperate plea to bring our individual lives together. I wanted it, but I wasn't sure that she did. At least not for the right reasons.

The mailbox was propped open with an oversized envelope inside. I grabbed it and tossed the brochures and informational flyers tucked behind in the recycle bin. I let Dexter lead me through town, but I knew where we would end up. As we rounded the corner in front of the bar, Dani and her wife were standing on the sidewalk. They'd changed out of their funeral clothes into casual jeans and jackets. I was glad for a bit of human interaction. They were looking at the tree behind the bar.

I stood beside them, tilting my head to see what was so interesting. "What are we looking at?" I asked.

"I was just noticing that all of the leaves have fallen off the tree. It seems really odd since there aren't any on the ground."

"Oh." I didn't know what else to say. "Hey, Dani." I did my best flip of a hand to wave with a fistful of mail.

"Hi, Wildwood. I'm surprised to see you here."

"Well, I'm not *here*, here." I waved my arm to point at the door of the bar. "Dexter and I are letting Shay rest."

"How's she doing?" Amelia asked. Her voice had a kindness, like a solemn prayer after hours of meditation.

"Not great, but she'd tell you differently if you asked her."

"Benton was pretty important to Shay." Dani looked at the entrance to the bar. "She was a great cop."

"I wish I'd had more opportunities to know her." The leash pulled my wrist, drawing me off balance. "I guess he wants to walk."

"Mind if we tag along?" Amelia asked.

"I don't as long as you're okay wandering behind this unpredictable animal." I didn't know what to do. Should we go back to the carriage house or just zip back and forth through the small town. I followed Dexter and Amelia and Dani were content to do the same.

"Can I ask you a question?" Dani interrupted the silence.

"Yeah, sure, go ahead."

She hesitated, and I wasn't sure she was going to ask at all. "Are you the one...?"

What did she mean? "The one what?" I could feel the tension crinkle the skin near the corner of my eyes. What one?

Was she digging for details? Did she hope I would reveal secrets I didn't know I knew?

Amelia jabbed her elbow into Dani's rib. "Don't."

"What?" I repeated. I didn't understand Dani well enough to guess what she was asking but Amelia wasn't amused.

"Are you the one that taught her magick?" The cop's fingers fanned out to cover her ribs before Amelia could elbow them a second time.

"Oh." I thought about the question, and I wasn't sure how to answer. "I guess. We were kids when I started messing around with light-work. I wouldn't call it magick, though."

"That's not how Shay tells it."

"Really?" I paused as Dexter stopped to sniff the ground and pick up a stick to carry as he walked. "How does Shay tell it?" I asked, curious to know how Shay told our origin story.

"She said you were her first and that she'd never forgotten how powerful you were."

"I was fifteen, and I was hardly powerful, but Shay was absolutely a first." Dani and Amelia laughed. "That's not a joke. I know you understand the magick world, but back then, I just liked the way it felt to have all of that energy moving through me."

"Sounds like a typical teenage exploration of boundaries." Amelia said.

"If your exploration included a cute redhead and harvesting the earth element. It was very typical." Their laughter was the perfect reaction to my answer. Dexter barked to get my attention as we stopped in front of the carriage house. "Would you like to come in?"

"Do you think Pierce would mind?"

"I'm sure Shay needs to rest," Amelia answered.

"Oh, just come on up. I'll check on her, and we can finish this conversation. I'd love to hear what Shay has to say." Dexter's nose pushed the door open wide enough for us to enter. His butt dropped to the floor, and he waited for me to unclip the leash. He didn't waste time hopping up the stairs. "I guess he's checking on her too?" I teased.

I took the stairs two at a time so that I could survey the apartment. It was tidy enough for company, and I was pleased to see Dexter greeting my favorite person sitting at the kitchen table.

"Hello, you," I said as I dropped the mail on the table.

"Hello, yourself. Did this handsome guy drag you out or vice versa?" Shay's cheek rose with a tiny smile, but I could see the redness around her eyes.

"I think we both needed to take a walk. I hope it was okay."

"It was perfect." She stood to come closer, and I noticed her lack of clothing.

"Dani and Amelia are coming up. You might want to put some pants on."

She walked a few more steps so she could kiss me on the lips. "Good idea." She brushed her hand across my cheek. "Thanks, love."

"Hey, Pierce." Dani stood at the top of the stairs holding out a hand to her wife. Shay stopped in front of the pair, waiting for Amelia to navigate the last step before hugging them both.

"Hi. How are you doing?" Amelia's skin was a beautiful copper tone, a stark contrast to Shay's pale complexion. She held both of Shay's cheeks, steering her face to direct eye contact. The intensity of the exchange left no room to question the depth of love between them.

"I'm the best I can be right now."

"And your magick?"

Shay's eyes opened wide, and she broke contact with her friend. "Dani, you shouldn't have said. . ."

Amelia interrupted. "Danielle didn't have to say anything to me. Regina is gone, and I've been in this family long enough to know what that means." She walked away from the rest of us and sat down at the table.

"Yeah, I guess you would," Shay replied.

I raised my hand to get their attention. "Hello, I know I'm the rookie here, but the three of you need to help me out. What are you talking about? What's going on?"

Dani walked around the table to sit beside her wife. "Amelia and I have been together most of our lives. You have to understand that if I know about fighting the evil in Bannock, she probably does too." Dani reached to hold her wife's hand.

"You're right. I don't know why I reacted like that." Shay walked closer, wrapping her arms around me. "The Forrests are my people. I may be a solitary practitioner, but they know magick too."

"Of course, they do."

"I didn't mean to panic," Shay said as she looked at Dani. "It's just been a tough week, and I feel so off balance and I'm going to go put on some pants."

I followed my girlfriend into the bedroom. "I didn't plan to bring them back. I hope it's okay."

Shay opened the dresser drawer and picked out a rolled-up pair of jeans. "It's good to have Dani here. With all of the changes going on for you and me, she's a good source of information." Shay kicked her feet into the jeans. "Plus, I need to do something about all of this crying."

I waited for her to zip her pants before stepping closer. "You loved her. You have every right to feel sad and to cry."

"Curling up in a ball. That's not like me."

"That much I know, but you've done more than lose Reggie in the last few days. It's okay to curl up for a minute or two."

Shay looked down at her hands. "Maybe just for a minute, but you and I have a lot of questions to answer, and that's not going to happen if I lay down again."

I circled her hips with my arms, lifting her body against my own. "Sweetheart, I love you, but if you need time, you should take it."

Her arms came around my neck. "I should, should I?"

"Yep."

She kissed me, and for a moment, I forgot there were guests in our apartment. The loud voice broke our mood.

"Hey Pierce, you putting pants on or taking some off!" I heard Dani yell.

"She never stops either?" I set Shay down.

"I think she's worse than I am." Shay turned to walk through the bedroom door.

"Goddess save us all. "

Amelia was sitting at the table watching her wife grab mugs from the cabinet. "The coffee fresh?" The pot wasn't even on.

"This morning. I'm sure it's cold." I said as I watched them navigate our kitchen.

"Would you like to go for coffee?" Amelia's voice had a comforting kindness. "Maybe take a walk for some fresh air."

"How about something to eat?" I asked, offering valuable distractions.

Dani picked up the duffle bag from the floor. "How about some target practice?" She dropped it on the table, rummaging through and pulling out two 9mm magazines and fanning them between her fingers.

"That sounds kinda perfect," Shay answered. I looked at Dani, Dani looked at Amelia, and we looked at Shay. "I'll make a pot of coffee. Wildwood and Amelia can make some sandwiches, and Dani can load up the armory."

"The armory?" I asked.

"The patrol car," Amelia explained. "The two of them are a little enthusiastic about shooting at the range." I handed her a loaf of bread.

"Not you?" I asked. I opened the refrigerator and stacked meat and lettuce in my hand.

"Definitely, not me." Amelia tilted her head toward the two cops. "Shay and Danielle are two peas in an extremely unique pod. I don't mind tagging along, though shooting isn't my thing. They can be very entertaining and a bit competitive."

"So, you just sit there by yourself and watch them shoot?"

Amelia opened the bag of bread and spread pieces out on the cutting board. "Not anymore." Her wink was playful and inviting and also a clear welcome to the family.

CHAPTER 14

Implications

Dani threw the duffle bag over her shoulder like it didn't have fifty pounds of guns and ammunition inside. I wrapped our food and put it in the cooler along with a few drinks. I watched Shay as she filled the thermos with coffee. The sorrow was still in her eyes, but I could also see hope in the flush of her cheeks.

"You take my car." Shay tossed the keys to Dani.

"Follow me." The taller cop was almost giddy; if giddy was a thing the two cops could be. I didn't know what to expect from this trio, but if today's experience was anything like the previous shooting range adventure, I was nervous about the show. What comes after demon guts splattered by a transforming dragon-dog?

The trunk of Shay's car was up as we exited the carriage house. Dani set the bag inside and opened the car door for her wife. I was staring; I couldn't help myself. They made a great pair. Shay was leaning against the driver's side door, watching me watching them. She waved to point at the patrol car. "There's a lot of history between them."

"I'm beginning to see that." I pulled the keys from my pocket as Shay opened the driver's door. She lingered in the space, and the breeze caught the tips of her hair. She tucked them away from her face, and I couldn't imagine a more beautiful person on the planet. I leaned in to kiss her, and a perfectly timed patrol car squawk caused our heads to bump. I looked at the car where I could see Amelia swat at her wife.

"So much for history," Shay said. Her kiss was a quick peck on my cheek as she ran around to the passenger side of the truck. There was a little pep in the way Shay pulled herself into the seat. Dani pulled away from the curb, and I made quick work shifting the truck into gear so I could follow. The exchange left a glow to Shay's cheeks and a smile on her face.

"Is this going to help?" I asked. The squad car was ahead of us, and although I knew the way, it was easier to follow.

"Spending time with Dani and Amelia?" Shay shifted against the corner of the cab, where the seat met the door. The pivot gave her a view of the dog behind us and me.

"Yes, and shooting." I made a quick glance over my shoulder at Dexter. His tongue was flapping out his mouth, savoring the ride in the back of the truck. "What if we stir up another attack?"

"We'll be ready this time." She patted the bag beside her. "We've got all of your forged weapons." She hitched her thumb toward the dog. "We've got Dex, and this time we've got Dani."

"You think Dani tips the scales in our direction?"

"She has years of experience surviving in Bannock, and I'm positive she knows how to stop an attack from just about everything non-human."

"So, you're telling me she's a good partner?"

"When it comes to the demon world, she's the best." Shay paused to look at me. "When it comes to the heart, you're the only partner I'll ever need."

I glanced at her, and the silly toothy grin made me laugh. "That's sweet."

"I mean every word." Her head fell against the glass, and she watched me drive.

I was quiet for a moment, thinking about the tattered targets at their shooting spot. They must have visited the firing range often before I arrived in Bannock. "The shooting range is where you blow off steam?"

There was no hesitation in her response. "It is."

"And you're an excellent shot." I wasn't asking a question but leading the conversation in another direction.

"I think you've witnessed that I'm very good." She said.

"Why did you have so much steam to blow off?"

"Ooh," she let out a sharp breath, "that's a tough question to answer."

"Too personal?"

"Not for you." She hesitated, and I wondered what memories were playing in her mind. "Being alone can be frustrating."

"Frustrating?" I thought about the word and the context it might hold, and then I thought about Shay as a woman who survived a brutal attack. I didn't say anything, but the sudden realization was evident on my face.

"You get it now."

I nodded. "I'm glad I can help you with that frustration."

"Me too."

The car in front of us turned down the gravel road. I watched the cyclops light in the rear window glow bright red before parking in the matted grass.

"We're here," I said as I pulled in alongside Dani and her wife.

"Are you going to be okay with us out here shooting?"

"I'll be fine." I shifted the truck into park, and before I could say another word, Dexter's paws were hooking over the window next to Shay.

"Hello, buddy."

His barking was the only response as he dropped away to greet our friends. Amelia had a book tucked under her arm, a paper bag clutched tight, but today her cane was not in hand. I wondered if she was recovering from an injury. "I don't usually stay out here while they play," Amelia said. "Would you like to come and sit with me in the cabin?"

I looked at Shay. "Do you mind?"

"I'm sure you'll have more fun with Amelia."

"I don't know." Dani dropped the duffle bag strap on her shoulder, crossing it over her chest. She pumped the action on the shotgun with a swing of her arm and started loading it with shells. She was ready to work out more than frustration.

"Let's go." Amelia hooked my arm and dragged us toward the tiny single-room cabin. "Danielle told me you'd been here already, so you know there's not much to do inside. I usually read a book, but if you're interested, I've got a deck of cards."

"I'm up for cards," I said.

"Perfect. Let's get inside before all the noise starts."

"They do this a lot?" I asked. I looked over my shoulder. Shay and Dani set targets, holding the paper in place while the other slammed a staple in the corners. I couldn't imagine the conversation taking place across the yard.

"Before you moved into town, they came out here at least once a week. I'm pretty sure Shay spent half of her salary on ammunition."

"You're not serious?"

Amelia shook her head. She was teasing, but she had no idea about the conversation Shay, and I had just had. "Not really, but the two of them could shoot the cap off a bottle and sit down and take a drink."

"Shay's a pretty good shot," I said.

Amelia opened the cabin door, and I followed her inside. "She needs to be. What they encounter around here; every shot must be perfect."

She moved around the cabin with an apparent routine. She pulled a lever on the wall. "This is my flag for Danielle. If I drop this, she knows I'm coming outside."

"That's smart."

She opened the curtain covering a cabinet and took down a lantern from the shelf. "The two of them can get very focused out there. Better safe than shot." She set the old kerosene light on the table before turning toward the cast-iron cooktop. She grabbed a few pieces of paper from a box in the corner and twisted them into sticks. She threw them in the stove, piled small pieces of tinder on top, dragged a matchstick across the vent pipe, and touched the flame to the lantern before dropping the match inside the stove. It wasn't cold enough for a fire.

"I usually make coffee. Would you like some?"

"I'd love some. Can I help?"

She looked up from the coffee pot. "Not this time. Next time, you'll know where everything is."

"Do you like coming out here?" I asked.

She set the percolator on the cast iron stove top and pulled out the chair across from me. She lowered herself and gripped her knee to slide her leg over. She noticed my stare, and I felt the heat of blush come to my cheeks.

"It's okay." She knocked on her leg, and it was evident that there was no flesh beneath her knuckles. "It's an old injury." She reached for the cards and opened the box. She removed the deck and started to shuffle it. "What's your game?"

I thought for a second. "Honestly, solitaire."

"Hmm." She looked at me. "That's going to be a little difficult for the two of us."

"I haven't played cards much, I'm afraid."

"Okay. Have you ever heard of cribbage?" She opened a drawer in the front of the table.

"I've heard of it but never played." I may not have had a ton of experience with card games, but I knew a set up when I got tangled in one.

Amelia placed the game board on the table and turned it over to reveal a tiny door in the back. I watched as she slid it with her thumb and removed plastic pegs. She pushed them into the holes at the end of the board. "Get comfortable, Wildwood. You're about to get your first lesson."

My body jerked when I heard the first gunshot in the yard. "Why do I suddenly feel like a target."

"Are you talking about the noise our girls are making or the game on the table?" She shuffled the cards one more time.

"I think my chances are better with the team outside."

The smile she gave was playful, but I could see mischief in the tiny wrinkles in the corner of her eyes. "I'll take it easy on you today."

"Thanks, I think."

She dealt six cards to each of us and began to explain the rules of the game. We took turns laying out the cards in our hands. I never knew counting could be so competitive. I heard the shotgun blasts outside and wondered if putting holes in paper targets was better than double skunking.

"That's fifteen for two?" It was more of a question as I laid out my hand. Her head tipped to confirm my points, and I moved my peg two spaces on the board, feeling like the champion of the world.

Amelia flipped her hand over. "That's fifteen two." She tapped the cards as she counted. "That's fifteen four." She was going slow, but the counting still confused me. "And I've got a double run for eight." I could already feel the pangs of defeat. "That's one dozen for me." She popped her peg halfway down the line.

I was feeling nostalgic for solitaire. "I sense an ass-kicking in my future."

Amelia's smile faded as we both turned toward the sounds coming from outside. The guns were silent, but I could hear Shay calling for Dexter. I walked to the door and opened it wide enough to see Dani kneeling beside Shay. "I wonder what's going on."

"With the two of them, it could be anything." Amelia moved the percolator from the cooktop to the trivet on the counter. "Let's go take a look." She dropped the handle by the door, warning the two women we were coming out.

"Stay inside!" Dani yelled, holding up a hand to stop us.

Amelia threw her arm around me, and we sidestepped behind the wall. Shay was quick to appear in the doorway.

"Dexter is at it again." She pointed to the stains on her chest and thighs.

"Demon?" I asked.

"A big one, just like the thing that attacked us the last time we were here." Shay opened the door wide enough to see Dani pile up the demon bits and pieces and holster the handgun she was holding.

"Is it from the mine?" I asked

Shay turned at the sound of Dani yelling outside. "Pierce, he's taking off."

"Damn it. Dexter!" The call didn't deter the animal from his full sprint toward the mouth of the mine. Before Shay could follow, he disappeared inside.

"What's going on?" I asked

Shay held up a hand to silence us and closed her eyes as if she was trying to listen. "He caught the scent of something."

"Don't disappear . . ." I was too late. Shay was gone, and there was no doubt where Dexter had summoned her.

Amelia stumbled back, thrown off balance in disbelief. "Did Shay just--?"

"Dexter just took her." I walked out of the cabin toward Dani.

Amelia was close behind me. "What do you mean he took her?" she asked.

"It's only happened once before, but they have some kind of bond."

"He's a familiar," Dani stated more than questioned.

"When he goes after something big, he takes Shay with him. Whether she's ready or not." I looked at the guns on the table. "Did she have any weapons?"

Dani picked up the shotgun and moved a box of ammunition. "Whatever she had on her body."

"Body armor?"

Her head moved from side to side. "No."

Amelia interrupted. "They're in the mine?"

"Dexter took off into the tunnels. There was no way to stop him."

"Do you think he's going to find the--" She stopped talking, and I turned to look at her.

"Find *the* what?" I asked.

Dani started pushing shells into the shotgun. "There's a tunnel in there, and it's not any place we want to go."

"I will guarantee you that's exactly where they're going," I said.

"Damn it." Amelia turned away, and I wish I knew her well enough to determine the focus of her concern. She walked closer to her wife. "Give me your spare."

Dani lifted her right leg and drew a small twenty-two from an ankle holster. "Sorry, love, that's not going to do much."

I ran to Shay's patrol car and reached through the open window to pop the release on the trunk. I grabbed the dark nylon bag and the demon forged axe. I had no idea what to do with any of it, but the anvil dust was inside the bag. If something happened to Shay, this would help her.

"Let's go!" Dani yelled.

I closed the trunk with a slam and ran to catch up with them.

"I'll take the lead." Dani said as she clipped a light to the top of her shotgun. "Stay behind me." She was looking at her wife.

"I got it."

Dani was five steps into the mine when I heard the paralyzing sound of a shotgun racking. She was loaded and ready to fire on the unknown. I was trying to sort out the thundering of my heartbeat against the silence that followed. The deeper we traveled inside, the darker it became.

"Danielle," Amelia whispered. "Do you have more light?"

"No."

I tucked the bag into my back pocket and held out my hand. I hesitated for a moment before deciding how many secrets we would reveal today. "*Ignis.*" The flame flickered in my palm.

"Whoa." Amelia reached to touch, and it flashed higher. "That's unbelievable."

I could see her curious eyes reflecting in my light. "I'm still trying to believe it myself." We walked side by side, staying a few steps behind Dani but close enough to watch her back.

We heard Dexter long before we saw the reflection in his dog eyes. I was looking at the body lying beside him, and my girlfriend pinned beneath it. "Shay."

"Dexter!" Dani yelled. "*Auferetur!*"

I scrolled through my limited knowledge of Latin. I hoped it meant-- kill this thing so we can get to Shay.

It didn't.

Instead, the fur transformed to scales, and the dragon threw flaming breath at the living demons in front of him. Dexter's talon gripped the demon corpse, and he sank his teeth into the shoulders, ripping the head from the body. He tossed it aside and flipped the corpse off of Shay. She was conscious but didn't say anything as her giant scaly partner dragged her closer to us.

"Goddess." I let out two quick breaths to calm myself. I could see the cut above her eye, but I was more concerned about the blood coming from her left side. "Oh, Shay."

She pushed up off the ground and cupped the wound with her hand. "I'm okay. It's just a scratch." She held up a bloody palm. "I'll be fine."

"Light your flame." I didn't intend to yell at her, but the adrenalin was pumping, and I was scared. I couldn't help Shay and hold my flame at the same time.

"Ignis." Her palm lit with fire bright enough for me to open the drawstring pouch and remove the bottle of demon scale.

I pushed Shay against the wall of the cavern. I needed to lift her shirt high enough to reveal the new wound. I wasn't thinking about the scars on her body or that Amelia might have never seen them. I just wanted to stop the bleeding. "Dexter!" I yelled for the dog. I had no idea if his presence was necessary for the magic to work, and I didn't have time to troubleshoot her wound.

"Oh, damn, that hurts," Shay said as I peeled the fabric from the slice just below her breast.

"She's going to need stitches." Dani glanced back and forth between us and the dark tunnel ahead.

"No, she's not." I looked into Shay's eyes. "You ready?"

Her lips pushed together as she closed her eyes. The tiny nod was all I needed. I filled my hand with the hammered scale of demons and pressed it against the seeping wound.

"Damn, woman!" Her yell echoed off the cavern walls. I felt the blood fill my palm at the same time Dexter was shoving his body against Shay, helping me hold her in place.

"What is that?" Amelia asked.

Shay's flame fell away as she threw her head back in pain.

"Dani, light," I called.

She ripped the flashlight from her gun and handed it to her wife. I held Amelia's hand, adjusting it to point to Shay's bare abdomen. "Shine it here."

"Pierce?" It was apparent from the direction of the light that Dani saw the old scars on Shay's body. It was also the reaction Shay feared, the sound I had made that first time I saw them for myself.

"Later." Shay winced as I pulled my hand away to look.

The wound was still bleeding. "I think I need to use more."

Shay's hand gripped my wrist. "Give it a minute. I can feel it working." Her voice broke as she took in a quick breath. "Oh, goddess, it hurts so much."

I looked at the massive German Shepherd pinned against us. "What did you do, Dex?"

"It was the demon."

"He brought you to it," I argued.

"That's his job."

I shook my head. She just didn't get it.

"It's like they don't understand what you're saying." Amelia interrupted. "It's not just Shay and Dexter. It's Danielle too." She leaned closer, watching as the wound bubbled blood and anvil dust together, creating a magic adhesive. "I've never seen that before."

"It's anvil dust from a demon, isn't it?" Dani asked.

My head whipped around to look at the cop. Her face was partially in shadow. "You know?" The response was a slow nod. "I guess you would."

Shay put her hand on my shoulder. "Let me up, honey." I stepped off enough for her to push away from the wall. Dexter's nose squeezed under her arm. "Good boy."

"Good boy?"

"Here we go," Dani said, and Amelia reached behind me to smack her wife's shoulder.

"What? He's only doing his job."

Shay was standing on her own. She touched the cut on her forehead, and her fingertips came back covered with blood.

"Let me get that too," I said and dabbed a smaller amount of dust to the wound.

Dani interrupted. "We need to get out of here."

I put the cap on the jar of anvil dust and gave it a little shake, noting that I'd used most of it. I waited for Shay to respond.

"No, we need to see what Dexter was taking us to."

"Do you think we can do that with better light, and maybe you could have more than your bare hands?" I interjected.

"Stay here." Dani pushed the shotgun into Shay's hands. I heard her boots clop away into the darkness.

"*Ignis*," I whispered, and the flame flashed from my palm. I could see the reflection in Shay's eyes. "How's the pain?"

"I'll be fine." She took the anvil dust and shoved it in her pocket.

"Care to share what happened?" I asked, forgetting that Amelia was standing behind me.

"Dex sensed the demons."

"There was more than one?" Amelia interrupted.

Shay dipped her head. "There were at least four. When I shifted to Dexter, I was disoriented. That's when one took a swipe at me."

"And Dexter stood on top of you?"

"Dex stabbed it." She made a hook with her finger. "With a talon claw thing, and it fell on me. You got here just in time for the squishy gooey part."

"Dex ripped the head off."

Shay rubbed the fur between the ears on Dexter's head. "Who's a good boy?" She said as I shoved her shoulder. "What? He loves eating demons."

I held the flame in the palm of my hand and watched my girlfriend and her K-9 partner exchange affection. The magick in the anvil dust was working, and as the healing properties took effect, Shay was able to stand on her own.

"Are you feeling better?" Amelia asked.

"I am."

I looked at the dark blood-like stains on Shay's clothing. "How much of that is yours?"

She didn't attempt to downplay the attack they'd just faced. "This is mine." She drew circles over the stains with her finger. "Dex ate most of the demon." As if on cue, we looked to see the dog licking the wall of the cave. Dexter did many things we couldn't explain, but this had to be the weirdest and most stomach-turning one.

"Is he licking the wall?" I asked as I brought the light closer.

"*Ignis*." Shay lit her flame, and we all watched as the dog ate tiny pustules clinging to the wall of the cave. We stepped closer, and I gagged a little as I realized what he was eating.

"Are those demons?"

Shay reached to poke one with her finger.

"Don't touch them." Amelia grabbed her hand.

"What are they?" I asked.

A bright beam of light flashed across the wall. Dani was back and carrying the gear Shay needed. The vest dropped at our feet as Dani responded. "They aren't demons, not yet." She noticed Dexter's teeth gnarl at the wall. "Is he eating them?"

Amelia answered before we could. "Every single one he can."

"I wonder what's going to happen."

Shay interrupted. "What are you talking about?"

"We never come in this part of the mine," Dani explained, trying to catch her breath. "When we were kids, there was an accident in here, and it's been closed off since."

"What kind of accident?" I asked.

"The kind that gave me this." She pointed to the prosthetic limb on her right leg.

"It was you?" Shay asked. "But--."

"It's not an easy story to tell, and maybe we can talk about it when we're out of here." Dani pulled the taser from the bag and handed it to Amelia. "This is better."

Shay picked up the vest and slipped it over her head. Dexter heard the noise and stopped eating the creatures growing on the wall long enough to see his partner nod. I felt like the odd one out. The humans in front of me had a clear idea of what was coming. I felt the darkness in more ways than I wanted to.

"Shay?" I tried to whisper, but the sound echoed through the cavern around us.

She stopped fastening the belt around her waist and looked at me. "Wil, I promise you that we've got this." Her gun remained in the holster. Instead, she popped the cartridge out of the taser and pulled the trigger. The tiny electric spark arced between the nodes, and the battery light was solid green. She flicked the safety on and pushed the cartridge back into place. Shay leaned close enough to kiss me and whisper against my lips. "We do this all the time." I grabbed her cheeks with my hands and kissed her hard.

"I'm scared."

"I know." She turned around. "Let's do this, D."

"I'm right behind you." Dani slapped her hand over Shay's shoulder.

"Dex!" Shay yelled, and the K-9 stopped eating the wall long enough to leap in front of them.

I thought about exploring caves and how exciting it might have been if the guts of demons weren't in our path. Amelia was walking beside me as if this was a typical Tuesday for the couple. I could hear the clicking of Dexter's paws as they struck the solid rock of the tunnel floor. The air was thick with the smell of the creatures growing on the walls around us. I wondered what Dex was focusing on that made him leave his snacks untouched. They were following a scent, of what, I didn't have a clue, and I almost wished I could stay in the dark.

"When was the last time you were in this part of the mine?" I asked Amelia.

"More than twenty years for me." Amelia stepped away from the wall. "Dani checks the tunnels often."

"Alone?"

"No, she would come out here with Regina."

I stopped to let the answer sink in. "Benton and Dani patrolled the tunnels? What for?"

"Shh." The sound came from the women ahead.

"As Danielle said, the story is for later." She held her hand to me, and we stayed five steps behind the cops.

The dog started barking the same time my feet fell out from beneath me. A hand came quickly to stop me from hitting the ground. I felt a rush of heat against my skin, like hot wind rolling off of desert sand. My hand pushed off the ground, and I stumbled against the slime-covered wall.

I closed my eyes as the dizzying force of earth energy knocked me back to the ground. Amelia was stronger than she looked as she helped me to my feet.

"Did you trip?" She whispered.

I shook my head, and the sensation returned. "Something's happening."

The beam of a flashlight blinded us. "You good, hun?" Dani asked.

"I'm good, but I don't think Wildwood is."

Dani walked closer to me. "Are you going to throw up?"

"Nah . . . I don't think so." I covered my mouth, regretting it as the demon seepage touched my skin. I pulled up the bottom of my shirt to wipe it away. "So gross."

"But you feel something?" Dani asked as Shay put out her hand to me.

"What happened?"

I wiped my hand on my pants before touching Shay. "There's something in this tunnel, and whatever it is, it wants me to know it's there."

Shay wrapped her arm around me, and we walked together. "Dex, *vigilant ad me*." On command, the K-9 transformed into his dragon self. His massive body grazed the sides of the tunnel, and I imagined his scales slathered in demon goo.

The deeper we walked into the cave, the stronger the pull toward the unknown. "It's got to be that way." I held Shay's hand, pointing the flashlight down the dark path.

"Dex, *ante*."

Amelia and Dani were behind us, and although their voices were low, I could tell they were discussing our current predicament and the scale-covered dragon ahead of us.

"I can't, Danielle." Amelia turned back.

"We have to stay together." She directed her flashlight beam toward the ground.

"You know what's happening. Go. I'll stay here, but I can't--"

"I'm not leaving you here."

Shay interrupted. "I don't know what's going on, but we stay together."

Amelia shook her head. "You just don't understand."

"You're right. I don't." Shay's voice was firm, commanding, and impossible to fight. "But Dexter will protect us."

Dani reached to take her wife's hand. "She's right. We didn't have a dragon last time."

Amelia pushed the hand away. "I'm good, but I'm staying behind you."

Shay and I turned down the tunnel, following Dexter. The deeper we walked into the earth, the tighter the walls closed around us. Dexter transformed back into his furry self, and although he wasn't as fierce, I knew he could be at a moment's notice.

"What are we walking into?" Shay asked.

"You ever poked a hornet's nest?" Amelia replied.

"I can't say that I have."

"Well, this is worse." There was no humor in her tone. Amelia was frightened, and I was too. Dexter stopped in front of a giant mass attached to the wall. His snout crushed against the rock as he gnawed the tiny creatures off.

"He's eating them again." Dani shined the light, and the furry animal kept crunching.

Shay stood beside Dex as she dug into the pocket of her vest and removed a tiny vile.

"Are you taking some?" I asked.

"I think I should." She scraped the container against the slime and jumped back as it resisted her movement. "These things are alive."

Dexter paused long enough to run his tongue across his teeth and snout. It was a feast day for him.

"They're also getting bigger." Amelia pointed out.

Shay screwed the cap on her sample bottle and called her dog. "Dexter." Her voice was scolding, and the animal responded with a bark. "*Ante!*" His ears perked up, and he was back on task.

I looked at the wall as we walked by. My hand raised toward the puckered space left behind by Dexter's snack. It was impossible to fight the compulsion to touch. My fingertip slid across the surface, and a thick paste of demon residue stuck to my skin. The reaction was immediate, like an injection of adrenalin, and my mind's eye twisted and turned as it raced through the tunnels of this mine. It was dark and light as I siphoned through vacant jagged abandoned holes in the earth. I couldn't stop the rush that tilted my balance as my hands slapped with full force into the demon-covered walls. The history of Maker magicks filled my palms, and I felt the funnel of energy overwhelm my senses. I couldn't see what was drawing me deeper into the earth, but I could feel it.

"Wildwood!" I heard Shay's voice as her hands gripped my shoulders. She pulled me away from the wall, but it was too late. The souls of the Makers before were calling me down into the darkness. I opened my eyes when I heard the feral sound of Dexter's howl.

"Go, Dexter! *Ante!*" I yelled before pulling away from Shay and running behind Dexter. I could see far enough in front of me to follow, and as my pace began to slow, the dog adjusted his gait. I could hear my girlfriend and the others, but I couldn't fight the lure of the energy of the Maker. Dexter leaped around the turning tunnel, and I listened to his growl.

The creature was twice the K-9's size, and I could smell the scent of the rotting secretion shedding from its taunt fleshy skeleton. It looked like my first, the gatekeeper buried beneath the circle in my carriage house. This one had both horns and eyes aglow like the dregs of glory-hole glass.

"*Ignis.*" I summoned the fire to my palm the same time the dog morphed into his dragon form. There was no space for the three of us, and before I had a chance to force a flame from my palm, Dexter was sinking his teeth deep into the creature.

This gatekeeper wasn't alone, and before I could move, Shay was leaping full force at the second monster. My Maker-forged hatchet cleaved deep into the demon's chest. It, and Shay, fell to the ground. A third demon attacked. As Shay pulled her weapon free, it slashed at her chest. The vest protected her from the strike, throwing the monster against the wall. I watched as she gripped her punch dagger tight before plunging it deep into demon flesh. A flame flashed from the wound as she tore her hand away.

Dexter and Shay were an impressive fighting duo, and I was in awe. When the tunnel fell silent, there was a pile of monsters at Dexter's feet, and he was sure to devour them before we saw daylight again.

I was holding light when Shay looked up from the corpses. "Are you okay?" She asked.

I did a quick survey of my body. "Yes."

Her hands came up to my shoulders. "What the hell were you thinking?" Her eyes were almost black, dilated wide to see in the dark.

"I don't know." I looked at my hands, covered with the remains of our demon attack. "There's something in here. When I touched the tunnel wall, I could feel it."

"It?" Shay asked. "What is it?"

"It's the fire of Brigid." Dani's voice broke the silence. She aimed her flashlight around the cavern as her wife stepped into the light.

"The goddess?" Shay asked.

"The first incarnation of the smith at work," Amelia explained. She grabbed both of my hands, asking, "You can feel it call to you, can't you?"

I didn't understand how she knew. "My heart is racing." I clenched my hands into fists, and when they released, I felt the burning sensation. "It's like a drug. It's so powerful."

Amelia grasped my shoulders. "You can hear the call because you are the Maker."

"What call?" Shay asked.

"The call of the fire goddess," Amelia said. "The earth-fire and every Maker that came before Wildwood."

"Calling her to what?" Shay kicked at the corpse before bending to remove her dagger from its chest.

"The tool of the Maker."

Their voices faded as my senses focused on the song of the goddess. I didn't understand how, but Dexter was in my head, and I knew he would also be at my side as I felt my body fade

257

from the trio of demon fighters. Seconds later, my physical presence appeared in the dark cavern, and I could not recall taking a step.

The shift in time and space was how it felt to be taken by a dragon to places unknown. Dexter's K-9 features faded. I reached for his collar, feeling scales and solid dragon armor. "What's here, Dex?" I asked, but the silence that followed made it clear that I'd have to figure it out for myself.

"*Ignis.*" The flame warmed the palm of my hand, and for the first time, I could see the open space I was standing in. The ground beneath my feet shimmered from centuries of quartz erosion. I stepped closer to the wall. I marveled at the surface etched with gouges that looked like marks from mining hammers and chisels, or maybe the desperate clawing of a savage ethereal creature.

My thoughts focused on the human-made excavation as my eyes took in the massive growth on the wall in front of us. Dexter saw it and launched a ribbon of flame that engulfed the wall. I dropped to the ground and crawled behind him to protect myself from the heat. The terrifying sound that followed was the absence of mercy. The creature inside woke to the presence of a dragon. Dexter lunged forward, and the cavern fell silent again. I had no idea how many demons the dog had eaten, and I was queasy from the thought.

"Wildwood." I heard the whispers before the flashlight beam skipped across the tunnel wall.

"I'm here." I didn't know how to explain where *here* was, but Shay found us in seconds.

Her hands clamped over my shoulders. "Are you okay?" She was out of breath, "Dex took you, didn't he?"

"He did."

She held my cheeks, pulling me in for a frantic kiss. Her hands traveled over my body, searching for injuries or a sign of a battle fought and won. "Are you hurt?"

"I'm not even sure I'm one hundred percent here."

"It's disorienting. I get it. Try fighting at the same time."

"I don't want to think about it. Dex did all the fighting, anyway." I took the flashlight from Shay's hand and directed it to the backpack on her shoulder. "Turn around. I want the candle holder."

"What are you thinking?"

"I have no idea, but I feel like the Maker has been in this cavern before." I opened the bag and removed my forged candle holder. Shay struck the handle with the blade of her dagger, and I saw a reflection in the demon steel. I stopped her hand. "The blade."

She held it closer to the flame. "It's blood from that demon. I was in such a hurry I didn't wipe it off."

She passed it to me, and I ran my finger over it. "There's something . . ." My fingernail caught the tiny fractures in the demon steel. "The blade is breaking." I swiped the dagger across my pant leg, trying to wipe the residue of a demon from the surface.

"How?" Shay held the candle closer.

"Damn it." The sound bounced off the tunnel walls. "I don't know. A few days ago, we were slicing through rocks."

Shay took her punch dagger from my hands and slid it into the sheath of her boot. She drew the taser from her holster, readying for whatever was coming next. "We can figure it out later." Shay lifted the candle holder until it was inches from the rock surrounding us. "Why don't you tell me what you're feeling in this cave. What makes you think the Maker was inside this part of the mine?"

"It's hard to explain. It's like a voice, but there are no words." I stood still and watched her zigzag the blue flame of the candle from the ground to the full extension of her arm. There were no symbols anywhere.

"There's nothing here, love."

I sat down in the dirt and pressed my hands to the ground. I could hear the echo of Dexter crunching another creature deeper down the tunnel. "There is something here. I just don't know how to find it."

"Dex brought you into this part of the mine for a reason."

With my eyes closed, it was easier to feel the call of the goddess. "Tell me what you know about the goddess Brigid."

I heard her footsteps crushing against the stones as she stepped behind me. "She is the flame keeper, and she holds it for the smith."

"The smith? You mean she bares the flame for the blacksmith, like me?"

Shay's hand touched my shoulder long enough for her body to lower behind me. She whispered in my ear. "Yes."

"And Dani thinks that the goddess called me here?"

"Yes." I could hear Shay's boots shuffle through the rocks on the cave floor as she settled behind me.

"Where are they?"

"Amelia wouldn't come this deep into the mine." Shay explained.

"What's that about?"

"She had an accident when they were caving. I think it brings up painful memories."

"Is that how she lost her leg?"

"Yes, I think it is," Shay answered.

I kept my eyes shut tight, and the woman I loved was behind me, her hands covering my own but I wondered about Amelia and Dani. What would lure them this deep into the earth? "Why would Dani and Amelia go caving in a demon-infested mine?"

"I don't know."

I tried to visualize the goddess Brigid, hoping to feel the energy that called me to this place. I remembered. "What did Amelia say about the tool of the Maker?"

"It wasn't much. She just said that there was one."

"What kind of tool would the goddess have?" I asked, almost sure I knew the answer.

"You know about the thunder god?"

"I do. Anyone with a comic book collection knows about him."

"The hammer of the thunder god is a tool of protection. For the goddess, her tool is for creation."

"What you're saying is that Brigid carries the hammer of creation, and for some reason, she called me into a mine full of demons to find it?"

"Yes, my love. I think that's an accurate summary."

"How am I supposed to find a hammer I've never seen; hidden by a goddess I don't know?"

Shay stood as Dexter returned. She kissed the top of my head. "Stay focused." The K-9's transformation to dragon form was an indication of trouble, making it impossible to concentrate on anything else.

Shay picked up the candle and smashed it in the dirt until the flame was out. She stuffed it into the bag on her shoulder. "We have to go." Her flashlight caught the edge of the cavern, and I could see the glow of a demon approaching. Shay's hand was beneath my arm, and she picked me up. "Now!"

She had years of experience fighting the horrors inside this mine. "I'm right behind you," I said.

"No, get ahead of us. We've got your back." She slapped the flashlight in my hand. "Go and don't stop until you're outside with Dani and Amelia."

"What about you?"

I heard the ripping sound of the Velcro on her vest. She was drawing it tighter to her chest. "Dex has my back. Just keep moving and follow the tunnels to the left."

I hesitated. "Shay."

Her lips crushed against my own. "I love you. Now run, and don't stop and don't look back." I turned around, and I could hear the slow rumble of a dragon's snarl as the monsters advanced on them. I steadied the flashlight, holding it tight in my grip. I'm glad she told me to keep left because I had no idea how to get out.

It felt like hours as one dark turn led to another. I stumbled into the chamber where we first encountered the slime-covered walls. I was almost out, but there was no sign of Shay or Dexter. I shined the light behind me, and as I cycled it forward, Dani was in my path.

"You okay?" she asked.

I was short of breath, but I huffed out an answer. "Yes, but Shay's still back there."

"You're almost out. I'll go and help Pierce."

I wanted to follow Dani back inside the mine, but I would only be in the way. I kept moving until I could see the light break through the darkness. Amelia was waiting for me.

"Are you okay?" she asked.

"I wish everyone would stop asking me that question," I yelled.

"Sorry." Amelia held a hand to me. "Let me help you to the cabin."

"I'm good." I walked back to the mouth of the cave. "I want to wait here for Shay." In the light of day, I could see the stains left behind by my traverse through the tunnels. I looked at my hands, covered in the charcoal-colored sap of demon blood. The streaks across my thighs were evidence of exposure to so much more. Removing the stains from my skin felt more important than standing in wait for Shay. "Can you help me get rid of the blood, or whatever this is?" I held my hands toward Amelia.

"Yes." She didn't try to move me. "I'll be right back."

As she walked away, the realities of the last few hours weighed heavy on my body. I steadied myself against a boulder and slid to the ground. When my hands hit the dirt, I could feel the tremble of energy move inside me. I don't know who the goddess Brigid was or why her call felt so strong, but I could sense her influence summoning me back to the darkness. I stumbled to my feet, and the crawl left tiny pebbles of earth clinging to the blood on my skin.

"What are you doing?" Amelia grabbed my elbow and pulled me into the sunlight.

I didn't know how to answer the question because I had no idea what I was doing. I felt the ice-cold washcloth rub across my forearms as I surrendered to Amelia's care. The transition between water on my skin and the haze of Brigid's call felt like the fabric of my soul separating from itself. The pain was unbearable, and I closed my eyes.

"You've got a cut on the back of your hand." She dabbed the skin, but I couldn't feel the wound.

"I'm not sure how," I said.

"Do you have any anvil dust?"

It took me a moment to clear my foggy mind. "Shay has it."

I heard the echo of gunshots and stared down the dark empty tunnel. Where were they? Why weren't they coming out? Amelia picked up the flashlight and adjusted the beam to shoot as far as it could reach. We saw the eyes of a dragon before we saw the reflection of one pair of human eyes. One pair. Where was the second, and who? I kept thinking who.

"Melia." Dani was calling for her wife. "Get the first aid kit, hurry, please."

I watched the trunk of the squad car pop open and turned back to see Shay flop from Dani's shoulder to the ground.

I crawled closer. "What happened?" I asked.

"There were too many. Shay stepped in front and took a hit meant for me."

"Damn it, why are you two always acting the hero?" Amelia dropped the first aid kit on the ground.

"We're hardly acting." Shay held up a hand, and Dani slapped a high five.

Amelia wasn't amused. "I'm glad you think this is so funny."

I felt the stones grind into my shins as I crawled closer to Shay. I patted her hip, searching for the container of anvil dust. "What happened?" I ripped the Velcro tabs from the four corners and lifted the breastplate off.

"Shit, it got crazy." Dani began. "Dex was on two of them when I got there. Pierce hit one with the taser and buried that hatchet in the chest of another." Her arms were waving, reenacting the motions as she explained the attack. "I don't know where these bastards were coming from, but they kept coming."

"You shouldn't have gone down in that tunnel," Amelia said.

"We didn't have a choice, did we!" Dani opened the kit, sorting through for a bottle of saline and gauze pads. Shay tried to sit, but Dani pushed her down.

"Let me up. I'm fine."

"You're hardly fine," I said. I started to lift her shirt to see where the blood was coming from. Shay grabbed the fabric, tugging it down, preventing me from revealing her torso. Her arm was oozing blood, and I wasn't thinking about the scars from her childhood.

"Stop." It was the first time she'd ever raised her voice to me, and it got my attention. I pushed away, and before I could get to my feet, she was pulling on my arm. "Wait, damn it, just wait."

"These two women love you." I pointed at Dani and Amelia, who were watching us. "I didn't mean to . . ."

"I know." She tried to sit, but the wound on her shoulder prevented the maneuver. "Damn it!"

"Stop being so stubborn, Pierce." Dani put her arm behind Shay to help her sit. "Let her look at the damn wound." She squeezed Shay's shoulder, and deep red oozed between her fingers.

"Fine." Shay pulled away and ripped her t-shirt over her head. "Stupid damn demons. Why couldn't you just eat them?" She glared at the dog, who was licking the remains on his fur.

"He ate about a dozen of those bastards today," I said.

I watched Dani and Amelia trying not to notice the scars on Shay's body. It was an impossible task, and I felt protective of my lover's privacy. "Can I have the towel? I want to wash the wound before I do anything else." I held out my hand. I opened the saline and dumped the entire bottle into the empty basin. I swished the towel, soaking it through before slapping it across Shay's wound.

"Woo, that's cold as ice."

"I think you'll live." I pushed the two sides of the wound together. It was a few inches long, and there was no way the bleeding would stop without stitches or my demon anvil dust. "Give me the anvil dust."

Shay patted the front of her jeans. "Don't you have it?"

"No, damn it, I gave it to you."

We didn't have time to go back and forth. Dani slathered the wound with disinfectant and taped a wad of gauze over it. "That'll get us back to the carriage house." She pressed Shay's hand over the dressing. "Pressure. Hold pressure and don't let up."

Amelia started collecting the supplies and tossed them back into the zippered bag. "Are you okay to drive?" She asked.

"I'm good. It's not like you're going to pull me over."

Dani had an arm under Shay, helping her stand. "Probably not." The walk to the truck was slow, and although it was just a shoulder wound, my girlfriend was weak.

I opened the door. "I'm going to speed."

Dani smiled as she pushed Shay in the seat. "I'll try to keep up."

"Dexter," Shay called her K-9 partner, but it came out as a weak whisper. I wasn't surprised when the massive German Shepherd bounced into the back of my truck.

As Dani closed the door, a feeling rang true; that my life as a demon fighter had just escalated to the next level.

CHAPTER XV

Hearthkeeper

I didn't have to worry about losing Dani during our drive back to the carriage house. She was leading the way with her lights flashing blue and red against my windshield. Shay's bloody shirt lay half draped around her torso. She wasn't asleep, but her eyes were closed, and she kept whispering Latin words under her breath.

"I love you, Wildwood." She must have been reading my thoughts.

"I love you too, baby." I looked up at the road before glancing at her. The stain of blood was growing in the hand Shay had pressed against the wound. I don't recall the drive or pulling into the parking lot of the carriage house. Dani was opening the truck as I jammed the gear shift into park.

"Get the door," Dani said as Shay fell against her.

Dexter leapt over the side of the wheel-well of my truck, doing his best to assist the two women inside. He looked more like a trip hazard, but I could sense the dog knew Shay was injured. I opened the carriage house letting Dani and Shay shuffle to the chair in my office. I wasn't thinking about anything but the jar of anvil dust on the shelf. Dani lifted the blood-soaked bandage, and my hand was shaking as I uncorked the bottle and poured more than half of the contents over her wound.

"Oh, damn. That hurts like hell." Shay slammed her head against the wall. "It didn't hurt that much when you healed my side."

"Maybe I used too much," I suggested.

"You have to wash it off. It feels like it's burning."

The anvil dust was bubbling and puckering as the wound seemed to drink it in. "Do you think you can give it a few more seconds?" I asked.

She clenched her teeth, and her eyes clamped tight. The reaction was different than the first time we'd used it. She didn't answer, and that's when we realized she'd lost consciousness.

"Shay." I tapped her chest.

"Let's lay her down. I'm sure the pain was just too much." Dani and I leveraged the redhead off the chair and worked our way one step at a time until we navigated to the bedroom.

"I don't understand why it's hurting her like this." We laid her across the comforter.

"I'm not sure either," Dani confessed. "Shay's read so much about demons. She's probably forgotten more than I've ever known. And I grew up fighting those damn things."

269

"Her mind is pretty fascinating." I grabbed a towel from the bathroom and a wet washcloth. I wanted to wash the wound. I noticed Amelia wasn't with us. "Where's your wife?"

"She's waiting for me. We have a history in the mine and watching Shay and the blood. It just brings back a lot of terrible memories."

"I didn't know." I started to wipe the dried blood from Shay's shoulder. It was evident that we could both see the old stabbing scars on Shay's torso.

"We don't always know about old wounds," Dani said. The tone in her voice filled with emotion, and I wasn't sure if she was talking about Amelia or Shay.

"I guess not." What else could I say? It wasn't my story to tell.

"I'm going to head out." Dani pitched her thumb toward the doorway. "Tell Pierce I'll talk to her later."

"I will," I said, and she turned to go. Dexter's furry snout plopped on the edge of the bed, and he started to lick at the bubbling blood on Shay's shoulder.

"Dexter." The visual of his tongue slathering across the oozy demon spawn in the cave was all I could see. I didn't want him to infect her wounds. I wasn't even sure how to wash a dragon-dog's mouth out with soap. "Come here, buddy." I hooked my finger in his collar and dragged him to the tub. "Get in," I commanded. It was a good thing that Dexter liked water and even better that I didn't have to hoist him in and out of the enormous porcelain basin. I lathered him from head to toe and brushed through his coat. The water washed across his body until it ran clear. It took longer than I expected.

"You're a wonderful dog-mom." Although I was startled by the sound of Shay's voice, it was also a relief to hear. She was leaning in the doorway, shirtless, but all I could focus on was the slice to her skin.

"He was trying to lick your wound." I wrapped the dog in a towel and fluffed his fur to dry it.

"That's a little gross." She said as she inspected the crusty combo of blood and anvil dust cracking off her shoulder. "It hurt like hell." She tried to raise her arm.

"You got sliced open by a demon. That's going to hurt."

"It's not the first time. I don't understand why this one was so bad."

"Could you be allergic?"

She walked closer, stopping in front of the mirror. "I have no idea." She twisted the handle on the faucet and scooped water to dump on the wound. As the dried blood and dust ran down her arm, I could see that my magick still worked.

"It healed," I said.

"I hope so after all of that."

I finished drying the dog, and he ran out of the room. I dropped the towel on the floor to catch the water prints from his paws. I stepped closer to Shay so I could inspect my Maker magick skills. I touched her shoulder. "It's like it never happened."

She looked in the mirror. "Our faces tell a different story." I noticed my reflection in the mirror. For the first time all day, I was staring at the remnants of our battle in the mine.

"I look like I've been at the forge for a week." I brushed at my cheek, smearing the dirt on my face.

She turned around. "You look beautiful." Her hands rested on my hips as she leaned in for a kiss.

"Are you sure you didn't hit your head, too?" I teased.

"Absolutely positive." She side-stepped the sink to turn on the shower. "Want to join me?" Her pants dropped to the floor.

"Is that a real question?" I kicked my boots off, and tiny bits of rock fell from the cuff of my pants. As I stripped my clothes away, I wasn't surprised to find an excessive amount of battle residue on our bathroom floor. "What a mess."

"It could have been worse." She said. I didn't want to think about the levels of danger that we'd avoided this afternoon as Shay stepped into the spray of water. She ran her hands through her hair. "This is the most disgusting part of the job."

"What? Demon guts in your hair?"

She lathered the bar of soap. "I wish it was just my hair."

I took that as my cue and climbed inside our shower. It wasn't a two-person space, but we made it work. Shay squeezed a handful of soap. "Turn around."

"Yes, ma'am." I did a quick twirl, and her hands began massaging my scalp. "Oh, goddess, that feels amazing." I held her hips to steady myself. Shay clicked the shower-wand on and rinsed the shampoo from my head. The water sprayed down the length of my chest, across my hip, and over my thighs. From this moment forward, a solitary shower just wasn't going to do it. She switched the diverter from shower to bath and filled the tub.

Shay reclined against the deep angle of the claw-footed basin. The old porcelain seemed to hug around us as I settled in between her legs. The water was quick to rise, and I was content to lay in her arms. Her hand rested on the soft of my belly, and her fingers made tiny circles on my sensitive flesh.

I nuzzled my cheek against her shoulder, and she kissed the top of my head. I didn't mean to close my eyes, but I did, and the image of fire appeared on the back of my eyelids. Maybe it was a reflection of the ceiling light, but it felt like something more, Brigid, the Maker's goddess.

"Did you fall asleep?" She asked.

"No, just thinking."

Her arms tightened as her knees popped out of the water. "About?" Her voice was warm against my ear.

"Brigid, and the tool of the Maker." I continued.

"Oh, that was. . . "

Her pause made me turn to look at her expression. "Was what?" I asked.

"Unexpected." She whispered.

I was intrigued. "Why do you say that? Explain, please." I turned sideways in between her legs.

Her arms came up to rest on the rim of the tub. "What do you know about the goddess Brigid?" She asked.

"Only what Dani and Amelia shared. You?" I asked.

Her finger trailed over my shoulder. "I read a book once."

"So, you know a lot then." I leaned back in her arms. I could feel her chest shake from a short laugh.

"You could say that."

"How about a lesson?" I ran my finger over her knee.

"Sure, but maybe not in here. The water's getting a little cold."

I leaned forward to release the plug from the drain, and Shay slipped out from behind me. I was content to sit until the water spiraled away.

Shay moved around the bathroom, taking a towel and drying off. I watched as she inspected her shoulder. "This is just; I don't know." She leaned closer to look at her side. All evidence of today's wounds had vanished.

"It's some kind of magick," I said as I stepped out of the tub and wrapped myself in a towel. I stared at the scars from her youth, wishing I could take them away with a little bit of demon dust. She glanced at me and caught my focus on her back.

"We can't undo the past."

"You can read my mind now?" I rubbed the towel over my head, shaking away most of the water.

"I don't have to be a mind reader to know what you are thinking. I've spent most of my adult life wishing them away." She ran her finger over the scar on her rib. "This is my body. The scars are a part of who I am."

"I know. I just thought, what if I could?" I opened my towel and wrapped myself around her.

She looked at our reflection in the mirror. "They are more than just marks on my skin. They're a chapter in the book of me."

I thought I understood the complexity that was Shay Pierce, but she kept surprising me. "You practically bit my head off when I looked at your stomach and shoulder in the cave."

"I have a right to . . ." She turned around, and my arms fell away from her body. "It's my story to tell. It's obvious to everyone I meet that something happened because my hands are impossible to hide. The rest, that's mine, and I get to decide who knows my story."

"I didn't mean to . . ."

Her finger touched my lips. "Shh, let me finish. I know you were trying to help. I know it was out of my hands but protecting myself is a reflex. I'm learning."

"Can your reflexes be nicer to me next time?" I asked.

"I'll do my best." Her hands combed through my hair, resting on the back of my neck. She pulled me closer and sealed the deal with a kiss. She leaned into my arms. "You want to talk about Brigid?"

My eyes were closed. "Who?"

"The goddess who has your number."

I was resisting anything that would take me out of Shay's arms. "I can't remember."

"That's funny." She took the towel from my hands, leaving me naked in front of her. I opened my eyes, and she was walking out of the bathroom, the two towels hanging side by side from their hooks on the wall.

"Hey!" I followed her into the bedroom, and she was pulling a shirt over her head. I took the opportunity to wrap her in a hug, lifting her off the floor. "Do we have to be in research mode all of the time?"

"After the day we just had. Do you have to ask?" I set her down, and she finished getting dressed. I was disappointed when she jumped into a pair of pants.

"I guess not." I waved a hand from the neck of her shirt to the middle of her thigh. "But do all the clothes mean we are going out?"

"Out into the kitchen. I'm hungry, and I might need a book for reference."

"Just one?" I made quick work of throwing on an old t-shirt and a pair of sweatpants. Shay was already putting a pan on the stove and opening a beer when I came into the kitchen. I sat down to watch her cook.

"What are you in the mood for?" She asked.

"I was in the mood for you, but I guess I have to wait for that."

She turned around to look at me and took a long sip of her beer. "Yes, you do."

"What's in the fridge?" I walked across the room to look. I opened the door. "There's no real food in here."

Shay bumped my hip to squeeze in beside me. "How have you survived?" She handed me a bottle of beer before opening the freezer door. "We've got two hamburger patties, no bread, and a sketchy head of lettuce.

"We might need some groceries," I said. "What's at the house?"

She laughed as she closed the doors. "Maybe the same but greener."

"Greener as in more veggies or greener as in advanced science experimentation."

"I'd say science experiment, one hundred percent." She unwrapped the beef patties and set them in the pan. "We could use the lettuce instead of a bun?"

"What's wrong with us?" I looked at the slimy half head of lettuce.

"You want to come with me to get a few things, or do you want to cook these burgers?"

I didn't want to do either. I wanted to climb into bed with my girlfriend and forget about the day. "You go, and I'll defrost these. Just grab some essentials." I turned the cooktop on low, hoping that they would defrost before they cooked through.

"What do you want with the burger?" She asked.

"You. Can I just have you?"

She smiled. "No, but I'll make it quick."

She was down the stairs and out the door before I could say another word. I wasn't worried about eating. I was concerned about the goddess and what she was calling me to find. I heard the thump of paws on the stairs, and Dexter was there, still fluffy from his bath.

"You want to take a walk?" He flopped down on the floor in front of the couch. "That's a first." The weight of his savage demon-feeding frenzy might have taken its toll. I gave a quick poke to the meat in the pan and thought about the goddess Brigid. I looked at the wall of books that migrated from Shay's place to mine, and I knew there had to be at least one that would tell me a bit about my goddess, Brigid.

The heavy crease on the spine caught my attention before the title. It was well-worn from reference, and I could just make out the gold embossed lettering, *Ceremonial Magick.* There was hardly any ceremony in the way it presented as I took it from the shelf. There were half a dozen pieces of ribbon hanging out from the bottom. I opened the cover, and the first page, scribed by a man named Arthur, was written in Latin. I pulled the first ribbon and flipped to a page marked *Rituals*, and I was glad to find that the opposite pages had an English translation. The book was written in the early 1800s when an index must have been an extravagance. I stood beside the stovetop and searched through the ribbon-marked pages for any reference to the goddess Brigid.

I split my attention between the sizzle of meat and the ridiculously tiny font until I found a chapter titled *Deities*—this section was co-authored by an anonymous occultist who specialized in celestial Magicks. I flipped the patties one more time and turned off the flame. On page 414, midway through the book, I found her.

I sat down beside Dexter and read through the two pages. Brigid had many names, all of which circled back to the idea of three goddesses in one. The goddess protected- humans and animals and all life. She was the quiet voice of inspiration calling you, like a poet to your destiny. But most of all, she was undeniably the keeper of the flame and watcher of the hearth. The drawing on the page was not complex. It was the silhouette of a magnificent woman but what caught my attention was her outstretched hand and the flame she was holding.

I heard Shay climbing the stairs and looked up from the page to see a brilliant smile crunching a stick of celery.

"I thought you might start without me." She set the bags on the table and walked over to the couch. Dex moved just enough to give Shay space to sit.

I closed my finger on the page so she could see the cover. "How many times have you read this book?" I asked.

She slid her finger alongside the edge, marking the page and taking it from my hand. "Sir Arthur E. Waine *Ceremonial Magick*. This book came from Benton."

"Really?" I was intrigued.

She nodded. "Benton gave it to me after we had a conversation about my scars."

"Why about your scars?"

"Thinking about it, it was our first serious conversation about magick." She rubbed tiny circles over the cover.

I didn't know what was more intriguing, the backstory of her relationship with the former cop or the new information about my goddess. "You're saying you've read this a lot?"

"I have." She held it to her heart before passing it back to me. "By the way, the E stands for Elinore." She crunched another bite of her celery stick.

I thought about it for a second. "Was Elinore a witch?" Shay's brilliant smile was the answer. I opened the book. "I was just getting to the story of Brigid, the triple goddess herself."

Shay ran her fingers through her hair, a frustrated sigh escaping her lips. "I don't know why I didn't put all of this together already."

"You have been distracted, saving lives, fighting demons, and becoming the Magick."

"Falling in love." Her head fell against my shoulder.

"I'm a distraction?" I asked.

"The best kind as far as I'm concerned." She said.

"Good to hear. So, what did you put together?" I asked. "By the way, I got far enough to read that she is a total badass. Not only is she the goddess of fire." I showed Shay the image on the page. "She's also the spirit of wisdom and transformation, of health and water and prophecy and the list goes on and on." I ran my finger over the long list of attributes, stopping on the last. "She is also the protector of metalworkers and the fire that blazes in their forge."

"It's like the universe made Brigid just for you." Shay kissed my cheek.

"Or I was made for Brigid," I said.

"I'm not going to eliminate any possibilities right now." She took the book and slipped a ribbon to mark the page. "We need to figure out what's calling you into that cave."

"It has to be her, or something left by her," I explained.

Shay stood up from the couch and moved to unpack the bag on the table. She filled a bowl with lettuce and started rinsing, taking an occasional bite from the pre-cut bag of veggies. What I wanted was a rare, juicy burger from Slammed, but I would settle for the half-cooked meat patties in the pan on the stove.

It didn't take long for Shay to turn the combination into a tasty stove top meal. She sat across from me as we ate, and I wondered what theories were turning around in her mind. "Penny, for your thoughts?" I said, regretting how corny the phrase sounded.

"Only a penny?" She smiled and took another bite of food.

"That used to be a fortune," I said.

Her eyes crinkled in the corners as she smiled. "I guess it did."

"So?" I prodded, wanting to know what she was thinking.

"I was just wondering how all of this happened to us."

"You mean, *all of it*, all of it?" I questioned.

She nodded. "We were kids when we met. We were apart for almost a lifetime. How does any of this happen?"

"You've got over a thousand books about magick and the occult, and you don't have a guess?" She scraped her fork across the plate, scooping up the last bits of her dinner. She took the bite of food, and I waited for her to finish chewing. Shay always had the answers. I expected her to deliver a grand speech.

"I don't know."

Her answer felt impossible to my ears. "Really?"

"When I was walking to the market, I was thinking about the tunnels and everything that happened today. Benton and Dani and what they've been doing down there." She stood up to take her dishes to the sink. She set them down and turned to talk to me. "They know what's down there, or at least Benton did."

I took my last bite and joined Shay at the sink. I turned on the water and began to wash the dishes. "Tell me about the goddess." I asked.

She bumped my hip. "Brigid?"

"Yes."

Shay stepped away to retrieve the book I'd been reading. "She has many names, you know."

I nodded. "Almost a dozen. I read the Christians tried to steal her and make her a saint."

"They did. Kinda funny to think about." She pinched the ribbon and opened the book to the pages on Brigid.

"The book says she watches over the hearth and the forge."

Shay's finger trailed over the Latin side of the page. "The hearth and the forge, kinda like the Magick and the Maker."

I'm sure she was thinking out loud, but I had to ask. "Do you think there is something for us in that tunnel?"

Shay turned the page and noticed the image of the goddess holding a flame. She held it up for me to see. "Does this look like anyone you know?"

"Maybe, I'm not sure. I've never seen you in a dress."

She closed the book. "You're hilarious, and you probably never will."

"Hmm," I pondered that for a second. I wasn't sure that I needed to see Shay in anything other than her superhero costume. I thought about her demon-armor vest and how it protected most of her body. She was going to have to jump in front of demons again. "You know this means we have to go back down into the tunnels," I said.

She nodded. "I don't like it."

"Could it get worse?" It was a silly question. I knew the answer.

"It could always get worse." She was quick to point out.

"We could prepare. Put together better gear and carry more demon anvil dust."

"Yes, and maybe this time we walk in together." She looked at the dog curled up on the floor. "His travel methods are disorienting."

"You've got a great way of minimizing complicated situations."

Shay walked to the shelf and tucked the book back in its place. "Let's make a plan. I can put together some tools and gear in the backpack. Can you make me some demon anvil dust?"

She never had to ask me twice to fire up the forge. "That's easy." I thought about working, pounding demon steel, and recalled the damage done to her punch dagger. "Can I see your knife? I just remembered that it looked cracked after you stabbed the demon."

Shay pulled it from the sheath in her boot and examined it closer. "It does look cracked." She handed the blade to me.

I walked closer to the light. "Could be the heat treatment." I was talking to myself out loud and didn't expect Shay to answer.

"Do you think it's breaking from intuitive reflection?" Shay asked.

"I don't know. Do you want it to break? Isn't intention part of that?"

"Of course, I don't want it to break, and when I'm defending myself, I only think about winning."

"It could be the heat from fighting and flaming. Maybe stabbing a room temperature demon messes with the hardness of the blade." I laid the dagger on the table. "Do you know what kind of demons we were fighting?"

"I'm almost positive they were like your gatekeeper." She opened the demon journal we'd been keeping. "This guy here— but the horns were small and no spire."

I walked to the bedroom to get the Dagger of Doom. "My blade looks good. Maybe use mine until I can figure out what caused the fractures."

Shay took her blade from the table and stuck it back in the sheath around her ankle. "I'd feel better if we both had one. Keep yours, please."

"If we can keep Dex from eating all of the heads, we can get more material, and I can make you a new one."

"One problem at a time. If we're going back to the mine, we should put together a better bag of gear." Shay took the backpack off the hook on the wall. She unpacked everything inside, laying each item on the table. "We should keep the candle." She started a pile. "I kinda messed the taper. Do you have another one?"

I opened the apothecary cabinet we'd assembled. "This one should work." I twisted the beeswax taper into the base of my demon candle holder.

"Flashlight, altar kit, taser, and two more knives." She fed each tool into the loops and pockets in the bag. "What else?"

I grabbed a jar from the cabinet. "Demon anvil dust."

Shay took it from my hand. "This is a big bottle."

"After today, I'm not sure it's big enough," I said, bumping her hip.

"It better be. This stuff hurts like hell." She buckled it in the side pocket.

"Better than the alternative." I looked at the contents. "You'll carry your gun, right?"

"I'll have my regular duty gear, yes, and my body armor."

I dropped a notebook and pen into the outside pouch. "Just in case."

"This should work. I'll hang it at the bottom of the stairs, and we can head out tomorrow after work."

I walked to the bedroom and waited for Shay to join me. "Do you think it's finally safe? Can we sleep for a little while?" I pulled back the comforter.

"I think I could close my eyes for a minute." She slipped under the blanket, opening the space of her arm for me to cuddle in beside her.

"This is good," I said before closing my eyes. Shay wrapped me tight to her shoulder.

"Yes, this is very good."

CHAPTER XVI

Exhumed

My eyes closed for a minute, but I couldn't fall asleep. Being in Shay's arms felt perfect, and I didn't want to leave the safety of her embrace, but I was restless. "Shay," I whispered her name, but she didn't make a sound. I lifted her arm high enough to shimmy out of bed. It was two-thirty on her clock, and I was aware she needed to work in a few hours.

I pulled on a pair of sweats and covered my feet with Shay's slippers. The wood floors of the apartment could get cold at night. Dexter was a balled-up pile of fur on the floor beside the bed, and he stretched his paws out as I walked by. Knowing I was awake, he followed me to the couch. "Can't sleep either?" I asked, and his big ears perked up, but he didn't respond. I stared at the shelf of books behind the furniture until I found

Celestial Magick. I stretched my arm, just short of reaching the book, before tumbling over the couch. "Shit."

"Honey, what are you doing?"

My face was close to the floor, and my hips draped over the arm of the couch. "I couldn't sleep."

"So, you decided to become an acrobat?"

I wriggled my toes in her slippers when I noticed her bare feet. I pushed up from the floor. "Tumbler, maybe. Did I wake you?"

She wiped her eyes. "The empty side of the bed did."

"I can't sleep," I explained. "I've been laying here trying to get my mind to just stop."

"Would you like me to make you something to help you sleep?"

"A magick potion?" I joked. Dexter rested his nose on my lap.

Shay shook her head and turned to open the door to the greenhouse. "I was thinking maybe some tea, but if you want to call it . . ."

I felt a cold silence wrap around me, pulling me away from my lover. My physical form faded from the couch in the living room to the foreboding darkness of the tunnel in the mine. I knew what was happening, but it didn't ease the adrenaline rush forcing my heart to thump against my breastbone. Dexter had shifted me back to the cave, back into the belly of the beast.

"*Ignis*," I whispered, and my palm flashed with a flame. I could see a familiar pair of eyes which confirmed that Dex was still in dog form. I was safe, at least for the moment. "What are we doing here, Dex?" I placed a hand on his head, between his ears. He took a step, making sure I stayed close to his side. He was leading me, with no weapon for defense and house slippers on my feet. I didn't plan to leave his side.

I heard the crunch of pebbles beneath my feet, and I could see the reflection of demon spawn pustules growing from the walls. Dexter did not pause to taste or even slow down to look. He was on a mission, and I was pleased to keep moving. I thought about Shay and how she would race here in her patrol car. I was more afraid for her than myself.

Dexter's nose snorted across my palm, and I read it as a sign to extinguish my flame. I was terrified to walk in the dark, but when the light went out, I could feel the energy that had pulled me into this tunnel only a few hours before.

"Show me," I whispered to the dog as I tucked two fingers around his collar. The pathway was narrow, and as much as I wanted to avoid it, I rubbed against the wall, trying to keep hold of my guide. I closed my eyes. It was unimaginable to believe, but I could hear the voice; Brigid and all of the powers of the goddess were calling me.

I caught the scent of smoldering coal just before it burst into a flame. As a blacksmith, I learned to tend fire before anything else. If I weren't standing in the tunnel of an abandoned mine, I would have believed I was feeding a forge. Dexter pushed against my thigh, and I followed him down a new tunnel. My eyes were adjusting to the darkness, but it was still difficult to see. His body turned to block me, and we stopped. The path stepped down.

"*Ignis*," I whispered again. The tiny flame flickered in my palm, and I bent to look at the ground in front of us. There was not a step but a thick solid mound of glistening white granules. I touched them with my finger and made my best guess. "It must be salt."

Dex snorted at my palm, and I clenched a fist to extinguish the flame. Why would there be a giant line of salt across our path? Was it holding something in or keeping something out? I heard a whisper, a voice foreign to my ears.

"The flame keeper."

I trusted Dexter as he led me through the tunnels. It felt like miles of walking, one shuffling step at a time before I kicked over another line on the ground. I stumbled and put my hand against the wall to catch my balance. I felt the slick blossom of a demon embryo in my hand, but I also felt the pull of Brigid and her flame. Dex nudged me with his body, forcing me around a sharp turn. Something about the dark space came to light, but there was no solid form to whatever was present. The dog stopped moving, and I realized that we'd come face to face with a cavern wall.

"Are you tricking me, buddy?" I asked the animal. I reached to pat his head, but the soft fur that lived between his ears was gone. I felt around in the dark. I was afraid to light my flame but also aware that I was alone in an empty cavern.

"*Ignis.*" My hand flashed with light. I hesitated to touch the wall, but I could see specks reflecting at me as I held the flame. It wasn't gold, I was sure of that, but I had no guess what it might be. I put my back against the stone and inched my way around the room. I moved, one short side-step at a time until the support behind me was gone, and I landed on my ass in the dirt. My fire smothered, and I was in the dark again. Alone.

"Wildwood?"

I heard a voice, but I didn't answer.

"Wildwood."

She called again, and I closed my eyes, believing if I didn't see her, this couldn't be real.

"I know it's you. Come closer."

It was impossible to fight the power of the Earth's energy, calling me into the cavern.

"Don't be frightened."

Who could ever say that to you and believe that terror wouldn't cycle from head to toe? My heart was pounding, and my hands trembled as I pushed off the ground. The voice was louder, closer.

"Who are you?" I whispered into the void.

I heard the crunch of stones and the shifting of movement. I flattened myself against the wall, trying to make my body as small as possible. There was nowhere to hide. I heard claws clicking against the ground. Where had my dragon-dog gone?

"Wildwood."

Was it possible? "Shay?"

"*Ignis.*" I know how a moth feels when the flame flashes because I ran with full force into her arms. I had no idea Shay's voice could steal my breath, but at this moment, all I needed was her. I felt the rigid steel of the demon breastplate hit my chest.

"Oh, goddess. I can't believe this." I was breathless, but I'd only taken a few steps.

"I'm here. It's okay." Shay opened her stance to balance my rush into her arms.

I felt Dexter lean against us. "Did he bring you too?"

Shay's arm came around my shoulder, and I could feel her breath as she spoke. "I pulled up to the entrance of the mine, and Dex was there, and then we were here." She started to pat my body. "Are you okay?"

"I am now. I guess." She stepped back so she could drag her light over me. "There are no demons in this tunnel," I explained.

"What do you mean?"

"I think Dexter brought me beyond them. Somehow we snuck past and-"

Her finger touched my lips. "Shh." She clenched her hand to extinguish the flame. "There is something else in here. Dex, *Ante*."

He didn't move. It was unlike him to refuse Shay's command. The only time I could remember him ignoring Shay was when he already knew the threat. There was definitely something else inside this cavern.

"There's a break in the wall somewhere over here." I held her hand and stretched out the other as I felt my way around the tunnel. There was only one direction, so we made our first move into the dark labyrinth. After taking a few steps, the path switched back on itself. We wound around two more times until a dance of light fell across the ground.

"Did you see that?" Shay asked, and before I could answer, Dexter was transforming into a dragon, putting himself between us and whatever was around the next turn. Shay drew the taser from her hip and pushed me behind her. My fingers gripped the backpack, and I felt a sense of relief, knowing that we had anvil dust just in case.

I was the last one to enter the cavern, and the sight of Dexter stretched out like a prayer warrior, and Shay's open mouth stopped me cold. There was a crack in the wall from floor to ceiling, wide enough for a person to fit inside. The flame pouring from the base looked white-hot as it ribboned over the opening, but the absence of heat made it possible to stand so close. I stepped forward, and Shay hooked my elbow with her hand.

"Be careful." She warned.

The gateway didn't feel like a threat, and I knew I wasn't in danger as I straightened my arm to hold her hand. "It's her. The flame is her."

"Her? You mean Brigid?" Shay asked.

"Wild—wood."

If angels could speak, I'd have thought my name flitted like the wind through delicate chimes. The sound of my name fell through the air.

I looked back at Shay. "Did you hear that?"

She shook her head. "I didn't hear anything."

"Brigid is calling my name." I reached to touch the flame dancing through the gateway in the wall.

Shay pulled me back to her. "Are you sure you should touch it?"

"I'm sure I won't survive if I don't." It sounded dramatic even to my ears, but whatever was on the other side of this opening was something the Maker should possess.

Shay took a moment to look around the cavern. "Before you go wild and touch everything, maybe we should look for some clues or direction as to what's in there." She slipped the backpack off her shoulder and dropped it to the ground. Dexter had transformed to his K-9 self and was sniffing the perimeter.

"It's the goddess, and she's calling to me. She's saying my name. Who else could it be?" I reached to touch the flames again, and this time Shay grabbed my wrist.

"Please don't touch the flame."

"It isn't going to hurt me." I held Shay's cheek.

"How can you possibly know that?" She asked.

"I just do." I kissed her. "Trust me."

"It isn't you that I don't trust." Shay dropped to one knee and opened the backpack. She pulled her knife from her boot to strike the blade against the candle holder. I stopped her.

"Wait, let me." I took the candle and held the wick to the flame coming from the wall. I don't know why but somehow; I knew what to do. The flash of bright white created fire twice the size of our tiny taper candlestick.

"Holy Goddess," Shay said. "That was . . ."

"Pretty wonderful." I gave the holder back to Shay. As the candle transferred to her hand, I saw the marking on my arm. "What the heck?"

She touched my forearm. "Glowing symbols, like mine at the old courthouse."

I slapped my hands over my eyes, realizing what was coming next. "I don't want to be naked." I didn't have to see her to know that she was smiling.

"I'll protect you. I promise."

What was it about magick and skin? Why was it necessary to continuously remove our clothes? I didn't mind it so much when it was Shay. I pulled my shirt over my head, and the collar dangled from my hand. "What do you see?" I asked.

Her cheeks flushed. "Your maker's mark."

"Stop looking at my chest." I covered the symbol over my heart. "We already know about this one. Do you see anything new?"

"The forearm symbol, that's the cross of the goddess. You're wearing Brigid's mark."

"I guess that would make sense." I turned around. "Anything on my back? Do I have a cool dragon like yours?"

"Uh, no. Not a dragon."

I turned my head, trying to see my backside. "What is it?"

"It's the most stunning flame tattoo I've ever seen." She pulled her phone from her pocket. "Stand still."

I was too excited to stand still, but she got a picture. "Oh, wow. It is pretty beautiful." The bright yellow glow dashed with orange and white peaks and valleys. One sharp point sweeping and flowing to move like the living flame in front of us. "Do you think it has anything to do with the huge flames coming from the wall behind us?"

"I do, but I'm also trying to understand how . . . and who . . . and so much more."

I took a step toward the fiery crevice. "I have to go inside."

"I guess you do, but I'm not sure I can go with you." She held my wrist, clinging to the collision of possibility.

"You're not the Maker."

Shay closed her eyes, letting out a long breath. "I'm not."

"Someone is calling me to go, and I have to do this."

"I don't have to like it." Shay put her hand on my shoulder. "Talk to me the whole time."

She started to unlace the drawstring straps from the backpack and pull the waistband string from my sweatpants, connecting them into a rope about eight feet long. She wrapped a loop around my wrist. "It's probably silly, but don't go further than this until you feel like you can come back."

"I won't take any chances. I promise." I kissed her. "I love you."

"I love you too, and you better come back." She grabbed me in a tight hug. "Don't you leave me."

I turned around and didn't hesitate because the desperate sound in her voice made me want to stop even though Brigid's call was impossible to ignore. I waved the back of my hand in front of the flame. There was no heat, so I fed my hand through.

Shay tugged the string. "Be careful."

I looked down at my naked body. "I'm going in with nothing. Brigid is my only protection."

"So mote it be, baby." She wrapped the end of the string around her wrist. "Go in, take a look, come back."

"Keep it simple." I summarized.

She smiled. "That's right, keep it simple."

The crack in the wall flexed as I pressed against it. I stepped through, having no expectation of what might be inside. The wave of flame was feather-soft against my skin. As I passed through to the other side, the glow of the fire illuminated the cavern. I felt a tug on my wrist.

"Talk to me," Shay yelled.

"It's so bright in here." Coming out of the darkness into a room lined with quartz crystals was like walking into the sun. My eyes squinted to adjust to the glare. I felt a jerk at my wrist.

"Is it fire?"

I tugged the string, so she knew I was okay. "There are crystals everywhere. It's amazing."

"And the Goddess?"

I gave my eyes a few long blinks until I could look around the cave. "It's just me in here and rocks."

"Focus on that voice again."

The string around my wrist was slack enough for me to explore. I didn't dare touch the wall's sharp edges, so I crouched down to inspect the piles of rock at my feet. I picked them up one at a time, but nothing called to me. I moved to another heap, stretching the cord that tethered me to Shay. As soon as I touched it, I knew. Buried beneath ordinary stones was a solid block of steel. It was mine the moment it touched my skin. The tapered eyehole bored through was void where the handle should be, but the scrolled artwork's craftsmanship was inspired. The block was more significant than any hammer I owned and was the treasure of skilled hands.

"It's here." I cradled it in my palms. "It's unbelievable," I yelled over my shoulder as I wiped at the tiny fragments of dust that collected in the artwork.

"What is it?" Shay asked.

I carried the hammer head back through the flames. Shay had pressed her palm to the wall giving me every inch of slack on her safety tether. "It's the head of a hammer." I began to explain. "I've never seen anything like it." I turned it over and over, trying to see each side.

Shay's fingers touched the etchings. "It looks like runes but not quite, maybe Pictish or Pics." Dexter's nose popped up between us, and he licked at the ancient metal. "Looks like Dexter approves."

"I hope so. I walked through fire for this."

Shay picked up my shirt from the ground. "Speaking of walking through fire, maybe you should put some clothes on so we can get out of here." She tugged at the string, pulling me close enough so she could untie my end.

I set the hammer head on the ground and pulled the shirt over me. The K-9 started to sniff at the metal chunk and lick it.

"Do you think he should do that?" I asked.

Shay grabbed his collar. "Dex." He resisted the pull and started licking it again. "He has been eating bits of demons all day. What's licking a hunk of metal going to do?"

I put on my sweatpants and kicked the slippers on my feet. "With the events of the last few days, I don't want to press our luck." I opened the backpack and dropped the hammer head inside. "Do you think we can just walk right out of here?" I picked up the bag and slung it over my shoulders.

"Dexter, how's about taking us home?" Shay asked. He started licking in between the pads of his paws.

"I guess that's an answer." I stepped close to the flames coming from the wall. I closed my eyes and held a hand to them. The bright white flash covered my arms and crept up my face. I have only ever felt completely devoured by one person in my life, but when the flame of Brigid covered my skin and wrapped around my body, I felt the magick of the Goddess flowing through me. The heat flashed to a blinding white and disappeared into the cavern. Before I could move, all of it was gone.

"Wildwood!"

I heard Shay call, but the weight of Brigid's energy was heavy in my body. My hands fell to the wall for support.

"Hey, can you hear me?" Shay put her arm around my shoulder, steering us away from Brigid's cave.

"I can. It's just that, the power—It's a lot." I leaned against her body.

"Can you walk? We still have to get out of here, and I'm not sure what's between us and the cruiser."

"Just give me a second to catch my breath. Have you got any of that moon water energy drink?"

Her nervous laugh was close to an answer. "I wish."

"Let's get out of here." I pushed her ahead of me. "I'll rest in the car."

She tugged the strap of the backpack and put me between herself and our demon-dog. "Dexter, *ante!*" He was up on all fours and did a quick perimeter check with his nose. I felt safe sandwiched between a dragon-dog and my fiercely protective Shay. As long as the two of them were walking and Dexter didn't transform, I expected an easy escape from the tunnels.

"Can you even see?" I whispered.

"Dex sees everything. I'll be fine. Just follow him."

"It sure would be nice if he just shifted us out of here."

Shay tugged at the strap on the backpack. "It sure would."

We zippered through the zigzag until we were at our original merging location. From this point forward, we had no idea what was next. I put my hand on Dexter's furry shoulders and was content to walk beside him. For some reason, I wasn't frightened, but I wasn't about to share that with Shay. The dog stopped, and I should have known why, but when he buried his snout against the wall, I could hear the crunching sound of juicy demon embryos popping in his mouth.

"Do you think that's a dragon thing?" I asked.

"I have to say yes, but I've also never had a dog to compare."

"Does it seem weird that there aren't any demons, I mean aside from the wall snacks?" I pointed at the dog.

"It's possible that shifting in with Dex doesn't leave a trace. I don't think it's going to be so easy to get out once we hit the cave we were in this afternoon." Shay explained. "I'm also unsure if those demons want what you've just uncovered."

"Brigid's hammer?"

Shay put her hand on my hip, just below the weight of the backpack. "If that truly is her hammer and it's the tool of the Maker. How did it get in that cavern?"

"That's a good question."

Dexter stopped in front of us, and I expected him to start licking the wall, but instead, he crouched down, ready to attack.

I bumped up against him, and Shay pushed against me. I didn't feel the spatial shift at first. I blinked my eyes for a moment, and suddenly I was standing outside the entrance to the mine. Dexter disappeared, and seconds later, Shay was beside me.

"We need to go." Shay pulled my wrist.

"He just shifted the two of us right past everything." I ran toward the squad car and looked back to see Dexter in magnificent dragon form, shaking the head off of a demon.

"Not quite everything," Shay said.

I lifted the handle on the squad car door and attempted to jump in the seat. The backpack snagged on the roof of the car and tugged me off my feet.

"Are you okay?" Shay was already starting the car.

I slipped the bag from my shoulder, and it gave a loud thump as it hit the floorboard. I wasn't thinking about anything but getting out of here, fast. I watched Dexter drag the remains back inside the mine. "Should he go back in there?"

Shay shifted the car into reverse. "I wish I knew." She rolled down the windows on her side of the patrol car and yelled to the dragon-dog. "Dexter, *reditus!*" She shouted the command for his return as her foot hit the gas, and we spiraled backward around in a half-circle. She hit the brake and shifted into drive. The entire maneuver left me slightly excited and a little nauseous. Our dragon came out of the cave at full sprint, his claws digging deep into the rock, firing him off the ground and into the air. In the twenty feet between leaving the ground and landing beside the car, he'd transformed back into his K-9 self. He squeezed through the car window, and Shay drove us away.

As the Maker of Bannock, I felt like I never got a moment to catch my breath and today was no exception. "That was insane." I looked over at my girlfriend.

"Just another day on the job for me."

Shay was playing it cool, maybe for my benefit, I wasn't sure, but there was no way our cave experience was like anything else. "It's not possible. We just found the hammer of the goddess Brigid. THE hammer!"

"And my dog ravaged another half dozen demons in that cave."

"You're acting a little too cool, don't you think?" I asked and watched as Shay switched her hand on the steering wheel. I saw blood seeping through the fabric of her sleeve. "Are you hurt?"

She looked at her arm. "It's nothing. I just caught it on the tunnel wall."

"The tunnel wall lined with demon embryos?"

"It's nothing."

I've come to understand that with Shay, nothing was probably something. "I want to look at it when we get home."

"Seriously, it'll be fine."

"What a crazy day." I let my head fall back against the seat. Shay reached across to hold my hand, and I was content to close my eyes for the rest of the drive.

"Crazy is right."

CHAPTER XVII

Fortuity

It was close to four in the morning when we pulled into the parking lot of the carriage house. My eyes were closed, and although my head was still resting against the seat, I couldn't shut down the thoughts in my brain. I felt the car stop and heard it shift into park.

"We're here, honey," Shay said as her hand patted my thigh.

I turned to look at her. "Can you magick me up the stairs?"

"I cannot, but I can carry you."

I thought about the last few hours and remembered that my girlfriend was bleeding. "Maybe I should carry you. How's the arm?"

She opened her door. "I told you, it's nothing." The dog pushed his way to the door.

I grabbed the backpack and followed Shay into the building. "Just let me take a look," I said as I turned on the lights. Before I could say another word, she was pulling her shirt over her head. I was distracted.

"You said you wanted to look at my arm." She snapped her fingers.

My eyes closed in a hard blink. "I did, but your shirt." Shay started poking at the slice on her arm. "Stop, let me." I grabbed her fingers, pushing them out of the way.

"So bossy."

"Go sit down and let me wash it out." I pushed her toward the sink in the back of the workshop.

"I've got a few hours before work. Can we just wash it in the shower?"

"I like the way you think." I dropped the backpack on the table and followed Shay upstairs. She was slow to remove her pants, trying to make light of the wound. I could see the gash as the water from the bathroom faucet washed the wound clean.

"See, it's just a scratch."

I laid my finger alongside the wound. "It's more than two inches. That is not a scratch."

She pushed my hand away. "Can you close it with anvil dust?"

"Now that it's clean. I will." I turned off the water and handed Shay a towel. I pushed a washcloth over the wound. "Put pressure on until I come back." I rushed to dry my skin and ran down to the office to get the demon dust. Shay was sitting on the end of the bed; her towel draped over her hips, fingers squeezed around her bicep. "It's still bleeding."

"If we didn't have this." I shook the container of demon scale. "You'd need stitches."

"I'm not a novice when it comes to those." She pulled the bloody cloth off her arm.

I poured a clump of the blue flakes into my palm and sprinkled a generous amount across the wound. The blood bubbled as it absorbed the dust, and the ripped skin began to close.

"Ooh." Shay shifted on the bed.

"Does it hurt?"

"It stings a bit, but that's the trade-off."

"I guess so." I capped the bottle and set it on the bedside table. When I turned around, Shay was brushing her skin with the blood-stained towel. "So impatient."

"I just want to climb in bed with my girlfriend. Is that so terrible?"

I kissed her. "Not at all." I took the towel from her hand and the one wrapped around her hip. I pulled the blanket back. "Climb in." I turned to take the towels to the bathroom, and when I returned, Shay was asleep. I pressed the alarm button, aware that she would get less than two hours to recover from the longest day of our lives together. The sheets were cold, so I pressed closer to Shay, and she wiggled herself into the curves of my body. My arm draped around her hip, and my hand snaked under to rest on her heart.

I closed my eyes and felt the pounding rhythm. I thought it was Shay's heartbeat against my skin. I tried to focus on the sensation, but it was more than the flesh beneath my hand. I rolled away from Shay and sat on the side of the bed, careful not to disturb the few hours of rest she needed. I grabbed a shirt from the drawer and a pair of sweatpants. I was sure the sound calling me was Brigid and the hammer of the goddess.

My bare feet were cold against the floor of the workshop. I kicked into a pair of work boots as I opened the backpack on the table. As soon as my hands touched the block of metal, the pounding stopped.

I shook the hammer head, getting a feel for the way it might swing as a tool. It needed a handle, but first, I needed to clear away what looked like two lifetimes of neglect. I set up a basin for water and put the block of material in the center. I twisted the cap off my homemade solution for cleaning metal; a combination of vinegar, dish soap, salt, and a sprinkle of baking soda poured over Brigid's hammer.

I'm not sure what I expected, but the debris didn't fall away. It held tight. I rummaged through my tools, searching for a miniature wire brush. It looked much like something you would clean your teeth with, but these metal strands would destroy your gums. I flicked the bristles with my thumb to test their strength. I hadn't used it for a while, but it felt like it would hold up, at least for this project.

The head of Brigid's hammer had two faces, and I started brushing the least soiled. I could see the tiny blemishes as I worked around the rim. I was patient, plunging the hammer into the basin to wash away the tiny chips of residue hit loose from the wire abrasive. I built up a rhythm, four or five strokes, and a dunk and swirl in the solution. I repeated the process until I cleaned away enough to see that this was not a striking surface—delicate scrolls of hand-tooled Celtic knots ribboned around the outside ridge. No one would ever use this as the working end.

I heard the sound of footprints on the floor above me and thought it was Dexter. A few minutes later, strong arms came around my waist. I noticed her wrist wrapped with a canvas watch band, and I could feel the gear on her duty belt press against my back as she hugged me.

"Did you sleep at all?" Shay asked as her chin rested on my shoulder.

"Not at all," I said as I turned the hammer so she could see my progress.

Her fingernail caught the edge of the scrolled etching. "That's beautiful."

I smiled. "Isn't it." I agreed. "I've been scrubbing this part for the last few hours. I have no idea what this coating is, but it does not want to come off."

"Maybe it's enchanted . . . or hexed?"

I set the hammer head back in the basin. "I didn't even consider that."

"What's it soaking in?" Shay asked as she stepped back.

"It's a mix I use for cleaning scrap metal." I held up the gallon container. "Why?"

"Just wondering."

"What are you thinking?" I asked.

"It requires some research and a book that's at the house. I'll swing by and grab it and stop back on my lunch hour."

"You know where I'll be." I waved my hand across the worktable.

Her finger hooked over the band of my sweatpants, and she pulled me closer. "I do." She kissed me. "I'll see you at lunch."

I held my dirty hands away from her uniform. "I love you."

"I love you too." She turned to leave. "Dex!" She called the dog, and he was at her side.

I didn't turn to watch her go. I plunged my hands back into the basin and continued to work the wire brush against the hammer. After another hour, I decided to mix a fresh solution and let the block of metal soak. It felt more like an archeological experience than a blacksmithing project. I made a pot of coffee and scribbled a few notes about our early morning excursion inside of Brigid's cavern.

I was killing time. I thought about using the hammer of a goddess and I realized it was useless without a sturdy handle. I flipped through the lengths of wood stacked on the shelf. I kept many pieces for knife handles, but a hammer's haft needed a balanced combination of strength and flexibility. I selected a rough-cut piece of hickory and set to work, shaping it to fit my hand and the eye of the hammer's head. Every step was necessary, and I took my time carving the perfect fit. I heard the handle on the workshop door and looked up to see that Shay had returned.

"I was pretty sure you'd still be here." Shay took off her hat and gave me a quick kiss on the cheek. Her feet kicked through the wood shavings on the floor. "You're making the handle already?" She asked.

"I am. I'm filling time because I wanted to let the head soak for a while."

"Not going so well?" she asked.

I set the handle down on the table and tapped my wire brush against the hammer head. "I thought it would be dirt or maybe rust, but it's neither of those, and I don't want to use anything that might damage the artwork."

Shay dropped a folder on the table. "Here's a suggestion." She tapped the cover with her finger.

"What's that?"

Shay sat down on my chair and flipped the file open. "I started thinking about where you found the hammer head and what might grow on it like that."

"Okay."

Her finger trailed down the page. "There are two references in this report about remains of unknown origin at a crime scene."

"What crime scene are you talking about?" I tried to flip the cover to read the name.

"That's not important." She folded a few pages over the top of the file. "The fire department had to use torches to melt the remains so they could contain the scene. So it got me thinking that maybe you could put the hammer head in the forge."

Her idea was a good one. "I like the way you're thinking, but there's one flaw."

She closed the folder. "I was worried it wouldn't be so easy."

"Yes, if we heat the hammer, we run the risk of destroying the hardness, and also, I have no idea what it might do to the etching that I've started to uncover. I'm guessing the images are on the entire thing."

"You're saying it's not going to work?" She asked.

"Sorry, love, I think it's going to be towels and brushes at a snail's pace on this project." I picked up the handle and held it over the contoured eye in the hammer head. "I've got a handle ready if that helps?"

"Maybe you can just put it on and hit the anvil a few times to vibrate that crap off."

"That's not such a bad idea." I pulled the hammer head from the basin. "Hand me a towel."

Shay folded the rag in half and held it out in her hands. I set it in the center, but the fabric collapsed, and the head dropped between Shay's feet on the concrete floor.

"Sorry, I guess I wasn't ready."

"It's not a big deal." I took the towel and grabbed the block of metal. I wiped away the loose particles and set the project on the table. "If you look at this detail." I pointed to the Celtic scrolling on the back of the hammer. "This is the work of a very talented artisan."

"I guess it's back into the bathtub for Brigid's hammer?" Shay asked.

I smiled. "Yes, I guess it is."

"Speaking of guesses, do you think that the hammer might have demon guts on it? Maybe it dried out, and that's why the dirt is so hard?" she asked.

"It would explain why my simple mix failed."

Shay swished her fingertips through the basin of solution and stopped to touch the artwork I'd uncovered. "What if we had a fire that didn't get hot?"

"What do you mean?"

Shay held out her hand. "*Ignis*," she said, and her palm flashed a beautiful blue flame.

"I didn't even think . . ." I held the block of hammer steel over her hand, passing it back and forth through the flame. I turned it over and tried to remove the hardened demon guts with the wire brush. Tiny flecks chipped away. "You are brilliant." I set the hammer back in the bath.

"Maybe, but you're doing all of the work." She closed her hand and rolled her wrist to check the time. "I've got to go back to work. I'll see you in a few hours."

"You have to go already?" I pinned her in the chair, stepping between her legs.

Her cheek raised in a tiny half-grin. "I'll be back soon, and maybe we can play with your new toy."

I leaned over her, giving her a slow kiss. Shay stood from the chair with ease, half carrying me off my feet. "Let me down. You'll get your uniform dirty."

"It'll be worth it." She stepped in a small circle reversing our positions, setting me down in my chair. "I think we both have work to do." She kissed me one more time before snugging her hat back in place.

"Thank you for helping me." I stood to walk her to the car. Dexter hopped up from his circle and led us out to the parking lot. I lingered in the doorway.

"We're partners." She watched Dex leap through the open car window.

"Yes, I guess we are."

Shay turned back to look at me. "I'll see you in a few hours."

"I can't wait."

She smiled, blew me a kiss, climbed in her patrol car, and drove away. I watched her go knowing that she would do anything to get back to me.

The next three hours were as slow as my morning work. Although the palm fire loosed the demon crud, I still had to brush it away, and the chore was tedious. I worked every side of the block of metal. Each revealing a stunning pictograph. It looked like the history of Brigid and the tale of the maker. The text was illegible for me. The characters resembled runes but with random hooks and slashes added. I'd have to wait for Shay to decipher Brigid's code.

I picked away at the bottom of the hammer, revealing what could have been a maker's mark. It was scored through with an X as though to erase the owner's existence.

As I looked through the eye, the hammer's top had a silhouette of the goddess herself. I'd imagined what she would look like, but this rendering was not the goddess drawn in my mind. The lines were long, and her body wrapped with a billowing single slip of a robe. The hammer's eye was centered with precision to penetrate her abdomen. I imagined creation as though her sacred body blessed each work forged by the Maker's hand.

Yes, the hammer of Brigid had a story to tell.

The last step in the cleaning process was to polish every surface. I looked up at the clock and felt like it was a race to finish before Shay walked through the door. I was excited for her to see how beautiful it was. I held the handle over the eye, checking the fit. I shaved a slight burr off the side and began to bond the two together.

Anyone who has ever hafted a hammer knows that a tight fit is most important. This hammer head was snug as I used its weight to cleave the two into one. I tapped the butt of the grip over and over. I was patient as I worked the head down until I forced a half-inch of material through the top. It was a perfect fit. I locked the two parts together with a wedge of metal. Brigid's hammer felt sacred in my hand like the mantle passed, and I was the rightful Maker.

I wiped the handle down with a light coat of stain and sealed it with linseed oil. It was the most beautiful hammer I'd ever held in my hand. I set it down on the face of my anvil and stood back to admire my work. It was the tool of my trade, and in its polished glory, I thought it quite impossible to use.

Perhaps it was peculiar, but I stood for a long time looking at the finished project, thinking about what the Makers might have forged with the hammer of Brigid. Had Jacob known of its existence? How did it come to be in the caves? How long had it been buried in the pile of demon waste? There wasn't a human soul on earth who could answer these questions.

There was a knock on the door and then a scratching which could only come from one animal I knew, but why would they knock? I turned the knob and opened the door to Dexter, who pushed past me, and Shay, with arms, loaded. "Hi honey, I'm home."

I reached to take a few of the items from her hand. "Hi, I'm so glad you are." I gave her a quick kiss. "You're going to be amazed at what I've done."

"Ooh, that sounds exciting—." She stopped, speechless in front of the anvil. The bags fell from her hand, and her eyes locked on the hammer of Brigid. Shay looked at me. "I've never seen anything like it."

"I know," I said.

Her jaw fell open as she walked around the anvil stand. "It's beautiful."

"I know." I didn't have any other words.

"Have you used it yet?"

I shook my head. "Honestly, I'm afraid to use it."

"Can I touch it?" She asked as though it was divine.

I picked it up and held it to her. "What's mine is yours." I gripped it tight, holding the handle for Shay to touch. If this was a legendary tale, there might have been choirs of angels or flashes of light from the heavens as I held it to her, but there was not. Shay ran her fingertips across the etchings and studied the straight lined characters.

"Do you think the Magick can wield the Maker's hammer?" She asked.

"I have no idea, but maybe you could look at the markings on the sides and answer that question."

I turned the hammer in my hand, noticing for the first time how the text intertwined with the ornamental scrolling.

"It's Pictish, I'm sure of it. That's funny because I ran to the house and brought a few books."

I looked at the bags on the floor by my feet. "A few?"

"I was driving through town, and I remembered the letters we saw on the hammer when we were in the cave. I just grabbed everything I had on written texts and glyphs."

"We're going to need another bookcase." I joked.

"Yes." Shay agreed, but her focus was on the surface artwork of the hammer. "This is so interesting." She pushed to rotate the head and noticed the damage to the mark of the previous maker.

"I thought so too." I picked at the circle with my fingertip. "Like someone was erasing the maker from history."

"Or something," Shay suggested.

"What do you mean?"

"Maybe this was done by a demon."

"If something erased the Maker, what happens if I put my mark in its place?"

She shook her head. "I have no idea."

"Are you feeling adventurous?" I asked as I shook the hammer in my hand.

"Maybe. What are you thinking?"

I walked to the wall and wheeled my torch closer to the anvil. "I'm thinking I'm going to heat this spot . . ." I touched the damaged circle on the hammer's head. "And set my mark in its place."

"You can do that?"

311

I raised my shoulder in a shrug. "I'm not sure, but I'm going to try." I picked up a towel from the box of rags. "Take this and soak it in water. Dump out the basin and bring it—"

She held up a hand to stop me. "Why don't you give me two minutes to change out of my uniform and put the books upstairs?"

"Oh, right." I laid the hammer on the anvil. "I'll get everything ready while you go change."

Shay picked up the bags and carried them up to the apartment. I rinsed out the basin and soaked the towel through with water. I wrapped everything but the area I was about to torch, hoping to keep it cool and dissipate the heat. I tied the towel in place with cotton cording to hold it all together. When Shay returned, I had the entire hammer bundled in a wet towel, and the only visible part was a space the size of a dime.

"That's an interesting swaddle you've got there." Shay pointed to my project.

"I don't want to destroy the hammer head or the handle. Wrapping it up should work."

"What should I do?" She asked, tugging a hat on her head.

I thought about her question. "You know, I have no idea what to expect. Maybe just stand behind me."

"You're going to be my shield?"

I put on a pair of torch glasses. "For the next few minutes, I guess I am."

I dialed the knobs on the tanks and squeezed the igniter. The torch blazed a solid flame, and I adjusted the flow, aiming the heat at the tiny circle on Brigid's hammer. The edge of the towel started to scorch, and steam poured from the folds as the metal turned from gray to orange.

"Shay, can you take some water from the quench bucket and pour it on the handle?"

She scooped enough to saturate the towel. It trickled down through the fabric to the metal of the head. My plan seemed to work as I watched the circle change to the perfect color for marking. I set down the torch, preparing to use a blank to strike a level surface, erasing the previous markings. When I turned to set the punch, the maker's mark vanished.

I looked at Shay. "That's strange."

"What's that?" She asked.

"The mark is gone." I tilted the hammer so she could get a better look.

"What do you think it means?" She was just as curious as I.

"I think it means we're guessing things right." The surface cooled just enough to prevent a perfect mark. "I'm going to torch the ring one more time. Heat it back up. Will you add just a little more water?" I asked, and Shay scooped from the quench bucket to soak the towel through.

I heated the circle again and turned off the torch. I could feel the heat through my glove as I adjusted my maker's mark die directly over the spot. With one swift solid swing, the mark claimed Brigid's hammer as my own. I felt the power of the Maker move through me, but it didn't stop. The rush of energy threw Shay against the wall, and Dexter morphed from a dog into dragon form.

A voice thundered from the workshop shadows. "It's about damn time, but *THAT* was unexpected."

The dragon-dog's tail whipped around to force his way closer to Shay. She lay unconscious on the floor. I dropped everything and crawled to her side. "Shay!" My hands wrapped around her shoulders to shake her body. "Shay, wake up." I brushed the damp tangles of red hair off her face. Dexter, in dragon form, was breathing over my neck. The force of my Maker powers changing him from his furry German Shepherd self.

"Maybe you should kiss her?" They suggested.

I looked up to find the source of the voice. "Who the hell are you?"

Thank you for reading book two of the Maker Series, the continuing story of Wildwood Blackstone, a lady blacksmith who finds adventure, demons, magick and love in the small ghost town of Bannock.

MARK OF THE MAKER (BOOK 1)

Wildwood Blackstone believed her dream of being a country blacksmith was coming true. When the town of Bannock hires her to restore their abandoned carriage house built in the 1800s, she can't wait to begin.

But there are more than ghosts in Bannock and shortly after her arrival she discovers this truth. When a childhood friend answers a call for help, Wildwood finds a part of her past that she longed to rediscover. Together they reveal Bannock's secret and uncover the Mark of the Maker.

THE MAGICK AND THE MAKER (BOOK 2)

Wildwood Blackstone longed for a life as a small-town blacksmith. She didn't imagine monsters or magick, and she never expected to fall in love with Shay.

Book two of the Maker Series finds the two women tangled together in the dark secrets buried deep in Bannock's small-town history. Is their commitment strong enough to carry them through? Who is the keeper of the Magick? When will Wildwood and Shay uncover the mystery behind the Mark of the Maker?

THE ORIGIN OF THE MAKER (BOOK 3)

Wildwood and her girlfriend Shay have uncovered Brigid's secret hidden deep in the earth.

Who is the stranger in the carriage house? How are they there? What do they know about the secret and the power it holds? Can Wildwood and Shay find the answers and keep fighting the monsters hunting them night and day? Find out in book three of the Maker Series. Origin of the Maker Coming in 2022.

MORE BOOKS FROM SHARON K ANGELICI

DEAR KANE; WHAT I WISH WE WOULD HAVE SAID

Do the words that we say in front of our children build them up or tear them down? This short story explores the consequences of hatred and bigotry when it applies, unknowingly, to someone that you love. There's a time in every relationship when a parent must let go of the dreams they have for their child, so the child can chase what they dream to become.

IMMORTAL HUMAN TRUTH

Immortal Human Truth is a collection of poetry written by the author as she traveled to promote her first book Dear Kane; What I wish we would have said.

Each section explores experiences with love, injustice, loss and triumph of the spirit.

SHE BELIEVED SHE COULD

What can you do in a single day? Why haven't you done it yet? Jump out of your comfort zone and dive into life as you follow the author on her journey to achieve 365 new experiences in 365 days

ABOUT THE AUTHOR

Sharon K Angelici, she/her, was born in the American Midwest, but her heart and soul belong to the mountains of Colorado.

She began writing as a child, using words to recover from trauma-induced depression. As a member of the LGBTQ+ community, she's an advocate for depression awareness and suicide prevention. In 2016 she published her first book dealing with both subjects, Dear Kane; what I wish we would have said.

Sharon is a full-time lover of life and all things Pagan and Magick. She's an artist and blacksmith, which inspired her to create her new Maker series. Book one Mark of the Maker released in 2020, and the second, The Magick and the Maker, to release in July of 2021.

Printed in Great Britain
by Amazon